A BEAM REACH

A NOVEL

STEVE MYRVANG
JOANNE JURGICH

Volume 3
of The Reach Series

Also, written by the authors:
Volumes 1 and 2 of The Reach Series,
A Broad Reach
A Close Reach

Cover Layout and Design
by Crave Design Studio
Artwork by Amy Scholten

Acknowledgements

While we did receive motivation from Barney, Paul, Sienna and all the other Reach Series characters to continue their story, it's with heartfelt thanks that we acknowledge the following folks:

To Shelly, John and the rest of the gang at Sand Castles who never missed a chance to ask when the next volume was coming out.

To our friends at Undercover Books who relayed their patron's complaints that we were taking too long to finish Volume 3.

To Julie, Damon, "Mitch", Phil, Tom, Joe, Unc, Gibby, Tim, Lolly, Paul, Annie and the many other readers who provided a needed spark at just the right time.

A special thanks to Dr. "Robdog" Roth, Sandy Caulder-Roth, Rod and Jody Mager, Luther Hintz, and especially, Bill Buck and Kirsten Casey.

Gratitude also goes to the island of Saint Croix; its inhabitants, its tropical splendor, cultural diversity and political absurdities. There is nowhere else we'd rather call home.

Prologue

Twin V-8 MerCruisers bit into the early morning Caribbean Sea. The foamy wake opened like a zipper, splitting the still waters of the Sir Francis Drake Channel down its middle.

He'd rebuilt the drive train and installed the radar and guidance system in the '86, Sea Ray Sundancer. Not wanting to draw attention, he'd left the worn exterior untouched.

Running all out, it took less than half an hour to pass Beef Island. Ten minutes later, Andrew Sherman pulled back on the throttle and approached Great Dog Island at just under 12 knots. The brightening sky reflected his mood. A huge weight had been lifted. Drawing in the warm salty air, he hadn't felt this good in years. The guilt he'd carried since staging his death had nothing to do with framing Buddy Falco. Having previously escaped prosecution for more than a handful of mysterious disappearances, Buddy's fifteen-year manslaughter sentence was well deserved. Andrew's guilt had been for another reason. His well-publicized disappearance had left T-Square Development bankrupt, with Paul Armstrong not only clueless, but holding the bag. He'd come to think of his former business partner as a younger brother. Leaving him in the lurch had been the hardest part of his decision to disappear. But their previous evening's chance encounter had given Sherman an overwhelming sense of relief. Paul was happier than he'd ever seen him. Tan and fit, living in the tropics with an incredible woman, his former partner appeared to be doing just fine.

Sherman cut the engines just off the island's northwest coast. Pleased there were no other vessels in the cove, he tied up to a white day-buoy and pulled his tank and dive gear from the aft hold. Inflating his BCD to counter the weight he would be carrying, Sherman checked his regulator and stepped off the swim step. Slowed by the 35 ten ounce Credit Suisse gold bars that he toted in the dive bag, he finned slowly, ten feet under the surface toward the island. Familiar with the route, he rounded a boulder that stretched twenty-five feet above the surface and made his way through a narrow passage. The water temperature dropped as he entered the mouth of a dark tunnel and switched on his headlamp. Though Andrew had made this run many times, he was never comfortable dropping through the blackness, deep into the bowels of the island. Six long minutes later he rose through a vertical chimney and broke the surface. His headlamp illuminated the bedroom sized cave as he removed his tank and set it on a large rock. Carefully edging his way along a narrow ledge, he located the familiar fissure which led into a second chamber.

The moist air was heavily scented with moss and decaying rat carcasses as he continued along the ledge to the far corner of the small cave. He set the bag on the ground and dropped to his knees. Straining with the effort he pulled away the last large rock, exposing a black plastic covered aluminum case. Unlatching the lid, his light sparkled off six rows of ten ounce bars, illuminating the walls and ceiling in a golden glow. Emptying his dive bag, he filled the final row with the bars he'd toted, bringing the total to 154. *Two million dollars*, he thought proudly. He ran his gloved hand over the booty.

If you'd believed Andrew's mother, his fascination with pirates was innate. An early reader, the well-worn copy of <u>Treasure Island</u> was dog-eared by his eighth birthday. It was only fitting that within days of his arrival in the BVIs, he was exploring the same caves rumored to have once concealed the loot of Blackbeard, Black Bart and other infamous privateers. Andrew admired their courage- attacking ships larger than their own, many times prevailing against superior forces. He felt a kinship with these men. Operating outside the law, he alone had taken down a powerful and ruthless gangster that the FBI hadn't even been able to touch.

There were much easier ways to hide two million dollars, but a buried treasure was most definitely the best match for his own swashbuckling panache.

1

Though skyscrapers rose higher, Wyatt had chosen The Space Needle. The iconic landmark remained the city's crown jewel since its 1962 unveiling at the Seattle World's Fair. Transfixed by the incredible view, he reached across the table and took Connie's hand. "Feels like we're sitting on top of the world." She returned his gentle squeeze.

Who knows whether it was Adam's spirit, fate, luck, or just the crapshoot of life that brought them together? But, two months after their chance encounter, Connie sublet her downtown condo and took up residency in Wyatt's modest brick Tudor on the north side of Queen Anne Hill.

Eighteen months earlier, if someone had told Special Agent Constance Hunter that she'd be leaving the FBI, she'd have told them they were off their rocker. In charge of the Seattle division for nearly a decade, it was only in the last year that she'd claimed a life outside of her high-pressure responsibilities with the agency. At 45, she had reached her position in the FBI riding a very fast track. A highly-decorated agent throughout her career, her insights and hard work had been instrumental in solving numerous federal crimes, as well as thwarting several national security threats. Her successful supervision and leadership over three hundred Seattle division employees had precipitated recent conversations in D.C. regarding her name being put forth as the first female Deputy Director.

The FBI didn't want to lose Special Agent Hunter. Taken aback by her decision to leave the force, her superior's response was as old-school as expected. "You quit and you can goddamn spend the rest of your life in a South Carolina detention center." When threats didn't work, the director, himself, broke the impasse by convincing her to hold off on her decision until after taking the six months of vacation she had on the books. She accepted the offer only after he assured her that he'd accept her resignation if she still wanted to resign after the six months.

Wyatt's selfish need to possess a larger portion of her life than her duties at the FBI would allow, was most often rumored as the reason for her early retirement. "It's insulting to both of us," Connie had complained one evening. "You're the most unselfish man I've ever known. Also, it makes me look weak; like I'm some kind of spineless wussy."

"Those are two words I'd never in a million years associate with you," he'd replied, laughing. "Really, Connie, who gives a shit what they think. Let 'em have their opinions. It doesn't affect us. You're just burned out. That's all."

It was hard, however, for her to let it go. She still felt the old responsibilities and associations pull at her. Up until Wyatt, her life had been all about her work. But the tragic death of her brother, Adam, had changed all that.

Connie had always been extremely independent. With no father, an alcoholic mother, and a younger brother to take care of, she was forced to grow up too soon. There hadn't been much room for fun in those early years. Later, while the strength and discipline she'd developed had set her on a trajectory through Harvard Law School to the FBI, there was still something missing. Adam had repeatedly begged her to take time off to relax and enjoy. "I need some quality time with my Big Sis. Let's do Iceland. We'll hike and find hot springs. You'll see things you never knew existed with all your FBIing."

After losing him, she vowed she wouldn't wait any longer. Deeply shaken by his death, her serendipitous encounter with Wyatt came during a solitary walk along Seattle's waterfront, at the depth of her despair. It had been a turning point for Connie and she truly believed that Adam's spirit had provided more than a small hand in bringing her and Wyatt together.

Wyatt's affable nature and simple, *live-and-let-live* approach to life had become the perfect antidote to her aggressive, take-charge personality. At six-six, Wyatt's easygoing demeanor could change abruptly when the job required his *you don't want to fuck with me* persona. It was a side of Wyatt that Connie had only heard stories of, as he quickly became her friend and soon thereafter her lover.

She found herself in unfamiliar territory. With only a few brief affairs in the past, the whole *sharing thing* was something she'd never experienced. But Wyatt was patient. He understood and gave her plenty of room. When she'd told him she was quitting the agency, he hadn't pressed her for specifics. Her vague explanation, "I've had it. It's time," sufficed. More than content with the evolution of their relationship, he was confident that any lingering barriers between them would eventually fall by the wayside.

As her controlling nature slowly yielded, she began to surrender to the trust and love, which, except for a few predictable setbacks involving his ex-wife, was deepening daily. For the first time, she shared painful stories from her childhood and cried in his massive arms over the loss of her brother. Still, she couldn't bring herself to tell him about Paul Armstrong.

Agent Constance Hunter's reason for leaving the FBI wasn't because she was burned out. Hell, with all the grunt work, all the late-night stake-outs and ass-kissing she'd done to get there, why would she quit now that she was in charge? Known only to her, not turning over the evidence she'd had on Paul Armstrong had violated her oath and undermined her capacity to lead.

The waiter arrived with their cocktails. Wyatt held up his Martini, "To you and to the best twelve months of my life."

Shit, she thought as tears welled in her eyes. *I can't go through the rest of my life bawling every time he gives me that look.*

"You OK?"

"Oh yeah. I am so OK. I just can't seem to turn off the waterworks." Smiling, she added, "Maybe they're right. Maybe I am a wussy."

"I kinda like the crying."

"Good thing. It seems like I've stored up years' worth."

"Also, the moaning isn't so bad, either."

Connie rolled her eyes and shook her head in feigned disgust. She liked the feel of her longer hair brushing across her neck. She'd always kept it short for the agency. The bobbed hair, heavy framed glasses and navy blue suits were gone; now just memories from her past. Wyatt complimented her often regarding this transformation, always adding that her best outfit was when she wore nothing at all.

His baritone voice refocused her attention. "So I got a call earlier today from a guy I met twenty-five years ago. Remember my telling you about when I wanted to be a desk jockey and they flew me to Atlanta for a course on computers?"

Connie nodded and sipped her drink.

"Well, he was coming up through the ranks of New York's Port Authority Police. Eventually, made chief. We used to check in with each other every year or so, but dropped out of contact after he got married and left the force. Anyway, he's flying in next week with his wife and a couple friends. Wants to meet us for dinner."

"That's great. What's his name?"

"Henry Johnson. He goes by Hank."

2

Paul couldn't understand it. His wife was an anomaly. She seemed to love everything about it . . . The anticipation, the early arrival, checking through security, even the inevitable delays and cancellations had little effect on her enjoyment. Sienna simply loved flying. At 35,000 feet, with Andy and Aunt Charlotte taking care of AJ and Red, there was nothing else to do but relax and enjoy the flight. Sipping her vodka tonic, she looked over appreciably at her sleeping husband.

She'd felt bad leaving so much for Paul to do the week before their departure, but covering all the required bases the three-week vacation from her restaurant required had her scrambling. Paul had picked up the slack around the house; cooking, cleaning, washing clothes and shuttling AJ to and from soccer practice, while still working late into the night finishing the permit drawings for a new client's residence. She lifted the open paperback from his lap, placed it in the seat pocket and turned off his overhead light.

Across the aisle, Hank sat next to Roxanne who was sniffling her way through a laptop movie. He leaned toward Sienna. "Our boy's out again? Think you might be demanding too much from him in the sack?"

"Very funny, Hank. So, what movie?" she asked Roxanne, who was drying her eyes and pulling out her ear buds.

"Titanic," she replied, blowing her nose.

"It's like her seventh time," Hank added. "Personally, I wouldn't choose a disaster film to watch on a transcontinental flight."

"It's not a disaster film. It's a love story, you oaf." Roxanne shot back.

"Maybe it's just me, but I like the kind of love story where—"

"Jeez you guys are loud." Paul stretched his arms and looked out the window.

"Well, if it ain't Sleeping Beauty. Anyone seen a kissing prince ride by?" Hank joked.

"How many gin-and-tonics have you had?" Roxanne asked her husband, suspiciously.

"That's not it. I'm just excited. We're about to land in Paul's former backyard and I can't think of a better tour guide for exploring this majestic and magnificent region."

"I'm guessing three doubles," Sienna speculated.

The idea of a three-week vacation without kids had been cooked up by Paul and Hank. Paul secured the enthusiastic support of Andy and Aunt Charlotte, who offered to cover for them with the kids. He'd picked them up at the Saint Croix airport the day before, with an impatient Andy broadcasting their status as "still shackin' up."

The pitch of the 757's engines lowered as the plane began its descent. Bunched at their windows, the four watched as the jet broke through a thick cloud cover. Sparkling lights separated by the dark patches of Seattle's Lake Union and Lake Washington appeared below as the pilot made a sweeping turn south over the Emerald City toward Sea Tac airport.

******

It was rare for Connie to sleep past sunrise. Today, the last to awaken, she threw on her bathrobe and followed the sound of his laughter. Wyatt greeted her as he and his teenaged daughter, Erin, sat at the kitchen table eating breakfast. "Morning, Sweetheart. Coffee?"

"Coffee'd be nice. Pretty early isn't it? When did you get here, Honey?" she asked the girl, bracing herself for the usual snarky reply. But today, Erin tried out a new tactic and avoided eye contact, pretending not to have heard the question.

"Erin, Connie asked you a question," Wyatt chided her, as he poured the coffee.

"Oh, a while ago, I guess." She stood and grabbed her jacket. "Anyway, I've gotta go. Kelly and I are catching a bus over to Bellevue to check out the new rock climbing center. Her boyfriend got a job there and he can get us in for free." She kissed her dad on the cheek, gave Connie a cursory scowl and quickly departed.

Although Connie had no trouble brushing off Erin's attitude, it bothered her to see Wyatt so affected by the surly seventeen-year-old. "It'll get better," she reassured him. "She's just going through a phase."

"I don't know how much of it's a phase and how much of it's Gretchen," Wyatt replied, referring to his former wife.

"Well, that one's a bit harder to answer. Seems like the lady still has a thing for you. Of course, I can't blame her." She moved behind him and massaged his shoulders. "It puts Erin in a difficult position, though. If she likes me, then she's not on her mother's side. Wow, you're too tight here, Mister. Relax."

"OK, let's change the subject then."

"Fine by me," she replied, working on his rigid trapezius muscle. "Now shut your eyes and let my fingers work their magic."

He was only able to stay quiet for a minute. "You know, I don't think it's that Gretchen wants anything to do with me, I just think she doesn't want me with anybody else."

Smiling, she leaned down and gently kissed him. "Good point, now be quiet, Wyatt."

The gradual relaxation of one muscle seemed to firm up another and the laughing therapist was soon fireman carried back to bed. Awakened by hunger pangs a couple hours later, Connie left a snoring Wyatt and returned to the kitchen for a toasted peanut butter and banana sandwich, a favorite of hers since childhood. Taking her meal and laptop out to the sun porch, she scrolled through her emails and found the weekly update from Carl Logan, an agent assigned to keep her abreast of the ongoing investigations she'd been familiar with. Nothing of interest jumped out as she perused the secured document until she read the afterthought Agent Logan had added as a postscript.

> *Salvador Boitano may be losing his grip as mafia leader. Informant says lack of retaliation for Buddy Falco's apparent murder, as well as his advancing years, has diminished confidence in his ability to lead.*

She recalled the evening in her condo when she'd linked the attack on Paul Armstrong's wife and two friends to the murder of Buddy Falco. She'd always been surprised how easily the mafia seemed to have bought the theory that Buddy and his two associates were taken out by a small-time island gang when a drug deal went bad. A major crime figure's murder

9

almost always resulted in a few murders in retaliation and that hadn't occurred. Now, with pressure mounting on Boitano, a rekindled search for Buddy's killer may be in the works. She replied to Agent Logan, requesting that he include a weekly update on the mob boss in his report.

3

After nearly a year of self-loathing and despair, Paul Armstrong's life was once again on an even keel. There were still times however when flashbacks made sleep impossible.

He took the hotel stairs down five flights to the lobby and left the building through revolving doors. Zipping his jacket, he pulled up the hood and made his way along the empty, wet sidewalk.

He hadn't left a note. If she awoke she wouldn't worry. It wouldn't be the first time. He knew it made her sad that he was still tortured and she was powerless to help. But Sienna didn't make demands or set timetables. "We're exactly where we're supposed to be. You'll get through it. I'm just grateful to have you back."

Walking helped. His insomnia had become less frequent. Tonight was the first bout in nearly a month. He turned off Union onto Second Avenue and headed north. Even in the heart of the city, the smell of evergreen trees sweetened the cool morning air and rekindled memories of his life before Saint Croix. Although grateful for his life now, the optimism he'd felt as a young man in this city had been replaced by a lingering sadness.

He veered west toward the waterfront and came back along Alaskan Way. His mood, as well as the sky, had brightened when he reached the hotel. Inside the lobby, a small Starbucks was already up and running. Leaving the elevator, he balanced the tray of two cappuccinos and almond scones in one hand and fished out the key card.

Expecting to find her sleeping soundly, he quietly entered the room. Instead, wearing a white terrycloth robe, Sienna came out of the steamy bathroom, toweling off her wet hair.

"I bring gifts, Fair Lady," Paul announced, holding the tray in front of him.

"You know, Paul, it might be nice if you'd ask me to join you on one of your night-time adventures. I've been waiting for you since I heard you leave," she motioned to the morning paper spread over the bed. "I hope you didn't wear yourself out." She slipped off the robe and let it drop to the floor. Taking the offered tray and setting it on the desk, she reached for his hand. "You look cold, Honey. I think I can warm you up more than that coffee."

Sienna laughed as Paul quickly peeled off his clothes, his earlier gloom now gone. "The socks," she moaned, as his mouth covered her nipple.

******

The thunderous pounding on the hotel room door jarred Paul awake. "You gonna stay in bed all day?" Hank asked, as he pushed past Paul into the darkened room and pulled open the black-out shade. Paul squinted at the sunlight and watched as Hank helped himself to the left-over scone.

"Sienna told me you took one of your *walk-abouts* last night. Oh, and by the way, they're down at the spa getting facials."

Paul rubbed his head. "Timeisit?"

"Noon. But really, it's 3 pm in Saint Croix. Come on Van Winkle, get dressed unless you plan on wearing that bathrobe outside. We've got people to do, things to see."

Muttering, Paul retreated into the bathroom for a quick shower and shave. Fifteen minutes later, he was scrambling east on Pine Street attempting to keep up with Hank's full head of steam.

"Hey Hank, where we going? What's the damn hurry?" Paul asked, pausing at a crosswalk.

"We've only got an hour and the girls will be looking for us. I thought we might drop in on the nearby pot shop and pick up some legal weed." Hank charged off again as the light changed.

Didn't see that one coming, Paul thought, catching up with him. "Why not wait until we get up to Barney's? I'm sure he's got plenty . . . and it'll be free."

Arriving at the dispensary, Hank held open the door. "Times are a changin' my friend. It's like the first moon walk. This is history we're taking part in. I used to bust people for having it. Now, it's legal to buy the stuff. Besides, we're on vacation and we're not seeing Barney 'til tomorrow."

After a lengthy explanation by the heavily pierced and tatted saleswoman on the effects associated with the different strains, Hank purchased two grams of *Kickass*, along with a small glass pipe and a Zippo lighter.

"So where you plan on lighting up, Cheech?" Paul asked on their walk back to the hotel.

13

"I hadn't thought of that," Hank replied, perplexed. In a minute his face brightened as he pointed over Paul's shoulder. "How 'bout over there?"

The sound of thousands of gallons of water tumbling over concrete ledges designed by Halprin Associates, had provided a welcome break from Seattle's downtown urban landscape for over thirty years. And now, Paul thought as he followed Hank up a secluded pathway behind one of the park's many waterfalls, a good place for an ex-police chief to get high.

Hank took two deep drags then offered the peace pipe to Paul.

"No thanks, I'm still experimenting with sobriety."

Hank laughed at the remark which turned into a brief coughing spasm. After which he commented, "You know; you really do have an unusual way of looking at things. How does this *experimenting* square with the occasional beer I've seen you enjoy?"

"And don't forget the special occasion, Martinis," Paul reminded him.

"Yeah. How does that work into your sobriety experiment?" Hank took another hit then continued, "Actually, I've been meaning to bring something up, but never really found the right time."

"And now that you're loaded, you've found it?"

"Exactly!" Hank looked down at the pool below and appeared lost in thought.

"Hank . . . You were saying?"

"OK, take the surface of that pond. Every falling drop creates a ripple."

"And?"

"Well, last year when you left the tracks; went over the cliff, lost it . . ."

"Yes, I remember."

"Sure you do. Of course, it's just that there are still ripples rolling around that I don't understand."

"Such as?"

"Not sure how to describe it, other than you seem different. More guarded . . . and what happened to all your music? I haven't even heard you play the guitar since you came back."

Neither spoke for several minutes. Hank turned and looked directly at Paul. "Is there something more going on with you? You can tell me, you know. Roxanne and I would do anything for you and Sienna. You know that. Right?"

While he never doubted Hank's loyalty to him, Paul had chosen not to tell Hank of the murders. He thought it would be too great a burden for the retired Police Chief to bear. After he'd pulled himself back from the abyss and regained a measure of control over his life, he had told Sienna and his life-long friend, Barney. Other than the two of them and Andy, who had helped dispose of the bodies, only the fish knew what had happened to Buddy Falco and his two associates.

Hank continued, "Look, I know a lot about this PTSD business. You guys went through hell when Sienna got attacked and everybody heals at their own rate. It just seems sometimes, you've given up on having fun. I'm actually glad you started drinking a little again."

Paul shrugged his shoulders. "I almost lost everything, Hank. I do feel like I need to keep a tighter grip on myself. I never want to go down that rabbit hole again."

"OK, enough said. I probably said too much already. Just remember that I'm here if you ever want to talk about things."

"I appreciate it, Hank. I really do."

15

"Looks like we've got a full day ahead of us." Hank stood. "The girls told me that they want to visit Pike Place Market before dinner . . . I know you're gonna like my buddy, Wyatt. Haven't seen him in years. He was in a bad marriage and his ex wasn't too crazy about me. Go figure. But he's out of that mess and it sounds like he's pretty serious about the gal he's bringing."

Paul shook his head and chuckled as Hank wobbled down the sidewalk in front of him. Soon, however, he stepped aside. "This stuff is intense. I think you better lead."

They found the girls sipping margaritas in the hotel lounge. Not realizing that Roxanne had already spotted him, Hank signaled Paul to silence as he crept toward her from behind. He placed his hands on her shoulders and whispered, "Hello Beautiful."

"Ricardo, I told you that my husband might return any minute. You'll have to be more patient."

Hank's THC fueled roar-of-a-laugh brought the girls immediately up to speed on what he'd gotten into. Sienna threw a questioning look at Paul who shook his head and smiled. "We'll need to keep an eye on Hank today. It's questionable whether he could have found the hotel on his own."

"It's true." Hank agreed, taking a seat next to Roxanne. "I'm a bit twitterpated."

Roxanne took his face in her hands, gave an exasperated sigh and kissed him fully. "That's OK, Hanky-Bear. We're on vacation. I might even join you and then we can look out for each other. But first, let's get something in that big stomach of yours."

Finishing their lunch, they headed up to their rooms, agreeing to meet in a half-hour for a cross-town walk to Pike Place Market.

******

Once in the room, Sienna and Paul called home to check on the kids. Aunt Charlotte answered and said that Andy and the boys were out picking mangoes. "AJ and Red found an old abandoned orchard yesterday about a half-mile down the hill, off Creque Dam Road. They took the ATV out first thing this morning."

Sienna's brow knitted. "I'm not sure I like the kids riding in that cart, especially on Creque Dam."

"Actually, Red's driving and Andy's in the trailer cart with AJ. But don't worry, Honey, most of their route is off road and you know Red's a much better driver than Andy."

"That's true," Paul chimed in, giving a thumbs-up sign to Sienna. "No worries. Did Rose go with them?"

"Of course, she'll probably eat more mangoes off the ground then they'll find in the tree. So, everything's great here. Now listen to your Aunt Charlotte, this is the time for you two to focus on each other. I mean, really enjoy each other! Now get back to your vacation and give Hank and Roxanne a kiss from us. We'll talk soon."

After they disconnected, Sienna sat motionless on the bed, staring blankly at the wall.

"Sienna?" Paul sat beside her.

"Seemed like Aunt Charlotte didn't want to stay on the phone. I'm usually the one that ends our conversations."

"And what? You think something might have happened and she isn't telling us?"

17

"I don't know. It just seemed strange."

"Well, if she had been covering something up, I think she'd have chosen a smoother alibi than Red driving the ATV with Andy and AJ bouncing along behind in the cart."

"Yeah. What about that?"

"You know what I think? I think that we've been under a lot of pressure and we're too used to having problems to deal with. I think she cut the conversation short because she wants us to forget about everything and enjoy three weeks of no responsibilities."

Sienna sighed and turned to him. He was drawn deep into the pools of her amber eyes. He put his arm over her shoulder and drew her into him. "Maybe I should ring Hank and Roxanne's room and lobby for another half hour?"

Smiling, she pulled back and dropped her gaze, "For sure, we definitely need to take more vacations."

The extension was gratefully granted. "We were just going to call and suggest the same thing," Roxanne giggled over Hank's Tarzan yell in the background.

Paul helped Sienna pull the sweater over her head.

"Watch the earrings, Loverboy."

4

Ducking inside from a sudden rain squall, Wyatt and Connie arrived first at the popular Seattle restaurant. Named after a major thoroughfare that passes through The Burgundy Region of France, the restaurant, RN 74, was three blocks from The Fairmount Olympic Hotel, where the two couples were staying.

Hank, Roxanne, Paul and Sienna arrived a few minutes later, shaking the rain from the two umbrellas that the wise hotel doorman had insisted they carry. The ladies used the restroom while Hank and Paul were led to their table. Wyatt stood as they approached.

"You haven't changed much," Hank noted, as the two men embraced.

"Neither have you. You're still full of bullshit," Wyatt replied, laughing.

"Paul Armstrong, I'd like you to meet one of SPD's finest . . . Wyatt Howard." The two men shook hands as Hank added, "But watch this guy, Paul. Wyatt's a smooth operator; the strong silent type. We need to keep a close eye on our women."

Wyatt started to reply, but Paul stopped him. "Don't worry, Wyatt. I pretty much ignore everything he says."

19

"Hey, that really hurt," Hank replied laughing, as the three men took their seats. "Where's this gal you've been telling me about?"

"Drying off in the lady's room. We didn't bring an umbrella," Wyatt replied, pointing a finger at his temple and firing.

"Well, they're all in there together. My guess is that they've already met. Seriously, you look great, Wyatt."

"Yeah, I hate to come off as all rainbows and butterflies, but . . . I guess love **is** best the second time around."

"I think we're all second time arounders," Hank added. "Right Paul?"

"One of my favorite songs," Paul agreed. "How'd you meet her?"

******

Reapplying her lipstick at the mirror, Connie briefly caught eyes with Sienna as she followed Roxanne into the restroom. *What an exotic, beautiful woman*, she thought. *Maybe an actress or a model?* But something else was pulling at her. The actress/model looked familiar.

"Good thing the doorman at the hotel insisted we take umbrellas," Roxanne said, opening her purse and moving next to Connie, while Sienna entered a toilet stall.

"Wish *we'd* thought of it," Connie replied. "You'd think people who live here would know better."

On a hunch, Roxanne put down her lipstick and asked, "Say, by any chance are you with Wyatt Howard?"

Smiling, Connie turned and put out her hand. "Yes, I'm Connie. And you are?"

"I'm Hank's wife, Roxanne. Sorry I didn't know your name. You know how men are. The only thing Hank told me was that Wyatt said you're the one he's been looking for. Of course, him being a police officer, we weren't sure if that was a good thing."

The two women laughed as Sienna joined them at the mirror and washed her hands. "I'd say, definitely a good thing. Hi Connie, I'm Sienna."

The name hit her like a freight train. Instantly making the connection, she fought hard to compose herself. Smiling, she missed a couple more beats before replying, "Sienna . . ." but stopped herself just in time before adding Armstrong.

Sienna didn't miss the reaction as she took the offered hand. She saw Connie's reaction again, as Hank introduced her to Paul at the dinner table. Quietly sipping a vodka Martini as Hank launched into stories of Wyatt and him in Atlanta, she casually studied Connie and wondered what to make of it.

"The computer class was usually out by four, so we'd jump on the Vespa that Wyatt was renting—"

"You two wide-bodies on a motor scooter?" Paul interjected. "That must've been a sight."

"Think what you want, Paul, but I'll tell you those southern belles loved it when we'd pull up to our favorite watering hole. We usually had three or four drink offers before taking off our helmets. Ain't that right, Cisco?"

"Right you are, Poncho," Wyatt replied, casting a nervous glance at Connie, who didn't appear to be following the conversation. He leaned over and kissed her cheek. "Hey Babe, just take Hank's stories with a grain of salt."

"No, no. They're great stories. I'm sorry. I was just thinking about an email that came in this morning."

"What do you do?" Sienna asked.

"I'm with the FBI."

"She's actually the special agent in charge of the entire Seattle division," Wyatt boasted.

Sienna felt the adrenalin coursing through her veins as she caught Paul's attempt to mask his own startled reaction to the disclosure.

"It may be more correct to say that I *was* in the FBI. I'm on a six-month furlough burning through some stored-up vacation time. When I'm through, I'm not sure if I'll be going back to the agency."

Wyatt took her hand. "If the FBI has anything to say about it, Constance Hunter will be back. They love her there."

"Agent Hunter. Of course, I've heard of you," Hank said. "I used to work with a bunch of agents when I was at New York's Port Authority. You have quite a reputation out here on the left coast." Turning to Paul he added, "They called her *The Bloodhound*. Said she could unravel a plot by just sniffing the wind."

Connie laughed and despite the situation, felt herself relaxing. "Only if I was downwind from the crime."

"So, what made you decide to take a furlough?" Hank asked.

"When my brother Adam was killed . . . almost two years ago now . . ." That was as far as she got. Wyatt took her hand as tears welled in her eyes. "I'm sorry. I seem to be doing that a lot lately." She dabbed her eyes with the tissue Sienna offered and continued, "Now, so much has changed in my life. Everything seems different. I love my work, but I'm ready for a new chapter."

Drawn to Connie's openness, Sienna reached over the table and took her other hand.

Looking directly at Sienna, Connie continued, "Adam used to say there are no coincidences in life and if we stay open, the universe will provide all we need." She gently squeezed Sienna's hand. "Everything happens for a reason."

A second round preceded the first course. Then, over dinner Roxanne and Hank described Windsol to Wyatt and Connie.

"Sounds idyllic," Connie said.

"We'd love to visit you guys down there," Wyatt added.

"Make it soon," Paul encouraged.

"Well, I've got a bunch of vacation stored up, and Connie already told you her situation. Would early next month be too soon?"

"No, that'd be great," Paul replied.

"Not soon enough," Connie and Sienna chimed in at the same moment.

Then laughing, they both added, "No coincidences."

*****

Conversation filled with plenty of laughter continued through the three-hour dinner. "So, what's next for you guys?" Wyatt asked Hank, as they sipped their Cognac.

"Well, we've rented a big SUV and we're heading up north for a few days . . . a little town called Quilcene. You know it?"

"Of course. I've passed through there several times on my way to the Olympic Mountains."

"We're staying with some friends who are also Windsol residents. Then we're heading out near the coast to a natural hot spring called Sold Your Duck, or some crazy thing like that."

"You mean Sol Duc. You'll love it. That whole region's incredible."

Turning to Paul, Wyatt asked, "Have you spent much time in the Olympics?"

"I actually lived with the friend that we're staying with in Quilcene after my first marriage went TU. I did a lot of hiking in the mountains . . . was good therapy."

"I agree. Nothing like sitting around a campfire after a long day of hiking. It's the best kind of therapy," Wyatt replied, looking questioningly at Connie.

"Oh yeah, you bet. Hiking and camping . . . definitely right at the top of my bucket list," a now slightly tipsy Connie replied sarcastically. "In fact, why wait? I think tonight we should just skip our shower, pee in the bushes and sleep on air mattresses in the backyard."

"Now that's my kind of girl!" Roxanne whooped. "I'm with you on that one, Connie. We love our big burly men but let *them* go commune with nature. You and I'll find a day spa."

Hank sighed, "It looks like if the guys take a hike one day, we'll have to leave the ladies to their creature comforts."

"Excuse me," Sienna cut in. "I'd love to have a spa day with Connie and Roxanne, but if there's a backpacking trip planned in the Olympics, not all of the ladies will be heading for the spa."

"A toast then," Connie said, "To strong willed women who know their own mind."

"And to the men lucky enough to have found them," Hank added.

"Very smooth," Paul chuckled. "You still working off the earlier damage?"

"My Hanky-Bear got over-served at a dispensary today," Roxanne explained.

"Hank smokes weed?" Wyatt asked, almost spitting out his Cognac.

Hank reproached her. "Jesus, Roxanne, you tell that to a cop and an FBI agent?"

"Relax, Hanky-Bear," Paul laughed. "Tell them about the moon-walk analogy."

"Well, I just think that times are changing and this whole legalization-thing is a momentous event of historic proportions."

"Like the moon-walk?" Connie guessed, barely holding back her laughter.

"You got it, Sister," Roxanne chirped. "The similarity was even more apparent at the Pike Place Market this afternoon when—"

"Wait, let me tell this part," Sienna joined in. "It was like he'd never seen a vegetable before. He might as well have been on the moon."

"Oh, oh . . . Wait!" Roxanne raised her hand. "How about that evangelical ministry group he assaulted?"

"In his defense," Paul explained, resting his hand on Hank's shoulder, "it wasn't really an assault so much as a respectful insertion of a differing viewpoint. And just to make sure there were no hard feelings—"

"He asked all five of them to join us for dinner this evening," Roxanne finished.

"I thought it would spark some interesting conversation," Hank whined defensively.

"But they didn't come," Connie observed, joining the roast. "Did they turn you down?"

"They asked if there would be liquor involved and all three of us shouted, 'Definitely!'" Sienna explained, now in tears, herself.

"Well thank god for booze then," Connie quipped.

"And the law," Wyatt added. "Or I might have had to drag his big ass downtown for a night in the pokey."

"They still call it the pokey?" Sienna asked.

"Only when we book a true desperado," Wyatt replied.

"Or an astronaut," Paul added.

"You guys are heartless." Hank held the door open as they exited the restaurant.

******

"You awake?"

"Yeah. Fun night wasn't it."

"I can't sleep. I think she knows about Buddy Falco."

"I'm sure she does," Paul turned over in bed to face her. "She's in the FBI."

"I mean, she knows something about *us* and Buddy Falco."

Paul thought for a moment before replying. "What makes you think that?"

"When we met in the bathroom, there was . . . something . . . a look in her eyes, like she already knew about us. I saw the same thing when you two were introduced."

"I'd like to say that you're being paranoid, but I saw it too. Also, there was something familiar about her. I felt like I'd seen her before. Did she look familiar to you?"

"No, not at all and you know I'm good with faces. But, remember when she was saying the thing about the universe providing and that there are no coincidences?"

"Yeah, she said her brother used to say that."

"Then she looked *right at me* and there was definitely a moment that we connected. She squeezed my hand when she said, 'Everything happens for a reason.' I really think she was sending a message."

The neighboring buildings cast a low light through the sheer drapes. Too dark to make out Paul's features, Sienna could tell by his labored breathing that his face was masked in worry. Speaking barely above a whisper, she continued, "Look, if you put it all together, maybe she knows that you killed Falco but wants us not to worry because . . . I don't know why . . . just not to worry."

"I love you, Honey, and believe me . . . I've learned to trust your intuition, but you may be reaching on this."

"Still, if she does know something, I just hope I'm right."

5

They took their coffees to the outside balcony and looked down as the last car boarded the ferry. The ship's horn blasted the deck crew into action as the clanking chain guards were wrestled into position. The engines' vibrations rumbled through the rounded steel hull, as they pulled away from Seattle's Pier 52.

"A million-dollar view for the price of a ferryboat ride," Hank said appreciatively, as their perspective of Seattle's skyline widened.

Following Paul up to the sundeck, they leaned against the guardrail, sipping their Starbuck's.

"That's Queen Anne Hill," Paul said, pointing north. "See that large building just below the towers on top? That's the old Queen Anne High School. It was converted into condominiums after the baby boomers grew up."

As the ferry continued across Elliott Bay, he pointed at the coastal edge of an adjacent hill. "I grew up south of here, but any kid growing up in the city back then could tell you about Perkin's Lane being a great place to watch the submarine races."

"What?" Roxanne blurted. "If they were racing underwater, how could you even see them?"

28

"Honey, he was joking. As hard as it is to imagine, he was probably implying that he was some kind of teenage Casanova," Hank explained.

"Oh . . . Well, that doesn't really seem right either." Roxanne punched Paul on the shoulder.

After a thirty-five minute crossing, the cars disembarked in Winslow, a small hamlet in the bedroom community of Bainbridge Island. With only coffee and scones fueling them, Paul drove to the nearby Streamliner Diner, an old Winslow haunt of his, for a hearty brunch.

"I'm really excited to finally see Barney's farm." Hank patted his full belly, after tossing down a steak and eggs breakfast.

"And to finally meet Joey and Brooke," Roxanne added. "How long of a drive do we have?"

When Paul didn't reply, Hank snapped his fingers. "Paul? Earth to Paul. Come in please."

"Oh . . . sorry. What was the question?"

"She asked if you were planning on driving the rest of the way commando."

"C'mon Hank," Roxanne laughed, taking her husband's arm. "Take it easy on Paul. You know these artiste types. They're always day-dreaming."

Enjoying the stroll back to the car, Sienna observed, "I love Saint Croix, but it's really nice to be able to walk on sidewalks and not have to watch your footing every second."

"That's for sure. You've got to be on high alert at home. The uneven steps and pavement aren't the only hazards. Those low arches could knock your head off at any second, if you're not paying attention," Paul added.

"True," Hank replied. "But I can tell you this . . . I haven't seen one chicken, rooster or runaway horse and I'm missing 'em. Saint Croix might be crazy, but it's my kind of crazy. This place is too perfect; just like out of a movie set. It really makes me miss our island's chaos."

"Does this mean Hanky-Bear wants to head home early?" Paul joked.

"Hell no. I'm having a ball." Opening the rear door of the rented SUV, Hank helped Roxanne in and got in beside her. "Hey Sienna, any idea what's rattling around in that empty head of our tour guide today? He seems a bit preoccupied."

"Maybe he's trying to figure out a way to stop your nose from sniffing up his business," Roxanne said, leafing through the O Magazine she'd bought for the car trip.

"Andrew Sherman and Paul entertained an investor at RN 74 a couple months before he disappeared. I think the dinner brought up some memories," Sienna ad-libbed.

"Oh, sure. That's understandable. Jeez Paul, I bet back then you'd have never guessed in a million years what your life would be like now."

"You got that right, Hank. I'm a *very* fortunate man."

Sienna leaned over and kissed him on the cheek.

"Watching you lovebirds is either going to make me carsick or get me too worked up for the drive," Hank kidded. "I might need to stick you two in the back seat and take over at the wheel."

Of course, Paul's distraction hadn't been caused by any association with the restaurant. He was still turning over the late night's discussion he'd had with Sienna. Long after she'd fallen asleep, Paul lay awake recalling their encounter with the FBI agent. Despite Sienna's take on Agent Hunter's message, he couldn't help but worry.

******

At the Scandinavian themed town of Poulsbo, Hank and Sienna changed places. Continuing north, the evergreen scented air they'd been enjoying through open car windows was replaced by the salty and sweet odors from the tidal flats, as they crossed the two-mile-long Hood Canal Bridge.

"There's a high and low tide differential of over fifteen feet in some parts of Puget Sound," Paul explained, nodding toward the seaweed thatched shoreline.

"I bet the clamming's pretty good up here," Hank replied.

"Clams, oysters, Dungeness crab, geoduck, they're all here for the taking."

"Maybe we need to develop a Windsol 2."

"The thought has crossed my mind. Although, I'm pretty certain Andy would want to build it in Eastern Washington and unless you'd want to bankroll the project, the location would be up to him."

"No thanks. I'm just fine with the spend less/work less approach to life. Besides, from everything Andy and Charlotte have said about Eastern Washington, it sounds like it's beautiful over there, too."

"I don't know that I could live there. I'd miss the saltwater. There are lots of lakes and rivers, but growing up near the sea is something that just gets in your blood. East of the mountains is drier and hotter in the summer and much colder in the winter. It's a lot more rural with orchards and farms everywhere. 'More room to spread out,' Andy likes to say . . . Well, I don't think we'll be looking at a Windsol 2 for a while anyway. After the last couple of years we've all had, taking on a big construction project just sounds like a lot of work."

"Speaking of work, that was quite a coincidence that I'd heard of Connie from the agents in NY. I know I said it last night, but I wasn't just blowing smoke . . . Connie has an amazing reputation on the force. She's probably not much over forty . . . Seems a little crazy to walk away from that kind of career. I don't get it."

"Yeah, who knows what makes someone tick."

"I can see why Wyatt's crazy about her, though. She's great, don't you think?"

"Yeah, she's terrific."

"Roxanne and I were talking last night about how well the six of us got along at dinner. Good chemistry with the group. So, what would you think about having them join us in Winthrop for a few days?"

Overhearing Hank, Sienna said, "I think that'd be great, if Kate and Carmen are OK with it. How about you, Paul?"

"Sure, I'd enjoy getting to know them better."

"I'll text Kate and ask her," Sienna said, pulling out her iPhone.

Kate's reply was immediate, "The more the merrier. We can't wait to see you guys."

Driving into the courtyard of Barney's farm, twenty minutes later, they were noisily greeted by a half-dozen mixed-breed dogs. Two of the larger dogs stood on hind legs barking excitedly through the open car windows before being shooed away by the big man himself.

"Go on! Get! Christ, my cattle ranch has turned into a fuckin' animal shelter and posy farm. See what women do to you?" Barney greeted them as they stepped out of the car, each steeling themselves for a smothering bear hug from the six-eight, three hundred-pound giant.

"I've got coffee and warm cookies fresh out of the oven," Claire shouted from the porch.

"You got a cold beer in there?" Hank countered.

"With cookies?" Claire shrugged her shoulders and turned back inside. "Suit yourself."

"She's really proud of her baking." Barney explained apologetically. "No worries though, Hank, there'll always be beer in the fridge as long as I'm above ground."

Roxanne winked at her husband. "Coffee will be just fine. Hanky-Bear can last at least until noon without alcohol."

Lagging behind, Hank threw Paul a WTF look. "Let it go Hank. It's just Claire."

It had been several months since Claire and Barney had been to their cabin in Windsol. Sitting around the big round kitchen table over coffee and cookies, Roxanne brought them up to speed on the island's latest news. "The Chinese are buying the oil refinery to use as an oil storage depot."

"Horse shit. That doesn't sound like it will give the island's economy much of a boom." Barney shook his head disparagingly. "Hell, I've been dubious from the start. You've got too many hands in the pot with Hovensa, the VI government, and the EPA all wanting what they want, reasonable or not. Don't see much good coming from all this for a long while."

"Actually, I'd like to see the whole plant taken down and the site cleaned up." Roxanne stood and refilled her coffee cup. "Put a cap on the site and build a big golf course or something."

"Golf? Since when are you a golfer?" Barney asked.

"I'm not a golfer. I'm just saying, I don't care what goes in there, but we need to move away from our dependence on fossil fuels. I'm real excited to see all the solar panels springing

33

up on the island. If I had anything to do with it, I'd put in a huge solar farm."

"I like that idea. But, the island needs jobs. Lots of our friends had to leave after Hovensa closed." Sienna reached for her second cookie.

"Well—," Paul started.

"Oh, here we go," Hank interrupted. "We just need to legalize pot on the island and we'll all be rich."

"Speaking of which," Barney said to Paul, "I'm back in the business. Had to put up another greenhouse 'cause Brooke filled up the old one with her flowers."

"What about Joey? When he moved in, you got rid of the plants and 'went legit' I think you called it."

"Yeah, well, he's nearly 18 and it's everywhere now, being legal and all. It was his idea. You'll see. The kid's really bright. Said he doesn't particularly care for the stuff, but is convinced there's good money in growing it."

"Actually, Joey had the idea, but I was the one who made it happen." Claire countered. "Even with Brooke, Joey and me on board, it took some well-crafted feminine wiles to convince Barney."

Hank raised his cup "Here's to wily women and their impact on historic events."

"It's still a federal crime," Barney explained, after the laughter died down. "But so far, the feds don't seem too worried about it. I think they're waiting to see what happens here and in the other legalized states before deciding which way to head on the issue. It's kinda like what happened with overturning prohibition; a few states led the way and eventually the rest followed."

"Speaking of Joey and Brooke . . ."

"They're making a delivery over in Langley and hope to be back by the time we head to Tex and Sal's for dinner."

"Flowers or pot?" Paul asked.

"Flowers, Amigo. As far as the pot goes, other than a few friends, we just sell to one distributor. He does all the running around to the dispensaries . . . Look, let's get you folks settled. Hank, you and Roxanne have the back bedroom. Paul and Sienna, Joey's set up a tent for you in the orchard."

"Barney! Stop it," Claire scolded. "The tent's for Joey. You two have Paul's old cabin. There's a nice queen bed in there now."

"Oh, the tent would be fine," Sienna said. "We don't want to put Joey out of his room."

"Don't worry about it. He's turned into quite the little backpacker. Actually prefers sleeping in his tent."

"I thought you said this kid was some kinda genius," Roxanne quipped, heading to their room.

6

Sally and Tex greeted their guests on the refurbished front porch of their craftsman bungalow. Sally, nearing her due date, waddled back into the kitchen with Sienna and Paul in tow. The rest of the group headed around the house to the backyard. Joey and Brooke challenged Claire and Roxanne to a game of horseshoes, while Hank and Barney followed Tex into the woodshed.

"It's been too long," Sally said, stirring the spaghetti sauce while checking on the garlic bread in the oven.

"You look great, Sal, but why don't you let us take over here? We should be waiting on you."

"That's OK. I figure that moving around is good. If she doesn't appear in the next week, I told Tex that I'm going to start jumping rope. I am *sooooo* ready for this to be over."

While the two women conversed, Paul stepped out to the screened porch and began setting the picnic table. Looking back through the window, his heart sank as Sienna laid her hands on Sally's belly. It had been just 18 months since Buddy Falco's brutal attack and the ensuing miscarriage of their baby girl. He knew that he had much to be thankful for, but at this moment all he could think of was the injustice. Tonight, he should be holding their own child, their daughter carried and

36

cherished for five months, only to be murdered by a kick from a madman. Paul swallowed hard, tasting the bile. His heart rate quickened. His hatred for Buddy resurfaced with the same intensity he'd felt when he first laid eyes on Sienna after the attack. Buddy and his crew were monsters and he was glad he'd killed them. *Fuck the bastards. Fuck them in hell. Bring on the entire FBI, I don't give a shit. I did the right thing and I'd do it again.*

******

With smoke streaming out his nostrils, Tex passed Hank the joint. "This pregnancy has been pretty rough on Sally. She was sick as a dog the first few months. Everybody kept saying that it would get better as she went on. But, she's been nauseous since day one and it hasn't eased up a whole lot. She tried a bunch of natural stuff to help, but the only thing that worked were these little bracelets that do acupressure on her wrists. Not being able to fly down to Saint Croix has really bummed her out, too."

"But the buns coming out of the oven soon," Barney said, taking the next hit. "The three of you'll be in Saint Croix before you know it." He handed the reefer back to Tex. "So Hank, how's our practicing teetotaler seem to you these days? Any signs of his dark past resurfacing?"

"He's still pretty much off booze, although he did have a couple Martinis last night at dinner. That was the first I'd seen him drink, other than an occasional beer and frankly it was great to see him let loose a bit."

"I agree. I don't think a few Martinis are such a bad idea. He still seems tight to me. Shit, why isn't he out here with us right now?"

37

Tex shook his head, "You two are such mothers. Leave him the hell alone. Considering what those two have gone through, Sienna and Paul seem to be doing great."

"Yeah? . . . I guess you're right. I've got plenty to worry about anyway with Claire adopting every stray dog in the county and now she's pushing for marriage."

"Not sure what to say about the dogs," Hank choked out, after quelling a brief coughing spasm. "But Roxanne and I have been wondering what's been taking you two so long to tie the knot."

"Easy there, don't go coughing up a lung. We just need to be careful. That's all. Things have been going great, but with this bipolar thing . . . I guess I'm afraid to add anything to the mix."

"She seems fine to me," Tex volunteered.

"And looks great too," Hank added.

"Down boy," Barney laughed . . . "Yeah, I can't see what she sees in an ugly goof like me."

"You're not really that ugly," Hank replied assuredly. "Hell, I still can't believe that Roxanne married me. Both ladies are plenty smart though. Maybe we're a lot hotter than we think."

"Maybe they just felt sorry for you two." Tex took a final drag. "I know I do, just listening to you."

Hank started toward the doorway. "I think we need to get back while we can still find the backyard . . . Get *back* to the *back*yard . . .Now that's funny."

Tex stood and pulled open the door to the woodshed, "Oh shit. It may be too late."

Barney's loud laugh announced their reemergence as the three amigos moseyed toward the kitchen for beverages.

Claire and Roxanne watched the parade pass in front of their chaises.

"A sheriff, a former police chief and a pot farmer smoking weed together in the woodshed," Claire observed.

"Yeah, maybe we *will* see peace in the Middle East."

"You know though, things never seem to go quite like you'd expect. I mean, I was married to Paul- the handsome, All-American nice guy. But turns out, *that's* my soul mate," she said shaking her head and pointing at Barney's huge, lumbering figure, as he ducked inside the house.

"Know what you mean," Roxanne agreed, returning Hank's blown kiss just before he followed Barney inside. "I met Red's bio dad at a health club. He was a fitness instructor. You could bounce a coin off his six-pack. He was a nice guy with a great smile." She leaned closer to Claire. "Sex with Curtis was certainly acrobatic if not intimate. I'd been told that I couldn't have kids, so Red was sort of a miracle. I'm truly grateful for the experience, but the relationship was never going anywhere."

Claire paused, then spoke quietly, staring down at her hands. "I could tell the first time I saw them together that Paul never loved me the way that he loves Sienna. I think he was always afraid to open up and really give us a chance." In the flash of an instant, her face brightened as she turned toward Roxanne. "So why should I feel anything other than happiness? Paul has Sienna and I have Barney."

Though Roxanne found the conversation and the sudden mood shift strange, she let it go. "Yeah? I can't imagine divorcing a man I'd been married to for as long as you two were and not having feelings that . . . well, might keep me from wanting to be good friends. I mean it is pretty unusual that you four are so close."

"Maybe some people might think it's strange considering the hell we've all gone through together."

"I wasn't around then, but from what I understand, it wasn't really you that was causing the trouble. You weren't completely in control."

"You're absolutely right. At first I felt guilty about what I'd done, but I've *completely* let all those feelings go. I can honestly say that in the last month or so, I'm feeling better than I have in years. I not only feel *zero* remorse, I think they're all pretty damn lucky that I haven't held a grudge."

Roxanne felt like she'd missed a step. "I'm a little confused, Claire, what grudge would you be carrying?"

"I could have gotten Paul back if I'd wanted to. That's all I'm saying."

"Hey Claire," Joey called out, "C'mon, it's your turn."

******

Paul found Sienna and Sally in the brightly decorated baby's room.

Sienna happily greeted him, "Come here, Honey, and look at the mobile Sally made from sea glass."

"Wow, great job, Sal. I heard that Tex built the rocking chair."

"The wood's from a big branch off a maple tree that came down in the backyard a few years ago and I made the cushion."

Sienna hugged Sally. "I'm so excited and happy for you guys."

"Thanks, Sienna. We can't wait to bring little Katie down to Windsol."

"I'll bet Aunt Kate is excited about the arrival of her namesake," Paul said.

"She's over the moon . . . Look I know they probably wanted to tell you themselves, but they didn't say I *couldn't* tell you."

"Tell us what?"

"Well . . . Kate and Carmen are both doing in-vitro with the same sperm donor."

"What?"

"That's only part of it . . . They're carrying each other's eggs."

Paul stood in confused silence, but Sienna figured the ramifications immediately. "So, if it takes in either one of them, the child born to the birthing mom will be genetically linked to the other mom. That's incredible!"

"I can't believe Andy didn't say anything about this," Paul mumbled, still trying to understand.

"He and Charlotte don't know. You know Andy. He'd probably have cancelled their trip to Saint Croix to babysit for you guys, just to stay here and wait on the girls, hand and foot. We missed you, and Kate and Carmen didn't want that to happen either. It's so early anyway, it's kinda crazy that they even told us, 'cause the chance of either one of them getting pregnant the first try is pretty slim."

"Knock, knock." Brooke announced herself, peeking in from the doorway. "I think we need to get some food in the woodshed boys' bellies."

While dinner helped level out the effects of the THC, it didn't keep Barney from extolling the many virtues of Washington State's pot legalization.

"Violent crime is down. Traffic fatalities are down. The big Mexican cartels are losing their grip on the supply. The only

41

ones hurtin' are the private prison companies. They'll be hit hard by the drop in victimless crime. You watch though, when they can't lock people up for using it, big corporations will start growing it. Then, we'll have to watch out for them rolling over us with some GMO shit-weed."

"Uncle Barney," Joey countered, "I think you're getting ahead of yourself. I'm pretty sure there hasn't been enough time to gather sufficient data regarding the effects of legalization on violent crimes and traffic fatalities."

"You don't, eh?" Barney replied, tapping his temple and smiling at Paul. "This kid keeps his Uncle Barney in line. What'd I tell you, Paul?"

"It's hard to imagine the Barnswollow genes kicking-in with brainpower. Must be from Brooke's side," Paul joked.

"That's what you think, huh? Well, you're probably right. I tell you, there are days when I can't remember how to spell fart."

"You can relate to that," Roxanne said to Hank. "Wait until you hit the back half of fifty like my Hanky-Bear here. Once he introduced me to a couple and completely blanked out on my name. 'I'd like you to meet my wife Rrrr . . .'"

"At least I minimized the damage."

"Hardly! He followed the 'Rrrr' with 'uff' and patted me on the ass. Hardly a successful recovery."

"Well, the governor seemed to enjoy it, even if his wife didn't."

"Atta boy, Hhhhhh . . . ank! Goddamn, I've missed you," Barney roared.

"Well, OK then." Sally stood slowly. "I'd say it's past time for some music. Joey, did you bring your guitar?"

"My acoustic's out in the car. I'll go get it."

42

Tex also left the room and returned with an old battered Martin, which he handed to Paul. "I found this in an estate sale. The bridge has been lowered so the action's pretty good."

Paul just looked at the instrument without taking it. The room went silent. He looked over at Hank who gave him an encouraging wink. Nodding his head, he let out a breath and took the guitar. "I'm seriously out of practice. Not sure I can keep up with *The Kid*."

It was the first guitar he'd touched since their baby had been killed. Sienna moved next to him as he pulled a flat pick, kept in his wallet. Rusty at first, his fingers moved tentatively through positions and patterns, once second nature to him. Practically every strum or pluck of a string was accompanied by an intense feeling of sorrow. He played at first with his eyes shut, not in concentration but in a futile attempt to hide his pain from the others, as Joey played melodic riffs off his chord progressions. Finally, the peak of his emotion passed. His reddened eyes opened. Joey was intently looking at the neck of his guitar. Everyone else in the room looked back at Paul with tears in their eyes.

"I'm that bad?" he joked. Then signaling Joey, he took over the lead.

Hank and Roxanne were first on their feet. Barney and Claire followed shortly after. The dancing, singing, and laughing continued nonstop until nearly midnight.

"Where's that all been hiding?" Hank asked, over a late-night beer on Barney's front porch. "It was like you were channeling Stevie Ray Vaughan, Jimmy Hendrix and Les Paul."

Barney finished rolling a joint and looked up. "We all knew you'd quit playing. Had us real concerned. Until tonight, I'd been worried that we were gonna lose you all over again.

43

And so . . ." he lit up the joint and held it out to Paul, "Welcome back."

"Thanks Barn, but I still have too much going on inside the old belfry to dissipate my lucidity."

Barney laughed. "Jesus, Hank. Did you hear that one? Ace here can't just say 'no thanks'. He has to rub our noses in his higher education and big words."

"For the life of me, I just don't know what he's talking about," Hank joined in. "Us old stoners must really bore him."

"You have no idea," Paul replied. "Shit, pass it here and fuck you both."

******

Paul awoke before Sienna. Feeling surprisingly clear-headed, he slipped out of bed and found Barney in the kitchen, bent over the gas range covered with sizzling pans.

"Grab yourself some coffee, Ace. I figured you guys could use a good breakfast to start your day. All this stuff is right off the farm. Brooke and Joey already ate. They're out loading the pickup."

They heard a slow shuffle coming down the hallway. Barney announced, "Looks like the smell of bacon was enough to pull Hhh...ank in here."

Unshaven and blurry-eyed, Hank entered from the hallway. "I hear voices. Need coffee." Hank barely nodded at Paul and Barney. He poured two cups of coffee and returned to the bedroom.

"Told him he shouldn't have added scotch to the mix last night," Barney chuckled. "He'd a felt a lot better this morning if he'd listened to me."

Paul took a chair and updated Barney on their trip. "So, we had dinner with an old friend of Hanks in Seattle. Guy's name is Wyatt Howard . . . He's a Seattle cop."

"And?"

"Well, his date and live-in girlfriend, is the special agent in charge of the FBI's Seattle division. It looks like they may be joining us for part two of this vacation. We're asking them if they want to head over and meet us in Winthrop."

Barney looked up from the stove. "Anything worrying you about that, Ace?"

"No, nothing really, I guess. She and Sienna hit it off. She's a nice woman." Lowering his voice, Paul continued, "It's just that . . . Sienna and I had this feeling that she knows something about—"

"Forget about it. If that were true, you'd have heard from her or the FBI a long time ago." Barney lowered the heat on the burners, covered the pans and took a seat next to Paul. "Seriously, Amigo, when are you going to let go of this thing? You didn't do anything wrong and there's no one out there coming after you."

"You'd think it would be that easy. But it's not. I'm not worried for me so much as I am for Sienna. I think she's concerned that I might turn myself in."

"Why would she think that?"

"I might have said something about hiding the murders from the law, when I have nothing to hide . . . pisses me off."

"What the fuck are you talking about?"

"If what I did wasn't wrong, then why should I have to hide it? Was what I did self-defense? You and I think so, but what does the law say? Maybe I should put it all out on the table for the courts to decide. I know it says that you can't kill three people and throw their bodies in the ocean."

45

"Listen, dumb-ass, if you ended up in prison, you'd never come out. Between Buddy's mafia friends and some horny hard-timer thinkin' your pretty-boy ass is the sweetest thing he'd ever seen, I think you'd realize pretty fast that keeping secrets hadn't been your worst option."

"You find my ass attractive?"

"Dammit, Paul. This is serious shit. Even if you got a medal instead of prison time for taking those scumbags out, that's not going to stop those guys up in Jersey. And don't think you're the only one they'll come after."

"You're right. I'd never do anything to put Sienna and AJ at risk."

Barney stood. "Well, just make sure Sienna knows that, so she can quit worrying."

Sienna sensed the tension as she walked in. "What did I miss?"

Barney greeted her with a hug then returned to the stove muttering, "Don't know how you put up with this meathead of yours."

"It is a wonder," she agreed. "Paul?" She asked, pouring her coffee.

Paul spoke in a hushed tone. "I was telling Barney about meeting Connie and the feeling we both had about her having knowledge of—"

"I told him there's probably nothing to it. You two would have heard something by now if there were. Told him to get on with his life and let the whole damn thing go. Then he says—"

"Let what damn thing go?" Hank asked, appearing, this time with Roxanne in tow.

"There you go again," Roxanne scolded. "It's impossible for anyone to have a private conversation without your antennae goin' up."

"I think private conversations are overrated anyway," Claire said, following Hank and Roxanne into the kitchen. "What's left to hide after everything we've been through together?"

"Thank you Claire. An excellent point," Hank seconded.

"You guys better sit down and eat if you plan on doing any hiking today," Barney said. "The plates are beside the stove. It's serve yourself, so have at it." They didn't have to be told twice as Claire nosed-out Hank for first in line.

Paul was relieved that Hank's curiosity over "the damn thing" seemed to have dissipated as they dug into Barney's farmyard breakfast.

"Oh, it looks like Joey's heading over to your alma mater in Pullman tomorrow," Barney said to Paul, placing two large pitchers on the table. "Bloody Marys and mimosas to help take the chill off."

"That's great," Paul replied. "Does he want to go to WSU?"

"Well, as the all-conference forward for the Quilcene Rangers his junior year, I'd imagine the Wazzu coaches will be showing him a pretty good time."

"So, I can tell he's a low-key kid, but does he seem excited?"

"Not really. I think he's going over only because I told him to. He really needs to go . . . if nothing else just to check it out."

"You think he wants to go to the Udub?"

"Honestly, he doesn't seem all that interested in going to college," Claire interjected. She patted Barney's arm. "But don't worry Big-Guy, there's still plenty of time. I'll work on him."

"Probably best if she and Brooke work on convincing him and not me. When I told him he was too smart not to go, he said, 'Well, you're not stupid and you didn't go.'"

"Well, he's got you there," Hank said, reaching for the pitcher.

"Anyway, he's heading to Carmen and Kate's after he checks out Pullman. He's going to help around the ranch for a week or so. It'll give you all a chance to spend more time with him. He's quite a kid. Now that he's filled out some, I can barely pin him with one arm."

Hank poured seconds for Roxanne and Claire from the mimosa pitcher, while Sienna refilled the Bloody Marys. Taking a long draw, Hank added cheerfully, "This is one kick-ass drink."

"The mimosa's good too," Roxanne chimed in. "Really does help take the chill off. I didn't realize it gets so cold here in the summer."

"Yeah, must be in the low sixties. Brrrrr," Hank laughed. "My island girl has a very narrow band of comfort."

"But would you exchange her for a different model?" she asked, snuggling against him.

"Not for a sixty-foot Sea Ray," Hank replied, kissing her forehead.

"He's still my smitten kitten." Roxanne wrapped her arms around his neck for a real kiss.

Still thinking about the morning's conversation with Barney, Paul barely listened. The serendipitous encounter with Agent Hunter was a chilling reminder that there was always the possibility someone would connect the attack on Sienna with Buddy's disappearance. Agent Constance Hunter may have her suspicions, but lacking evidence, had probably decided to leave it alone. However, if one of Buddy's associates from the mob ever put the two events together, a hunch might be all that was needed.

7

Erin frowned as Connie's white Infinity slowed and pulled up to the curb.

"Where's Dad?" she asked, once inside.

"He had a meeting at the precinct that ran over and asked me to pick you up. I thought it might give us some girl time. How was school?"

"Ridiculous, as usual."

"Yeah? Why ridiculous?"

"The boys are jerks. The girls are snobs and my teachers are stupid."

"Wow, the trifecta. Sounds like a great time."

"Yeah right."

They rode the next ten minutes from Capitol Hill to the top of Queen Anne Hill in silence, until Connie suggested they stop for an espresso at the bistro often used for school carpool drop-off and pick-ups. She took Erin's indifferent shrug as a positive response and pulled into a vacant parking space.

While waiting in line to order, Connie noticed three men enter and separate toward different sections of the crowded bistro. She immediately recognized the pattern and sensed Erin's anxiety as one of them approached.

"So if it isn't Little Miss Perfect. Who's your foxy friend, Erin? Aren't you going to introduce us?"

"Beat it Shane."

Sizing him up, Connie noticed the dilated pupils, bloodshot eyes and even at a distance could smell the foul odor of rotting teeth. He was obviously hard into the meth he was trying to push.

"Hey Bitch, didn't your parents teach you it's not nice to be rude?"

Connie felt her own muscles tighten as Erin spun around and faced him. "What'd you call me?"

"Ask your friend here," he replied, jerking his head toward Connie. "You should be careful who you spend your time with, Lady. This girl's a real loser." He leered at Connie. "Not too bad, Grandma. You lookin' for some fun?"

While Erin stood mute, clenching her fists, Connie weighed her options. The room became silent. She realized that with his two sneering cohorts in the room, there was potential for collateral damage if she put Shane's face through a wall. Instead, she smiled and quietly suggested that the two of them head outside to discuss the matter. Confused but intrigued, he followed her.

Once outside and away from the door, she turned abruptly and moved into him. Standing toe to toe, they were about the same height, but he suddenly felt quite small. Even though her smile remained for the benefit of the voyeurs inside the bistro, her voice hardened.

"Here's the deal you little shit." He blinked and stepped back. "I could make things very tough on you and your gang of meth-heads." Agent Hunter had dealt with many bullies who, like Shane, counted on fear to control people. Her hand shot out and grabbed his crotch. Squeezing hard she continued, "I promise if I ever hear about you bothering any of these kids again, I'll make sure it's the last time."

Other than the initial scream, he was too afraid to make another sound. She gripped him harder. Sweat washed across his face. It took a long minute, but her message finally registered.

"Please stop." He whimpered. No longer playing for the crowd, he burst into tears.

"Stay here," Connie commanded. Sweeping open the door, she flashed her badge wallet and pointed at his two compatriots. "You two, out here. Now!"

Reaching Shane, now a blubbering heap on the sidewalk, his cohorts jerked him to his feet. With a shoulder under each arm, nobody looked back as the posse quickly vamoosed.

Erin smiled, "He may never be able to have kids."

"Well, we can only hope. Still feel like a latte?"

"You bet," Erin replied, enthusiastically holding the door open. Connie accepted the gesture, with a surprised nod.

"On the house, Mam. I've been trying to get those tweekers out of here for over a month," the barista commented, handing them their drinks. "I've almost come over the counter myself a few times, with that punk mouthing off the way he does."

"Hopefully, he won't be back." Connie gave him a card. "I'm on leave, but give me a call if they show up again."

"I'm Abe," he said, extending his hand. "Will do, and as long as I own this place, your coffee's on the house."

Driving home Erin chuckled, "Well, that story'll be buzzing around the home-room for a few weeks."

"Sorry it turned into such a big deal. You OK with how I handled it?"

"More than OK. It was really cool. He's always been trouble. He used to go to our school and got kicked out last year for selling drugs."

"Really, he looks 30. It's sad to see."

"Yeah, I suppose. But honestly, he was an asshole before the drugs; always saying mean things, picking on smaller kids. He mostly left me alone because of dad. Must have been really pasted to have come at us the way he did."

"Well, make sure you tell your dad or me if there's any more trouble."

Erin chuckled.

"What?"

"You really surprised him when you grabbed him. I think he'd worry more if I told you."

"With an addict, a warning is more likely to be remembered if it's accompanied with pain. It kind of breaks through the haze."

"So, are you and dad going to get married?"

The comment caught Connie completely by surprise. She looked over at Erin. Seeing the serious expression on her face, she knew she was waiting for an answer.

"We've talked about it. I think we'd both like to."

"You're no spring chickens you know. I wouldn't wait too long."

"Yeah, thanks for reminding me. That little twerp called me Grandma."

"Well, I bet he wishes he hadn't."

"So, you'd be OK with it?"

"I don't care. It's none of my business, but you seem to love each other. Why wait?"

******

It had already been a challenging day. Exhausted, Wyatt knew it still wasn't over as he parked on West McGraw outside his home. It was their night with Erin. While Connie seemed to handle it just fine, Erin's rudeness usually resulted in a shouting match between father and daughter, with Connie withdrawing into their bedroom with a cup of tea and her laptop.

Right out of the chute though, something was different. Opening the door, he thought he heard Erin laugh. Not sure what to expect, he announced his arrival, "I'm ho-ome."

"Hey Dad," Erin jumped up from the stool and gave him a hug. "Connie and I had quite a day."

"Well . . . tell me about it," Wyatt replied, throwing a curious glance over to Connie, who was pouring three glasses of Cabernet.

"You tell us about your day first." They kissed as Connie handed him his glass.

"My day was just great. I spent half of it interviewing victims of a telemarketing scam and the other half filling out my report." He took a sip of his wine. "The meeting after work was OK though. It was kind of a rap session between us old hats and the new breed just coming in from the academy."

"Sounds really exciting, Dad. Connie grabbed Shane Goldfarb's nut sack."

Her timing was perfect. Wyatt inhaled a small portion of the wine and barely blocked the rest from squirting out his nose.

"Oh my god, Daddy. Are you OK?"

"Yes, fine, fine. Now . . . What!?"

Connie served up the spaghetti while Erin described the afternoon encounter in detail. "You should have seen how cool she was through the whole thing," she concluded.

"I'll swing by and let the owner know if Shane shows up, I'll gladly pay the little creep a home visit," Wyatt fumed.

Connie started to reply but Erin jumped in, "That's what's so cool. You're this big guy who obviously can take care of himself. But, Connie, isn't as tall as I am and she completely destroyed the guy."

"Small but mighty," Connie joked.

Wyatt laughed, "Remind me to stay on your good side, Crusher, I mean Connie."

Erin started clearing the dishes. "You two relax. I'll clean up."

"Thanks Erin." Connie led Wyatt into the living room.

"What did you do with my daughter? Really, where is she and who is that in the kitchen?"

"You know what she asked me?"

"How to make a boy cry?"

"No, seriously. She asked me . . . told me actually, that she didn't think we should wait to get married. Said we weren't getting any younger."

"Wow! What did you say?"

"I told her that I thought we'd both like to. My worry is that this might be temporary amnesia and once her mom finds out about our plans, Erin will be pressured back into her earlier perspective."

"I don't know. I'm going to hope it's permanent. Just in case, maybe we get married in Saint Croix next month and bring Erin with us."

"Strike while the iron's hot?"

"At least before the aliens return my daughter."

8

It was mid-morning by the time the vacationers were on the road. When Paul pulled onto Highway 101, Roxanne leaned forward from the back seat. "I had a pretty strange conversation with Claire last night at Tex and Sally's."

"And I'm just hearing about it now?" Hank complained, sitting next to her.

"Sorry, Hank, but you weren't really in a receptive mood last night for a serious discussion."

"She's saying you were stoned out of your mind, Hanky-Bear."

"I understood what she was saying, Paul. Sheesh, can't a guy have a little fun once in a while without the fun police kicking down his door?"

Sienna turned in her seat. "What'd she say?"

"Well maybe I misunderstood her, but it sounded like she still has the hots for Paul and thinks she's owed a thank you for not stealing him back from you."

"She said that?"

"Pretty much. She also said that she feels better than ever and has zero guilt over what happened when she was manic."

Paul dropped his head and groaned.

56

"Eyes on the road there, Mister Armstrong," Hank cautioned. "Not worth rear-ending that fuel tanker ahead of us."

"Anything else? Did she seem spun up at all?" Sienna didn't attempt to mask the concern in her voice.

"No, not so much spun up. I'd say self-righteous would be a better description. I had said how amazing it was that the four of you could be so close with her having been married to Paul. She said that after all you'd been through together, you were lucky she didn't carry a grudge."

"WHAT?!" Paul's knuckles whitened as he tightened his grip on the steering wheel.

"Has Barney said anything to you about this, Paul?" Sienna asked. "She's obviously building up to something again."

"Not to me and she seemed OK when I talked to her. Are you sure you didn't misunderstand her, Roxanne?"

"I'd like to think so, but no, it's not possible."

"I think I recall Barney saying when we were in the woodshed that Claire was on him about getting married."

"And?"

"And he was holding off, out of concern that the bipolar business might heat up if too much was going on in their life."

"Do you think we should tell Barney about her conversation with Roxanne?" Sienna asked.

"I'd say no," Hank voted. "It's not really any of our business. Barney can take care of himself and Claire too, if it comes down to it."

"For now, I agree with Hank." Paul shifted forward, stretching his back. "Let's see how it plays out the next time we see them; which probably won't be until fall on Saint Croix. In the meantime, I'll check in with Barney by phone every week or so. I think he'll tell me if he's concerned."

"OK then. How much longer before we get there? If you guys are gonna take a 12-mile hike, hadn't you better be on the trail pretty soon?"

Paul looked at his watch. "We should be alright, Hank, if we can start before 2:30. Remember, it stays light until 9:00. I'd say we have another hour before we arrive at the cabins and a half-hour later you can drop us at the trailhead."

"Sienna, are you sure you want to do this? Twelve miles up and down a mountain sounds like torture to me. Wouldn't you rather come with Hank and me out to the coast and stick your toe in the Pacific Ocean?"

Sienna laughed. "Actually, I'm looking forward to it. I did quite a bit of backpacking in the Cascades when I went to school here. I've never been in the Olympic Mountains. I hear they're beautiful."

"So is the Pacific Ocean, Sweetie, and you can drive your car right to it. Suit yourself, but when you're halfway up the trail and wondering what the hell you were thinking, just remember that I tried to talk some sense into you."

******

Fresh mountain air filled their lungs as Paul and Sienna hiked through the six mile, 3,500-foot vertical climb. Reaching the High Divide Trail, they headed northwest until Sienna spotted a large flat rock just off the trail with a clear view into the Blue Glacier of Mount Olympus.

"We could have our lunch here, Paul."

"Or we could lay our blanket over here." Paul walked toward a grassy knoll, barely visible through the scrub brush about 35 yards back from the trail.

"You got ideas, Mister?" Sienna asked, following him.

"Always," he replied, bending a branch out of her way.

"Does this have anything to do with your walking behind me for the last two hours?"

"Hey, I looked at the ground occasionally, too."

They slipped out of their hiking clothes quickly.

"I'm cold, Paul. Warm me up."

******

"I bet that brought a few groundhogs out of their holes." Sienna giggled, resting her head in the crook of his arm. "You sounded like you slammed your finger in a door."

"Me? There were so many birds taking flight from your screaming, it looked like an early migration."

The ensuing wrestling match ended, as usual, with Sienna's strong legs wrapped around Paul's abdomen.

"OK, OK, I give."

Sienna released her hold, jumped up and pranced around naked with her arms above her head. "Winner, and still champion!" Dropping next to him on the blanket, she kissed him on his mouth. Slowly moving down his neck and chest, she asked, "Did I hurt you? Are you injured, Sweetie?"

"Nothing hurt but my pride . . . A little lower please . . . I have wounds that need tending."

The sun had dropped noticeably lower by the time Paul moved their packs and blanket to a trail-side lookout. He brought out the cheese, bread and nectarines from his pack, as Sienna rejoined him.

"I've enjoyed traveling with Hank and Roxanne, but next time, you and I need to take a vacation alone." Sienna kissed him languidly.

"How 'bout we find a carrier pigeon and send Hank a note to pick us up next week?"

"Think we'd find enough to keep us busy?"

"I'd be more worried about finding the pigeon."

Across the wide forested valley, they looked down on the blue glacier. A circling bald eagle's screech drew their attention upwards, as the majestic creature rode the warm air currents, searching for prey.

"I can't believe I'm finally up here with you." Paul wrapped his arm around Sienna's shoulders. "This is one of my favorite places on earth."

"Well then, it's fitting you should be here with your favorite girl." Sienna rested her head against his shoulder.

Paul felt the vibration on the ground before hearing the voices. "Horses," he explained, as Sienna shot him a questioning look.

"Good thing they didn't come fifteen minutes earlier. How many are there, Tonto?"

"Maybe two or three, Kemosabe."

The horses had already sensed their presence before the three riders rounded a bend and came into view. The two women following the male rider, however, seemed startled as Paul and Sienna stood.

Smiling warmly, the lead rider greeted them. "Hi, Folks. I'm Kent." Resting the reins over the big, gray Appaloosa's withers, he pulled a canteen off his belt and turned in his saddle. "You ladies like to step down and stretch for a bit?"

"Are you kidding me?" The rider closest to him grumbled, while waiting to be helped off the horse. "My ass is so sore that my feet've gone numb."

"No problems here," the rear rider volunteered, climbing down from her horse. "It's your bony little ass that's the problem, Terry."

"Easy for you to say Ms. Plus-Sized. All kidding aside, you can't tell me that you wouldn't rather be riding a cowboy than one of these creatures."

Paul stood silent, but Sienna laughed at the comment and walked toward the group, as Kent carefully pulled the whiner from her saddle. "Those are beautiful horses, Kent. Are you an outrigger?"

"Yes Ma'am. I have a ranch down in the Elwa River Basin. These ladies hired me for a weekend ride. Seems a lot longer though," he added in a low voice, watching Terry moan and groan her way through a series of back stretching exercises.

As they conversed, the rear rider approached Paul who smiled and greeted her. "Hi, Jan."

"Hi, Paul."

"What are the chances?" Paul said, glancing over at Sienna who was now busy helping Kent tie up the horses.

"Well, I can't say that I'm totally surprised. I've kind of been looking out for you. Terry and I have made this our annual pilgrimage since my divorce."

"I didn't know you were married. Actually, I didn't know anything about you. You did leave a note though."

"So . . . is she your wife?"

"She is. I see Terry is still complaining."

"Yeah, but you've got to give the girl credit for coming. She's not what you'd call outdoorsy and this is our third year since you and I . . . met."

61

"Seems longer to me."

"So, you finally found your mystery man," Terry said, joining them. Then looking back at Sienna added, "Looks like you're too late though. Does this mean we can do a spa in Sedona next summer, instead of dragging my ass through this god-forsaken wilderness?"

"I don't know, maybe. But, I have come to love these mountains. My first trip up here, meeting you, Paul; the entire experience gave me the boost I needed to leave a marriage that needed ending. I never really expected to find you and now that I have, I'm truly happy for you." She leaned forward and kissed him on the cheek.

"I'm glad we met as well, Jan. Now let me introduce you to Sienna."

******

"It was quite a coincidence, you two running into each other again. Are there many other Jans combing the mountains? Imagine me thinking that I was the only one besides Claire whom you've bedded."

"What makes you so sure that Jan and I—"

"You're so transparent. Don't even try. It's OK, you had to have gotten your chops somewhere. Maybe, someday, I'll tell you about some of my experiences."

"No thanks." Paul threw a rock out over the edge. They listened for several seconds before it hit and clicked its way down the face of the cliff.

"I'm really looking forward to seeing Kate and Carmen," Sienna said.

"You know, while I can picture a pregnant Carmen being very happy, it's difficult for me to imagine how Kate will survive being slowed down by a pregnancy."

"I'm sure Kate can handle anything that comes her way. She's like Andy."

"Yeah, you're right. There's no quit in that woman."

Paul stood. "Well, it would be easy to stay here longer, but I didn't bring headlamps. You ready to go back?" When Sienna didn't reply, he thought he knew the reason. "Look, Honey. It was a one-night thing. I—"

"Relax Casanova," Sienna laughed, then grew serious. "That's not it. I was thinking about meeting Connie and what she might know."

"And?"

"Let's look at this thing rationally. There's no way she could know what happened, unless you, Andy, Barney or I talked. There were no witnesses, no evidence, no bodies floated to the surface. So, there's really nothing for her to go on."

"That's absolutely true."

"Still, I know I didn't imagine her surprise when we met and there was definitely a message she was trying to deliver. I'm just not sure what it was. If they join us in Winthrop, we might find out. Hank said she was called *The Bloodhound*. Maybe she put together the connection between Falco's disappearance and the attack on Barney, Claire and me."

"Maybe, but it would only be a suspicion. Also, if she'd made the connection, she probably would have had me brought in for questioning. She might even have interviewed me herself. She wouldn't just . . ." Gasping, Paul's head dropped, his arms fell to his sides.

"Paul? What is it? . . . Paul!"

63

His face was as gray as the cloud bank rolling toward them from the coast. Drawing in a deep breath and letting it out slowly, he turned to her. She saw only the devastation behind his futile effort to appear strong. "It'll be OK, Sienna."

"What? What are you talking about?"

"Honey, she did interview me . . . and I told her everything."

9

The pilot's voice came over the sound system as the strawberry blonde served the three men their beverages. "We're passing just east of the Bahamas at an altitude of 45,000 feet. Our current air speed is mach-point-eight or just over 600 miles per hour which should put us on Saint Croix in less than two hours. Sit back, relax gentlemen and let Miss Candie know if there is anything she can do for you."

Salvador Boitano scowled at his ghost-like reflection in the Gulfstream G450's porthole window. *When the fuck did I get so old.* A blanket of clouds stretched unbroken below. Across from him, stuffed tightly in luxury seats, Vincent and Anthony giggled like school kids as they rock-paper-scissored for the first go at Miss Candie.

The jet was a flagrant example of the wealth Salvador had amassed during his lengthy tenure as head of the New Jersey syndicate. With all the pumped-up security and endless delays, Sal refused to fly commercial. Even after acquiring the jet, he avoided flying whenever possible. Intuitively it didn't seem safe putting your life in the hands of a glorified bus driver, hurtling through space at close to the speed of sound. Still, the jet was an impressive perk for the politicians and lobbyists he'd pocketed. Flying with one or two Candies and crew to all corners of the world had often been an impressive cherry on top of Sal's appreciation for their cooperation.

Startled by the jet's sudden drop in elevation he gripped the armrests. "Shit!" Then realizing they weren't going down in flames, he bellowed, "Vincent, go tell that fuckin' asshole that if he does that again, his next flight will be out a ten-story window."

"Don't worry, Boss, that's just turbulence. The pilot can't—"

"He can fly around the goddamn turbulence then, and I don't need you to . . ." he stopped himself, took a deep breath and waived Vincent off. "Oh fuck-it, never mind."

Sighing, he turned and pulled the blind down, laid the seat back and shut his eyes. *Damn Sylvie anyway.* He recalled her words before taking off. *'I'm warning you Sal, this better be a quick trip. If you back out of another marriage encounter weekend, I'll cut off your shriveled balls and use them for earrings.'*

In their fifty years together, she'd never spoken so disrespectfully to him. He didn't need it; this new backbone of hers. Rubbing his temples, he tried to block the fast-building migraine.

******

On October 12, 1967 a 24-year-old Sylvia Vizinni had arrived in New York, intent on leaving her Palermo family's Cosa Nostra ties behind. Initially, she'd refused the advances of the dark eyed, *bel ragazzo* who'd discovered her serving cannoli at a Bronx bakery, but his humor and perseverance overcame her resistance. Six months later, the chiming bells in the tower of St. Nicholas of Tolentine announced Sylvia's marriage to Salvadore Boitano.

66

It was both of their dreams, that their children would lead respectable and prosperous lives. Sal had promised Sylvia that he would legitimize the holdings of the New Jersey crime syndicate. But after the trauma of three late-term miscarriages, Sylvia was unwilling to try again.

Lacking progeny, fear of imprisonment remained his primary motivation for an *appearance* of legitimacy. He did have Sylvia to appease, but her interest in him had waned with each discovery of his numerous affairs. Besides, she knew well enough that moving from prostitution and drugs to gambling, even if it was legal, wasn't any better in the eyes of The Lord. With the realization that her past had now followed her from Sicily, she retreated further from their marriage into the only place she found solace, The Catholic Church. For over forty years, they slept in separate rooms, ate separate meals and voted for different presidents. Only during family and required social gatherings were they together. Still, she felt it a sin to divorce and he liked the back door the marriage gave him if one of his girlfriends got too clingy.

But by the time Sal hit seventy, a forklift would have been needed to lift what Viagra couldn't. His interest in chasing tail disappeared and in a moment of existential terror, he followed his wife back to St. Nicholas of Tolentine for confession. Like Jesus, Sylvie added her stamp of forgiveness to his troubled soul. For the past five years, though devoid of any physical intimacy, they had enjoyed a more caring, nurturing relationship, as Sal slid fearfully closer to life's end.

The sickening and well-publicized confessions of a pedophile priest, who'd often heard Sylvia's daily confessions, was almost cause enough. But when an elderly nun opined that God knew Sylvia would have been an unfit mother to the three babies she'd lost, that was the final straw. The reverberations from the slamming mahogany door echoed through the empty church's narthex like a bomb. Sylvia left her Catholic Church for the last time.

For Sal, apart from the social ramifications associated with the abrupt termination of their regular church attendance, he was elated. It didn't surprise him that there was something else going on under that pious prick's robe and the Catholic Church always made him nervous anyway. Although he'd taken communion and occasionally confessed selected sins to hedge his bets, Sal was much less terrified with the notion of *dead is dead* than *heaven and hell*.

But the pagan honeymoon didn't last long. Pastor Edmond was a former Catholic Priest, excommunicated when he and Sister Kathryn Kane gave up their vows of celibacy. Together, Eddie and KK led a group of fed-up Catholics in the formation of a small worship and support group. Preaching God is love and there's nothing evil about homosexuality or condoms, it was Pastor Eddie's mission to bring Catholicism out of the catacombs and into the twenty-first century. Employing familiar vestments and rituals for the subliminal Catholic still simmering within his fold, his fevered sermons challenged his flock to *Become the light of God.*

Sylvia was ripe for the mission. But for Sal, it was just another thing to endure. He grimaced through his wife's tearful emergence from her baptismal dunking in Pastor Eddie's arms . . . born again.

Encounter weekends were offered by Pastor Eddie and Sister KK as *An essential integration of God's love into our daily lives.* On two previous occasions, Sylvia had attempted to drag Sal to a quarterly-held marriage encounter weekend, but the lengthy period between each session had given him ample time to develop iron-clad excuses. When notified of a special session offered in two weeks, Sal had suspected that it had been concocted at Sylvia's behest, but nevertheless succumbed to the trickery.

******

The investigation into the disappearance of Sal's nephew and two associates had been dropped a year earlier by Saint Croix's Police Department, without turning up a single suspect. The theory that Buddy had been taken out by a gang of drug pushers might have been believable to Sal, if Buddy had been on Saint Croix by himself. God knows, he could piss people off, and the idiot did love his coke. But Stinger and V were with him. Stinger wasn't much protection, but V, that fucker was a different story. Nobody could come close to pounding on people the way V did. It just didn't make sense. No way could a bunch of punk-asses have gotten the drop on V.

Up until now, Sal had been content to ignore his suspicions. His life was much less complicated and his blood pressure had dropped twenty points since the disappearance of his idiot nephew. But blowback from the lack of retribution had been building as opinions circulated marking Salvadore as too old and too weak to head the syndicate. He needed to talk close-up to the people who had last seen Buddy alive. Most often the *threat* of violence was sufficient to make people talk, but in this case his boys might just push in a few doors and slam a few heads to loosen up some tongues. To dispel any opinions to the contrary, Salvadore Boitano was still *The Man* and it was time for someone to fuckin' pay.

69

10

Hank stepped out of the car as Paul and Sienna emerged from the trail, wearing a look of gloom and doom. "You guys look exhausted. What's the matter? You get rolled by a Sasquatch?"

"Didn't see Big Foot this time." Paul loaded their day-packs into the back of the SUV. "Twelve miles over a 3,500-foot vertical climb is a long day. The downhill part's always the hardest for me."

"How was the drive?" Sienna asked, climbing into the back seat. "Did Roxanne stick her toe in the Pacific Ocean?"

"Oh yeah. You know my woman. Nothing was gonna stop that from happening. But, we forgot to pick up rain gear like you suggested and got soaked. We spent most of the time at a restaurant in La Push drinking coffee while our clothes dried out over a radiator."

"That's too bad. So, did you get a hold of Wyatt about joining us in Winthrop," Paul asked casually.

"Yeah, he said that he'd get back to me after he talked with Connie. His teenage daughter, Erin, would also be coming."

"Joey might like that," Sienna said. "Brooke told me that he and his girlfriend split-up."

"I guess they've had a break-through with Erin. Wyatt was telling me that up until now she's been rude and bitchy to Connie; you know, like the stepmom thing. Yesterday she saw Agent Hunter take down some punks at a coffee shop and now she thinks Connie's the coolest."

"Yeah, she is cool, alright," Paul replied, barely listening to Hank's banter.

"Well, I'm sure it was just a matter of time before she'd win the girl over," Hank added to break through the silence.

They drove up to their rental cabins. "We'll give you a couple hours before heading over for dinner. Jesus, maybe you guys should take a nap or something."

Once inside, Paul and Sienna collapsed onto the thin mattress. The Sol Duc cabins were extremely sparse, as Paul had warned Sienna and the Johnsons when they planned the trip. But Roxanne gave it her blessing when she was assured they were clean and had indoor plumbing.

"Paul, we're going to have to pull it together. That was uncomfortable for Hank. I'm sure he thinks we've had a big fight."

"You're right. Look, we shouldn't assume the worst. Like you said, there was something positive in Connie's message to us. Maybe she **was** trying to tell us not to worry."

"Exactly. The fact that it's been over a year and she hasn't done anything about it . . . there must be something else going on that we don't know about . . . But I have to say, I just can't believe that you didn't recognize her. How could you spend an hour with her in the Dallas airport and not remember what she looked like?"

Paul rolled on his side to face her. "I was really drunk and she looks different then I remember. I think her hair was shorter. I do remember her telling me that I reminded her of her brother who'd been killed. Maybe it has something to do with that."

"One thing's for sure . . . she hadn't planned on meeting us. She was as surprised as we were . . . I really did like her though, and I think it was reciprocal."

"Who wouldn't like us? We're really fun." Paul took Sienna in his arms. "You know what I say, Honey?"

"What?"

"Fuck-it. It's all out on the table. Now we can just talk to her straight-up when we get to Winthrop and find out what's going on."

"You seem to be handling this pretty well, Paul. Frankly, it's a little irritating to me."

"I'm irritating you because I'm not flipping out?"

"Yes. I'm freaking out here and I'd really appreciate some company."

******

Hank and Roxanne were half-way through their cocktails when Paul and Sienna joined them at the dining table in the main lodge.

"Well, you two are looking better. I told Roxanne how that hike must have kicked your butts. That was it, wasn't it?"

"There you go again, Mr. Snoopy. If there was anything else that happened and they wanted to tell you about it, they would."

"Well, one amazing thing did happen," Sienna volunteered. "We ran into one of Paul's old girlfriends. She was riding a horse on the High Divide Trail."

"Well, well," Hank chuckled. "So, was this someone you met before Claire?"

"No, it was after my divorce."

"Really. Where did you meet her?"

"Actually, up here."

"Apparently, she's been wandering the trails looking for him ever since," Sienna interjected, rolling her eyes.

"No wonder," Hank replied laughing, "I guess, once they get a taste of single malt, it's hard to enjoy a mixed blend? Isn't that right, Killer?"

Paul winced, almost like he'd been slapped.

Surprised by Paul's reaction to just another one of his ribbings, Hank apologized. "Hey, Paul, you know I'm just kidding. Nothing serious intended here." He took a sip of his drink. "So was this a long-term thing with the mountain woman?"

Roxanne cautioned. "OK, Hanky-Bear. Let's leave our boy alone, or we'll be bringing out your checkered past for examination."

Sienna knew what had startled Paul. He was a killer, but not of women's hearts. A wave of sadness passed through her as she again realized the suffering he continued to endure.

"That's OK, Roxanne, it's just Hank being Hank," Paul said flippantly, "and no, Hank, it was just for one day."

"And one night, I assume."

The mother lion emerged. Sienna started to steam. "Seriously Hank, that might be something you'd ask him when the two of you are alone, but you might consider that both Paul and I may not want me there to hear any of it."

"Excuse me, but you brought it up. What's the big deal anyway? We all have a past with old lovers and ex-spouses. Why don't you two figure out what we can and can't talk about, and when you do, let me know." Hank stood and stalked out of the room.

"Ah Jeez," Roxanne sighed. "Now he'll probably pout for an hour, before realizing what an ass he can be. Think I'll stick with you guys. He'll come around."

Both Paul and Sienna felt bad. They were used to Hank snooping in places he wasn't welcome, but it was the "Killer" metaphor that had stirred up Sienna's anger. "I should apologize. I could have handled it differently."

"Don't worry about it, Sienna. But, I do want to bring up something he's been saying to me for a long time that might explain why he's so nosey with you two." Roxanne leaned in and spoke quietly. "When Paul came back with you last year, Hank told me that he thought there was something Paul was keeping from him. It's been quite a while since he's said anything more about it, probably figured if there was, you'd tell him when you're ready. But for some reason he felt it again when you met Connie and Wyatt. You have to understand; his entire career was built on reading people's reactions and it's impossible for him to turn it off."

"I know that about Hank. That's how we met . . . His sticking his nose into our business when Stinger turned up at Cooper Island Beach Club."

"Yeah, well . . . I thought that might explain why he's been a bit overly nosey." Roxanne stood. "I think I'll go find him and see if I can trim down his pout to fifteen minutes. I mean, come on guys, we're on vacation."

Sienna watched Roxanne leave and then turned to Paul. "Maybe keeping him out of the loop hasn't been such a good idea. If an FBI agent who only met you once didn't—"

"Maybe we should post it on Facebook . . . Sorry, but seriously, Sienna, the more people who know, the more chance someone will slip up."

"It's Hank, Honey. He's had our back ever since we met. I think his wondering and guessing may lead to a serious rift if we don't bring him in on it."

11

Pinpricks of worry ran over Connie's scalp as she read the single line from Agent Logan's email.

This afternoon, Salvador Boitano and two associates embarked by private jet for Saint Croix.

She thought only briefly before sending an email to FBI Agent Brad Harper, on Saint Croix. Pushing back from her desk in the makeshift office she'd set up in a back bedroom, she considered the potential ramifications to Paul and Sienna. She brushed aside the moral and agency conflicts that had kept her in limbo, as she quickly came to the realization that, no matter the cost, she needed to advise them of the potential threat. Although she was certain that Sienna had picked up her subtle message, were they ready to open up to an FBI agent? Was she willing to acknowledge her complicity in forestalling Paul's prosecution? At dinner, she and Sienna had exchanged cell numbers. Shrugging her shoulders, she reached for her Blackberry, but stopped when she heard Wyatt enter through the back door.

"Lucy, I'm hoo-ome." His singsong attempt to mimic Ricky Ricardo always made her smile.

"Hi Honey." Emerging from her office, they kissed and she led him into the kitchen. She pulled two glasses and a bottle of Glenlivet from the cupboard.

"Great idea," he toasted, as their glasses clinked. "It's been quite a day. I got a *'You take her'* call from Gretchen this afternoon. Seems like there's been a clashing of the minds, or hormones more likely, and Erin's gotten the boot."

"OK . . . Well, her living with us could be a good thing, Wyatt."

"You sure?"

"What's the alternative? Look, we'll make it a good thing."

"How'd I ever talk you into signing up for all this?"

"I told you, I think my brother had something to do with it."

"Here's to Adam then. Man, I owe him, big time."

"That's sweet Wyatt, but you may want to recount your blessings when you hear what I have to say."

"No way, Missy. There's nothing you could tell me that would . . . Oh, before you start, Hank called right after I got off the phone with Gretchen."

"Yeah? How's the vacation going?"

"Sounds great. Paul and Sienna were taking a hike and Hank and Roxanne had just gotten back from the ocean. Anyway, he asked if we'd like to join them in Winthrop over the weekend. I'm thinking it might be a good idea for the three of us to do something fun together. Hank says there'll be a seventeen-year-old boy there. Joey, I think's his name."

"Actually, I was just about ready to call Sienna when you got home. I think when she hears what I have to say, they'll be cutting their vacation short."

Wyatt set his drink down, a look of concern spread across his face. "OK, I'm listening."

She thought briefly and decided to tell him everything. "You remember Buddy Falco's disappearance?"

"Of course." His concern shifted toward a look of confusion. "Somewhere in the Caribbean, wasn't it? A drug deal gone bad?"

"Well, the disappearance closely followed his attack on Sienna and two of their friends."

A light of understanding sparked. "Oh shit." He drained his glass. "Go on."

"A kick from the attack caused Sienna to abort their child. Buddy's mob-boss and uncle, Salvador Boitano, has been taking heat over the lack of a reprisal for Buddy's apparent murder and—"

"He's got Paul in his sights? He thinks the architect did it? No way."

"This is the part you might want to sit down for," she said, refilling his glass.

******

The black, late model Range Rover idled in front of the private hanger, a half-mile west of Saint Croix's Henry Rohlsen Airport's terminal. The slender driver bit nervously at his stubby finger nails. George Clay was not Francis Gardner's real name, but it matched the Colorado driver's license and credit cards he'd carried on his Saint Croix arrival, two weeks earlier.

He'd easily located the four, unsuspecting subjects and spent the first week becoming familiar with their daily schedules and activities. Afterwards, the remainder of his time was spent behind the tinted windows of the Range Rover,

78

across from a popular west-end beach, peering through hi-powered binoculars at string bikini clad sunbathers and cruising the red-light district in Christiansted.

Prepared as he was, his chronic anxiety jumped several notches as he spotted the private jet taxiing towards the hanger, near the west end of the runway. Francis jumped out of the SUV, as the three men approached, and darted around its front. Practically bowing, he held the door open for Salvador Boitano. He pushed the rear hatch release for Vince and Anthony, who dropped luggage in the cargo hold before wordlessly cramming their giant frames into the back seats.

"How far's the villa?"

"We should be there in twenty minutes, Sal."

Francis's eager efforts to engage Sal in light conversation regarding the flight down were summarily tossed off, "Just try and get us there in one piece, Francis."

Arriving at the villa, he punched in the key code and followed the metal gate in as it swung open. He wheeled through a circular drive and pulled alongside the Jeep Wrangler he'd be driving now that Sal was on island.

Scrambling outside, he hooked his knee on the corner of the front bumper and painfully limped around to Sal's door. The mob boss scowled as his tiny feet touched the ground. "I don't have all fucking day, Francis."

"Right, Sal. Sorry, Boss." He carried Sal's luggage through the front door, into the vaulted entry. "Your room's the big one upstairs. Vince and Anthony's are down the hall."

"Now listen up." The boss patted Francis's breast pocket after dropping in a folded hundred. "I'm gonna need a rest. This heat ain't good for my heart. You come back and pick us up around five after it cools down a bit." Sal pushed his mirrored sunglasses above his forehead. He almost broke a smile as he looked past the carved mahogany stairway in the grand lobby, out to the pool through the tall glass doors. "The AC feels good. The place looks fine, Francis. You did all right." He sighed and found a cushioned chair. Pulling out an embroidered handkerchief he wiped his forehead. He peeled off two more fifties from a wallet sized wad of bills. "Go buy yourself some pussy, but make sure you're back by five. I don't want to spend any more time on this fucking rock than I have to."

"Thanks. Gotcha. Don't worry, Boss. I've got everything covered."

12

Sal and his boys were already waiting in the shade of a large mango tree when Francis pulled the Range Rover back into the drive court.

"So, how far to this place?"

"Take us about twenty minutes, Boss."

"I heard it's just an outdoor joint with a kitchen."

"Most of the beach bars are open down here. A.C.'s crazy expensive."

"Cheap-ass low-lifes. Skip on air conditioning, bugs swarming your food. Let's not take any longer with this than we have to."

Fifteen years ago, Sal had brought sixteen-year-old Francis on board as a favor to the kid's mother. Francis's dad, Luigi, had worked for Sal and was gunned down by an enraged spouse after finding Luigi's dick in his wife's mouth.

At first, he'd just used the kid for running errands, but then realized that Francis possessed *street smarts* and often relied on him for a second opinion when planning a course of action. Sal could be rough on him, praising him one minute then berating him the next. Francis wasn't anything like Vincent and Anthony. They'd been his muscle for over five years, since the suspicious disappearance of his former bodyguard, Tiny. With

Vincent and Anthony, there was nothing more going on inside than what was visible outside. It was easy to keep them happy; food, computer games, pussy and money, in that order. Francis was different. Sal knew that his placid demeanor was a front, but didn't really want to know what it was covering up. All he cared about was that the kid's unremarkable appearance blended in well and he was reasonably proficient at carrying out orders.

"So, we'll go in like we're tourists," Sal said, as they turned onto the island's north shore, coastal road. "This Armstrong guy must be a pretty crappy architect if he needs to tend bar on the side."

"Only does it Fridays. I think he goes in because of his wife owning the place."

"The old ball and chain. I know it well. OK, he and I'll have a little talk. Maybe give him something to think about and get an idea what else he might be capable of."

"I don't know, Boss. The impression I got is that he's just a pretty boy. Lives in kind of a hippy commune . . . you know, peace, love and all that shit."

"Yeah, I've been reading your reports, but I'm still thinking he might be our man. Remember, Buddy did attack his wife. I'm not sure that the guy's all peace and love."

"OK, good point," Francis agreed. He turned into the parking lot at The Green Flash. "But if you don't think Buddy, V and Stinger could've been taken out by an island gang, no way Armstrong could have done it by himself. He must've had help."

"I expect to have some answers shortly. With a little encouragement from the boys," Sal said, nodding toward the back seat. "Our hippy, pretty boy architect might prefer talking, over having his face remodeled."

Francis led Sal and his boys up the wooden steps into the outdoor dining room. A jolt of anxiety coursed through him when he saw the heavyset, black man tending bar.

Sal gripped his shoulder. "That doesn't look like Armstrong."

"He's probably in the back with his wife," Francis replied nervously, as the hostess seated them at their table.

Shortly after their drinks arrived, Sal signaled a waitress. "So, where's the owner and her husband?"

******

Francis hated himself for wilting under Sal's icy stare as the mob boss threw a C note on the table and stood leaning towards Francis, with his hands on the table. "Give me the keys, Francis. Pay the bill and we'll talk about this out in the car."

Francis knew he was in for it. He'd fucked up. The Armstrongs and Hank Johnson, three of the four jerk-offs that Sal wanted to *interview* were gone. The fourth, Andy Meyers, was only on island part time. Still, it was the best hope Francis had at this point.

He fought the compelling desire to run into the surf across the street and swim the 40-miles to St. Thomas, but forced himself instead to climb into the idling SUV. With ears still ringing after Vincent's vicious slap to the head, he was finally able to cut into Sal's tirade.

"Look, I know where they live. Maybe this Andy Meyers character's there."

"He'd better be, Francis," Sal growled, offering Francis a handkerchief for his bloodied ear. "He'd better be."

******

Andy was careful not to press up against the sharp thorns as he squatted behind the bougainvillea waiting for the *damn deer* that had been launching night raids on his beloved vegetable garden. AJ and Red, crouched near him, suppressing giggles as Andy shushed them. He'd only caught a glimpse of the creature the evening before, as it sprang back into the bush after gorging itself on the tomatoes. But now, spotlighted by the full moon, he was surprised by its size.

"He's a beaut, boys. Got himself a six-point rack for sure," Andy whispered. *Back in the day, I'd-a put a 45 through his eyes. Carry him out strapped to my mule.*

The buck edged forward toward the garden. "That's it, just a little farther," Andy coaxed as the animal approached the motion detector's field.

The sudden flood light's illumination and hissing of the broadcast sprinkler, sent the deer bounding into the brush. The heavy stream of water doused Andy, knocking off his straw hat as the boys jumped back laughing uproariously. Sputtering and cursing, Andy pulled himself out of the sprinkler's range.

Aunt Charlotte, hearing the commotion from inside, quickly appeared by his side. "What in the world?" she asked, as Andy wiped his glasses with a wet handkerchief.

Still shaken, Andy managed a chuckle. "Guess that buck wasn't the only one surprised. That sprinkler pert near knocked me on my ass. Thought I showed those boys how to direct it away from us."

"I'm guessing you did," was her simmering reply as she glared over at the boys. AJ looked down at the ground while Red continued laughing.

"Now wait, you don't think—"

"We'll find out," she replied crossly. "Boys, get over here. Now!"

"Wait, Char. Calm down, even if they did it on purpose, it was just a practical joke. No harm was done."

"Andy, I lost one man to a heart attack, I'm not ready to lose another. This might have been funny if they had done it to Paul, but you're 82 years old for Pete's sake."

"OK, but let's go light on them. I'll be damned if I want them to think of me as fragile."

"Fine, you talk to them then." AJ sheepishly arrived with a giggling Red in tow. She shot AJ another look and left.

AJ was the younger of the two boys by 6 years, but with Red's mild Asperger's, he was their spokesperson. "Papa, are you OK? I didn't think the sprinkler would hit you that hard. We're sorry. Aren't we, Red?"

Red's freckled-faced grin was replaced immediately by a solemn expression. "Hank says jokes aren't funny if somebody gets hurt."

Relieved that he needn't add anything more to the subject, Andy replied, "Well, thanks for your concern boys. I'm a tough old bird, but next time, I'd appreciate you letting me in on your prank before you decide to try it out. Now, you kids can stay out for a couple more hours if you'd like. Just stay inside the gate."

Andy heard the phone ring as he stepped onto the porch and took off his wet T-shirt and pants. Inside, concern had spread across Aunt Charlotte's face as she handed him the receiver. "It's Gigi from the restaurant."

"Hi Gigi. What's up?"

"Hi, Andy. I was just telling Char about the four men who just left. They were asking questions about Paul and Sienna. You know, like they were friends or something. I told them some things that I was thinking afterwards I shouldn't have."

Andy groaned, and dropped his forehead into the palm of his hand. "What'd you tell them?"

"I'm just so used to everybody knowing each other's business on this island . . . I slipped up . . . I told them that Paul and Sienna were on a vacation for three weeks with Hank and Roxanne . . .I think I may have also mentioned that it was an adults-only vacation and that you and Char were watching the kids while they were away."

"Jesus, Gigi!" Andy saw Char's startled reaction to his outburst and calmed himself, before adding, "You should know better than that."

"I know. I'm sorry. Is it bad? Are you gonna be OK?"

"It's all right. What's done is done. Don't worry about it, we'll be fine. Thanks for letting us know. If they come in again, try and call me before they leave."

"It's the mafia, isn't it? What should we do?" Aunt Charlotte asked, after Andy disconnected with Gigi.

"Well, for sure we're not going to get all worked up about this. I've stood up against a lot tougher men and I can guarantee you that they won't set one foot—"

"Andy, calm down. I'm not worried about us. God knows, with the amount of practice you do at that little gun range of yours, it's about time you got a chance to shoot somebody. But, it's not just us that we need to think about. I'm calling Sienna and Paul to see if they want us to take the boys over to her parents."

"No, Char, that'll ruin the rest of their vacation. There's probably nothing to worry about. No one can get through the front gate. I'll keep watch tonight. You know I can take care of them if need be."

"Oh, that's just great. I'll tell Sienna that you're standing guard with your ammo belt, machine gun and a bowie knife. She won't worry a bit."

Fortunately, despite Andy's fully engaged protector instinct, the irony wasn't lost on him. "OK, call 'em."

Looking up at the ceiling and muttering something about a gunfight at the O.K. Corral, Charlotte shook her head and picked up the phone.

"Well, I guess we'll just have to figure out what to do ourselves for now," Andy said, after Aunt Charlotte was unable to reach Sienna or Paul and left voice messages.

"Let's get the boys packed. Maybe we'll hear back from them soon. If not, I think we should drive the boys . . .Wait, a minute. Today's Friday. They're at Sol Duc. There's no cell service up there, but Sienna left me the number for the main lodge."

13

The hostess approached their table. "Excuse me, Ms. Armstrong, you have a call at the main desk."

"It's probably Barney. He mentioned that he and Claire might come up tomorrow," Paul guessed.

But the worried look on her face when she returned a few minutes later wasn't from talking with Barney.

Paul set his menu down. "What is it?"

"It was Aunt Charlotte. Salvadore Boitano and three men came into the restaurant this evening asking questions about us. Gigi told them we were on vacation, but that the boys were still on island. We need to fly home immediately."

Paul threw two twenties down on the table for the drinks and apologized to the waiter. "Sorry, something has come up."

They found Hank and Roxanne, walking back toward the dining room.

"Hey Paul, I'm sorry about all that back there—"

"We have to get back home. Salvadore Boitano and three of his gangsters were at The Green Flash tonight asking questions."

"About what?" Hank and Roxanne fell in behind them.

Paul stopped Hank, as the girls continued toward their cabins.

"There is something I need to tell you."

"You know that anything you tell me is between just the two of us and, whatever it is—"

"Boitano may have guessed that I killed Buddy," Paul's voice broke as he added, "and if he did, he'd be right."

"Jeeeesus, Paul. How in the . . . Does anybody else know?" Seeing Paul's hesitancy, he continued, "Look, you don't have to tell me that. Christ, I missed this one by a mile. I thought it was another woman or something." He took a couple deep breaths. "OK, Paul. I'm here for you. When are you gonna believe that?" He set his hand on Paul's shoulder. "We'll be ready in ten minutes."

Twenty minutes later, Sienna braced herself while watching for bars on her cell phone, as Paul sped through the tight turns of the Sol Duc Hot Springs access road onto Highway 101.

"When you get cell coverage," Paul directed, "see what American might have going out to Miami this evening."

"It's eight now," Hank said, from the back seat. "How long before we make it to Sea Tac?"

"We'll be there in about three and a half hours."

"I don't think any flights can leave after midnight. That's cutting it too close." Hank read the approaching green highway sign. "Port Angeles, 28 miles. Is there an airport in Port Angeles?"

"Good idea, Hank," Paul replied. "I think it's called The William Fairchild Airport."

"I've got bars," Sienna announced, opening her maps app for directions to the airport. The chime from an unknown caller, interrupted her search. "Hello?"

"Sienna, it's Connie Hunter. I've been trying to reach you. I have some information you all need to know. Salvadore Boitano and two associates have landed on Saint Croix. I believe that Boitano now thinks Paul had something to do with Buddy Falco's disappearance."

Sienna groaned and pushed the speaker button before replying, "Connie, you're on speaker. We're in the car heading toward the airport in Port Angeles. We got a call less than an hour ago, from Charlotte and Andy who are taking care of the kids. Boitano and three men were at my restaurant asking questions. They know we're on vacation and the kids are still on island. We're trying to catch a flight to Miami this evening."

"That's good. I can help you. I know a pilot up there who owes me a few favors. Stay off the phone and I'll get right back to you."

"Thank you, Connie," Roxanne gushed, with tears welling in her eyes, but Connie had already disconnected and was on to her next call.

"It'll be OK. Don't worry Honey," Hank reassured Roxanne, his arm held tight around her shoulders.

Only a few minutes passed before Connie got back to them. "You're all set. Al Maurer will meet you outside the terminal in half an hour. You'll be at SeaTac in an hour. In the meantime, I'll work on getting your flights booked through Miami to Saint Croix."

"We can't thank you enough, Connie," Sienna's voice quavered.

"Try not to worry, Sienna . . . I've contacted an agent in Saint Croix who's probably paying Salvadore a visit right about now."

Twenty minutes later, their luggage was loaded into the rear of a Cessna, CJ3+. Once they'd cleared The William

Fairchild airspace, Paul leaned into the cockpit and thanked Al for dropping everything.

"Not a problem. I'm just happy to help. I'd do anything for Connie. Agent Hunter and I go back a long way."

"Oh, shit. I just realized we flew off and left the damn rental car at the airport, with the keys in it."

"Not to worry. My girlfriend, Gretchen, will return your rental car. We'll spend a night in the city and fly home tomorrow. Now the four of you just sit back and relax. I'll have you there in plenty of time."

******

Standing beside their car, Connie and Wyatt waved as Al finally cut the engines, following a lengthy taxi across the tarmac that seemed to last nearly as long as the flight.

"Jump in," Wyatt said, helping Paul and Hank with luggage. "We've got about fifteen minutes before they close the flight."

Connie's badge, along with an American Airlines agent, expedited them through the TSA checkpoint. The flight was still boarding when they arrived at the gate. They'd been so rushed it wasn't until the four turned to thank Connie that they noticed her carry-on.

"After all, you guys did invite us down. Wyatt can't make it, but I think I'll tag along, if you don't mind. I might be of some help and we probably have a few things to talk about."

"Ah . . . sure," a surprised Paul replied, while Sienna, Hank and Roxanne took turns hugging her.

14

Paul fell into the window seat. Sienna took the middle with Connie on the aisle. Hank and Roxanne continued past them toward the back. Twenty minutes after takeoff, the cabin lights were shut off as most of the passengers attempted to catch a few hours of sleep during the five-hour, red-eye flight.

Sienna leaned toward Connie. "Paul remembers meeting you."

Connie smiled. "He was sucking down the Cuervo pretty fast, but I figured eventually he would."

"Please don't take this the wrong way. After all you've done for us tonight, I feel embarrassed even asking."

"Is it something like, am I a friend or an FBI agent?"

Sienna weighed what she might say next. Before she spoke, Connie turned to her. "Look Sienna, I'm already in way too deep to be anything other than your friend."

"OK . . . You mentioned that you aren't sure you'll return to the FBI. Does this have something to do with your decision?"

Connie nodded her head.

"Can I ask why?"

"Why I didn't bring Paul in?" She leaned forward and looked over at Paul, who was already asleep. "It was a couple of things. When I set him up at that bar, I wasn't expecting that outcome. I went with the intention of arresting him. But when he shared his story. . . I could only think of my brother and our endless discussion regarding right, wrong, good guys, bad guys and the grey area that he worried I could never see. Also, I knew that if I'd started an investigation, it's very likely Paul would have been murdered before the trial."

Sienna started to reply, but Connie held up her hand. "There was something else, too." She shook her head slowly struggling to find words. "Maybe I'm working through some kind of mid-life thing. Wyatt says I'm blossoming, but sometimes it feels more like I'm going nuts." Still shaking her head, she concluded, "Sorry Sienna. That's really all I have right now."

A few minutes passed before Sienna asked, "What was Adam like?"

"Adam was wonderful. He was sweet and gentle, but would never let go of something if he believed he was right. He always seemed to find something to laugh about, especially when the joke was on him. Also, he was so open . . . not just with me, with everyone. There wasn't a sneaky bone in his body. With Adam, what you saw was what you got."

"I think maybe Adam and Paul had more in common than looks," Sienna said, softly. "It's the lying that's really eating at Paul."

"That's part of what I was trying to say. When I met Paul, his voice, the phrasing of his sentences, the self-deprecating humor . . . it was like being with Adam. At one point, he referred to himself as *bad news*." She paused to collect herself. "Adam referred to himself as, 'Your bad news brother' in his last voicemail to me."

"Sounds like a wonderful man."

93

"He was. I still feel so sad that I didn't get a chance to tell him how much he meant to me. Towards the end, we fought a lot. I felt like he was always giving me a hard time. He thought I'd lost myself to the agency . . . He was right, and I see that now."

"I believe he knows how you felt."

Connie wiped a tear off her check. "Thank you, Sienna. Actually, I agree with you. Ever since he died, I've felt closer to him than ever. It's like he's leading me. That's how I met Wyatt. I was having trouble sleeping after his death and would take walks along the waterfront. One night, Wyatt just appeared. Told me I shouldn't be walking alone. He's been beside me ever since."

Now it was Sienna's turn to tear up. "That's so beautiful."

Connie laughed, "Aren't we a pair? Do you think we'll need a box of tissue every time we talk?"

"Probably."

"So how did you and Paul meet?"

Sienna turned on her attendant light. "Let's see if anyone's awake back there. I could use a drink."

"This was a good idea," Connie said, clinking glasses with Sienna, after the flight attendant delivered their Glenlivet.

The two women took long sips before Sienna continued, "I was engaged to another man when Paul came into my restaurant. He didn't tell me until later that he had come down to help Andy, who's my first husband's father, reconnect with me. Andy and I had gotten off to a bad start. The breaking point came when Aaron's mom died and we decided to move to Saint Croix. Andy felt that Aaron had abandoned him. Even though Aaron was an only child, there was no reason to stay. Andy had become a bitter drunk, bent on making Aaron as miserable as he was. Aaron never saw his father again. When Andy came down to Saint Croix for Aaron's funeral—"

"How did he die?"

"He was killed in a small plane crash. At the funeral, I said some terribly hurtful things to Andy. I wanted him out of my life and didn't want to tell him I was pregnant with his grandchild. When he left island, I thought I'd never see him again . . . A few years later, he met Paul on a trail ride in Eastern Washington and thought that Paul might be able to help bring us back together."

"It appears he was quite successful."

"He'd kept Andy hidden until after we spent a night on my boat, just holding each other." Seeing Connie's eyebrows raise, she explained, "Oh I wanted to, but I knew he was keeping something from me and didn't feel like making love until I knew what it was."

"Smart girl."

"I don't know if you've picked this up or not, but Paul goes in for the dramatic."

"I'm not surprised. Most romantics do."

"So, he has me walk down to the end of a deserted beach to meet the mysterious man he'd come to Saint Croix with and it was Andy. He apologized. I apologized. We cried, hugged and talked for an hour. Having Andy back in our lives has been a blessing for all of us."

"I imagine for Andy as well."

"You'll love him and Aunt Charlotte. Come to think of it, you and Wyatt will love all the Windsol folks and I'm sure they'll feel the same. Anyway, Paul and I married. Paul adopted AJ. I was pregnant and life was near perfect. I guess you know what happened next."

"Pretty much. I'm so sorry for your loss." She finished her drink. "The world's a better place without those thugs. I wish I'd been the one who'd taken them down." Connie leaned over and looked at Paul still sleeping soundly. "Paul just isn't the type who could let it go."

"He still has nightmares, and I know it's always in the back of his mind. I'm not surprised he referred to himself as 'bad news' when you met. Between his drinking and the PTSD, he was a mess. He's careful with his drinking now, and we're doing fine." Sienna adjusted the blanket that had slipped down from his shoulder. It's just that I don't see the carefree, goofy Paul anymore. I understand why, but I kind of miss him."

"Sure, I get that. It's true that time heals most wounds, but there are certain things that we never forget. I still remember the first man I had to kill and there have been too many since then. Even though it was kill or be killed, it still works on you."

Neither spoke for several minutes before Connie said, "Adam had adopted the tag, *your bad news brother* after I'd complained about his bombarding me with endless examples of individuals' rights being violated under the guise of patriotism and homeland security."

Sienna thought for a few moments before asking, "Did you ever worry about Adam? I mean before the accident. There are some bad people out there and Paul, well, I don't know if he gets it yet. Even after all we've been through."

"Absolutely. People can be real assholes and even before our mother took herself out of the picture with her booze and little pills, I was always looking out for him, afraid he'd piss someone off, saying whatever came to his mind."

"I worry about Paul. He's so *Dudley Do Right*. I think he'd actually enjoy having his day in court."

"We can't let that happen. Although I think he'd get off for justifiable homicide, Sal and his gang would never abide by the verdict."

******

Sienna realized after several minutes of silence that Connie too had dozed off. Although having Connie on their side was reassuring, the fear she had felt in the hospital following Buddy Falco's attack had returned. Her happily-ever-after hopes when Paul returned from Cabo had never truly materialized. She looked down at him lovingly and thought of how he'd stepped up to protect his family. Shutting her eyes, she searched for something that would take them out of the mafia's crosshairs, for good. She'd been too weak and fragile to be of any help back then. She wasn't weak now."

15

"Hey lighten up, Francis. You fucked up, but nobody's perfect . . . 'cept me. Eh boys?"

"That's right, Boss, just you and the Lord," Vincent's raspy voice replied from the back seat.

"Well, don't sweat it, boys. Sylvie says we're all saved in the end." But Vincent's attention had already been diverted to Anthony's efforts at reaching the fourth level of *Zombie Carnage*, their newest video game purchase.

Despite his patter to the contrary, Sal was still pissed that neither Paul Armstrong nor Hank Johnson were on island. His simmering desire to punch Francis in the face was downgraded with a hard slap across the beleaguered driver's shoulder which still allowed Francis to keep the SUV on the road. Feeling a bit better, he resumed his discourse. "OK then Francis, we'll pay this Andy Meyers a visit tomorrow. I can't imagine it'll take very long before word gets back to Armstrong and Johnson. With their kids down here, my guess is the wives will have them back within a day or two max." He turned back to Vincent and Anthony. "You boys smell FBI at the restaurant?"

"Thought maybe I'd stepped in somethin'." Vincent laughed at his joke.

"You mean the two sitting at the bar?" Francis asked.

"What do you think the FBI was doing there Francis?" Sal quizzed.

"Well, assuming it was the FBI, I'd say keeping tabs on us."

"Oh, they were *fibis* all right. Who else would it have been? They've got nothing better to do. Tail me all over the fuckin' world . . . But that's OK, it tells me something."

"What's that, Boss?" Anthony asked.

"It tells me that we're not the only ones thinkin' this Armstrong putz might have had something to do with taking Buddy down. Yessir Boy's, I think we're onto something." Francis flinched as Buddy's open palm slapped hard on the top of the dashboard.

"Thing is, Sal, if it was Armstrong, I still don't see how he did it," Francis said, turning into the rented villa's driveway.

"Keep it running Francis. You can pick us up in the morning. We're done for the night." Buddy let himself out of the car. Still holding the door open, he thought for a moment before adding, "I intend to ask him that, just before his accident. I hear that more people are killed by falling coconuts than sharks down here. That's just one idea, Francis, see what you can come up with."

"You got it, Boss."

Sal slammed the door muttering, "Meantime, I got to deal with Sylvie, who's gonna be royally pissed I'm missing another of her fucking marriage encounters."

"What the . . .?" Francis's hand shielded his eyes as he squinted through the high beams of the arriving SUV. Vincent and Anthony drew their guns even before the two occupants climbed out and stood facing them from behind their car doors.

"Sal, I'll bet your boys have no permits for those guns. If they put them away now, I'll pretend I didn't see 'em. This is a friendly visit."

"Who the fuck are you?"

"I'm FBI agent, Brad Harper," the tall slender man said, as he and his partner shut the car doors and approached the group.

His muscular partner flashed his badge wallet. "I'm Agent Wilson."

"That's not necessary, Agent Wilson. I've been around so many FBI agents that I smelled you two back at the restaurant. No offense, of course," he added smiling. He nodded at Vincent and Anthony who both scowled as they slowly holstered their weapons.

"Of course," Wilson replied. "For me, it's the same with murdering slime-bags, present company excluded . . .of course."

"Of course," Sal replied, through clenched teeth. He flashed briefly on having his boys open fire on these arrogant assholes, but quickly thought better of it. "So, what brings you two out on a night like this?"

"We thought you might appreciate a warm island welcome. It's your first time down here, isn't it Sal?" Agent Harper asked.

"Yes, and thank you. I'm thinking I like the place so much already, and with you coming by to welcome us, I'll be coming down again, soon and often. Probably'll sail down with the missus next trip."

"I'd suggest waiting awhile," Wilson advised. "We're in hurricane season. There's the risk of damage to your vessel if we have a storm."

"Excellent. I'll take it under advisement. Well, I'd ask you in for drinks, but this hot weather has me turning in pretty early."

"OK, have a nice evening." Agent Harper handed Sal a business card. "It's a small island. Don't be surprised if we run into each other again before you leave." The two agents returned to their car.

Francis stepped out from behind the heavily tinted windows of the SUV as the agents drove out through the gate. "What was that all about?"

There were times when Salvadore Boitano hated his life and this was one of them. He'd survived a very long time by avoiding direct confrontations with anyone related to the law. That's why he took such good care of his boys. They were the ones who carried out the threats and beatings required for the darker side of his operations. Now, here he was with two newly minted, punk-assed FBI agents in his grill, serving him warning that they had him, not Vincent, Anthony or Francis, in their sights. He shook his head and headed for the house. There was nothing he could do about it. With all the flack he was getting back home, he had to personally see this through to the end. Armstrong had to go. Simple as that.

"You just do as I tell you. You fucked up once, Francis. Better not do it again."

Francis climbed back in the car, the taste of blood still fresh in his mouth from the earlier drubbing. Driving away slowly, he ground his teeth together. "One day, Old Man. One day."

16

Spilling out the elevated gangway at the Miami airport, the weary travelers stumbled into the American Airline's Admirals Club. Somewhat rejuvenated after showers, Paul and Hank found an isolated area they could talk, while the others catnapped and conversed in the lounge's large comfortable chairs.

"So, why did you wait so long to tell me?"

"I didn't want to burden you with it, Hank."

"Did you think I'd turn you in?"

"I wasn't sure, with you being a former chief of police. I'm still not, quite frankly. I wouldn't blame you if you felt you had to. Do you?"

"You know that you really are a dumbass sometimes. I'd confess to killing 'em before turning you in."

Paul dropped his head, relieved. "Sienna said you wouldn't, but I know that you've spent your life enforcing the law."

"Yeah, but this is different. The fact is, if you were brought up on charges, you wouldn't stay alive long enough for a trial."

"There is that. Also, I worry about my family and friends."

"With good reason. I worked around those creeps and their codes for most of my professional life, and even though Salvador Boitano comes off as this benevolent family patriarch, he's a ruthless killer who wouldn't hesitate making an example of you, your family and friends."

"I'd do it again Hank. I will do it again if I need to."

"How did you do it the first time? Those were dangerous killers. Hell, you saw what they did to Barney."

"I guess they didn't think I had it in me. When I pulled the gun on them, I think they hesitated because they couldn't believe it was happening."

"Did you have any help? Barney wasn't in any kind of shape after the attack."

"Andy, helped me dump them off the reef."

"It's probably best I didn't know, at first. I might have held back on helping the Saint Croix police investigation which might have aroused suspicion. But you should have told me when you got back from Cabo."

"Again, how would that've helped anything?"

"That's just what you do with real friends. I've known you were keeping something from me. It's not right to keep a good friend guessing all the time. Who else knows?"

"Barney, Sienna, and Connie."

"Oh shit, Connie knows? How did that happen?"

******

Before their early afternoon departure to Saint Croix, they lunched at Sushi Maki which Hank and Roxanne had found in the airport a year earlier.

Hank tried to lighten Sienna and Roxanne's mood, which darkened as they drew closer to Saint Croix. "With

Connie's agents contacting Sal, there's nothing to worry about with the kids."

They joined the line of passengers boarding their flight. Sienna took the seat toward the rear of the plane, so that Connie and Paul could sit together and continue an earlier discussion regarding security measures.

Her elderly seatmate greeted her, "Are you on vacation?"

"No, actually I'm returning home from a vacation. How about you?"

"I'm flying to Saint Croix to surprise my husband, who came down on business a few days ago. He was supposed to be home this evening, but, his work's taking longer than anticipated, so I thought I'd pay him a visit. We've been married for a very long time, but life just seems to have passed us by so fast, sometimes it feels like I don't really know him at all."

Sienna, already preoccupied with her own problems, wasn't keen on listening to her chatty neighbor's marital challenges. She pulled a Sky Mall magazine from the seat pocket. "Well, I wish you the best. It's a beautiful island with plenty of remote beaches for long walks. Should give you guys a good chance to reconnect."

Once in the air, both women ordered herbal tea from the beverage cart. Something about the silver-blue curls framing the woman's warm smile and kind eyes encouraged Sienna to pick up on their conversation. "I apologize for not being more social. I have a lot on my mind."

"Oh, no apology is necessary, Dear. I think we all have too much on our minds. There's so many distractions these days with TV's and computers. Hardly anybody goes to church anymore. It's certainly not like it was when I met my husband. Things were much simpler then. Are you married?"

"Yes, my husband's sitting with a friend up near the front."

"My husband and I have been married for nearly 52 years."

"Wow, congratulations."

"Well, thank you. But you know it hasn't been easy." She thought for a few moments. "He's a slave to his work. He always has been and I guess I knew that when we married. Still, early on, he made me feel that I was a priority. But all that seemed to change after the three miscarriages. Once we gave up trying to have children, things just never seemed the same between us." She sipped her tea. "Is this your first marriage?"

"I've been married twice. I lost my first husband in an . . . accident. I was pregnant at the time and raised our son alone until I met my husband, Paul."

"Any children with Paul?"

Sienna felt a familiar sadness. "Yes, but I lost the baby, late term."

"I know how awful that is. I'm so sorry."

Sienna felt a bond form between them. "Thank you. You know, I'm so fortunate to have been loved by two incredible men. But like you said, it hasn't been easy. In addition to streaking by, life can sure throw in some painful punches."

"Yes, it does. Yes, it does. I know it's none of my business and I don't mean to pry, but you seem troubled."

Sienna couldn't speak; the stress of the last 24 hours finally caught up with her. Tears filled her eyes. "Excuse me, I haven't slept much in the last two days."

"Of course." She offered Sienna a tissue. "I've lived a long time, Dear. Like I said, I've never had any children, or of course grandchildren, so I can't speak from experience . . . But, it must be very difficult to keep a family on track these days. I may not be able to help, but if you'd like to talk about it, I'd be more than happy to listen."

"That's just it, we're on track. My husband, my son and I have a great time together. It's just . . . there are some very bad people in the world." Sienna realized that she had to be careful. "I guess I'm just having a bad day."

"These people you're referring to . . . do they live on Saint Croix?"

"No, I think they're mostly from New Jersey." Sienna chastised herself. *What are you going to tell her next? That a mafia boss has flown to Saint Croix because he thinks my husband killed his nephew?* Sienna straightened in her chair. "I'm sorry to have burdened you with this."

"It's no burden at all. You're such a sweet girl, I'm sure everything will work out."

"Thanks. I'm sure it will. By the way, I'm Sienna Armstrong."

"What a lovely name. I'm Sylvia. But you can call me Sylvie."

******

While waiting to disembark, she thought of the phone conversation she'd had with Sal the previous night. "Sorry Sylvie. One of the parties I was meeting on Saint Croix was called off-island. I need another week to finish up my business down here." Sensing how upset she was, he'd added, "Look, we don't need any advice from Pastor Eddie. You and I could

106

write a book on marriage. I promise when I get home, I'll take you out to dinner. Some place real nice and we can talk about it."

"I'll notify Pastor Eddie that we won't make the retreat," she'd replied stiffly.

There was a click on the line and mistakenly thinking she'd hung up, he spewed, "Yeah, you do that *You Wacko Old Bitch.*" Sylvie'd been too stunned and hurt to respond before he'd disconnected.

******

The passengers grabbed their luggage from the overhead bins and began clearing out. "Goodbye, Sylvie. Good luck and I hope we run into each other before you head back."

"Thank you, Sienna. You never know."

Despite Sylvia believing that her marriage was beyond saving, Pastor Eddie had managed to convince her to fly to Saint Croix. "Forgiveness is the pathway, Sylvia. As his wife, it's God's mission that you lead Salvador to salvation. Go to him. Help him find the path to righteousness."

She knew who the *bad people* were and enough about the circumstances surrounding Buddy Falco's disappearance to piece together Salvador's reason for coming to Saint Croix. Her husband's bus ride to salvation had left the station years ago. His path was a hate-filled campaign levied at a loving family. An operation to bolster his image, by avenging the disappearance of a nephew he'd hated. *It's the work of the devil. Evil incarnate.*

Dazed, she walked toward the terminal. *How could I ever think he was anything but a murderer? When one of his henchmen pulls the trigger, he's just as guilty. What am I doing here?*

107

Disoriented, she stopped and leaned against a concrete column inside the terminal. "Are you OK, Mam?" A tall, sandy-haired man gently took her arm. "It's hot today, especially if you're not used to it. Can I help you over to a bench?"

Sylvia was about to reply when Sienna approached. "Sylvie, I see you've met my husband, Paul."

"Hi Sylvie," Paul said, taking her hand. "Thanks for being such a good listener for Sienna. It's tough for us right now, but meeting someone as nice as you has really lifted her spirits."

"You are blessed to have such a wonderful wife. I'm certain that you and your family will be watched over and protected from that horrible man."

Sienna caught a questioning look from Paul, before handing Sylvie her business card. "I hope everything works out with you and your husband. You should bring him by our restaurant. We'd love to meet him."

"Thank you, Sienna. But no promises. As you know, he and I have some important issues to work out."

The two women hugged goodbye as a black SUV pulled up to the curb. Paul brought Sylvie's carry-on to the rear of the Escalade. The driver, a thin, dark-haired man wouldn't make eye contact, as he took the bag from Paul and jumped back in the car.

Rejoining Sienna, Paul asked, "What did you tell her?"

"Just that there were some bad people in the world causing us problems."

"It's odd that she would say *that horrible man*. Did she give you her last name?"

"No. Why?"

"I don't know. No reason."

As Francis pulled away from the curb, Sylvia looked back at the couple. *It's not Sal that God sent me to save.*

17

During their Miami stop-over, Sienna had briefly notified Andy of their arrival and mentioned, in passing, that they were returning with an FBI agent. Decked out in cowboy boots, blue jeans and a red and white checkered sports shirt, the spry octogenarian warmly greeted Connie. "Welcome Agent Hunter. Mi casa es su casa."

"Thank you, Andy." Connie took his offered hand. "I've heard a great deal about you from Paul and Sienna."

"Oh, is that right? Most everything I've told them is made up, so I wouldn't bank too much on anything you've heard."

"I'll remember that," she replied, laughing.

"Where's Aunt Charlotte," Sienna asked.

"She went to pick up the kids from your folks. Figured we could fit you all in the truck's crew cab this way and besides we thought you'd be pretty tired and it'd save you the trip." Sensing Sienna and Roxanne's worry, Andy reassured them, "Listen, Char knows to keep checking her rear-view mirror. Anything looks suspicious, she'll high-tail it to the police station in Frederiksted. It just ain't right, you guys having to cut your vacation short from worry. No sir, it just ain't right at all." He repeated this to himself several times, as Paul drove them to Windsol.

A relieved Sienna spotted Aunt Charlotte's Prius as they passed through Windsol's entry gate. Aunt Charlotte appeared on the porch as AJ and Red ran at a full gallop into their parents' open arms.

"There's chili and cornbread back here when you get settled," Andy shouted, as the group headed toward the cabins.

"This is Barney and Claire's cabin," AJ explained to Connie, as he and Sienna led her through the front door. Sienna opened the sliding door onto the outside balcony terrace. A nice breeze flowed through the room.

Connie set her bags in the bedroom and joined them outside. "Wow, now that's a view!" she exclaimed, taking in the uninterrupted expanse of the Caribbean Sea. "Is that St. Thomas?"

"Yes, it is," AJ replied, knowledgeably. "It's forty miles away, almost due north and that's St. John just to the east. On a clearer day, like after it rains, you can see Tortola and Virgin Gorda over there," he added, pointing further to the south. "We've been to all those places on our sailboat."

"My friend, Wyatt, loves to sail. Maybe we could all sail over there one day."

"That'd be great," AJ replied enthusiastically. "'Cept, we'll probably need another boat. But that's OK, because my friend Red's parents have a bigger boat. So, if they came, we could make it work."

"Honey, let's let Connie get unpacked." Sienna said. Turning back to Connie she added, "We're so glad you're here."

"Me, too. Any chance Barney'd let me keep this place?"

"AJ, you go ahead, I'll meet you and your dad at our cabin in a few minutes."

"Roger that, Mom."

Watching AJ skip away, Connie smiled. "That's one great kid."

"Yeah, we think we'll keep him."

The two stood quietly at the guardrail enjoying the warm breeze and view until Sienna asked, "Did you and Paul come up with any ideas about dealing with Boitano?"

"I actually spent most of the time convincing Paul that he shouldn't turn himself in. He thinks, and I agree with him on this point, that if he were in prison, Boitano would try to reach him from inside and wouldn't pose a threat to any of you."

"That just can't happen," Sienna moaned. "If we lost Paul, I don't know what—"

"Yeah, I know what you mean. The boy kind of grows on you. So, like I told him, I think the most effective way to deal with the situation is to make sure Sal knows that we're watching him. He's usually much more insulated than this; dining with politicians, while his boys take care of the dirty work. It may work to our advantage that he's down here proving that he's still top dog. He knows he's exposed and now front and center in the FBI's sights. He may be having second thoughts about all this. Retirement may start looking like a more attractive option. Two agents already visited Sal at his rental villa. Also, Paul and I discussed avoiding predictable patterns and for the time being, Hank or I will accompany any of you whenever you're out. None of this is a guarantee, but that and keeping our eyes open until Sal and his goons leave the island is all I've got for now."

"Like I said, Connie, we can't thank you enough. I'm so grateful for your help, but—"

"I know. We're still just marking time, waiting for Sal to make his move. It's not enough for you to feel very safe, but—"

"It's the best we can do for now?"

"I'm afraid so."

"Well, then, since there's nothing more to be done, I'll try not to worry and trust that somehow it will all work out the way it's supposed to . . . We'll see you up at the great house when you're ready." Sienna hugged Connie warmly before leaving.

Connie punched in Wyatt's number. He picked up on the second ring. "Hi, Honey. How was the trip?"

"Long and mostly sleepless. I'm staying in Barney and Claire's cabin, sitting alone on this big comfortable king-sized bed, and really missing you."

"This is the only time we've slept apart since our first night together. I don't really like it much."

"Me neither. How's Erin doing? I bet she's enjoying her one- on-one time with you."

"Actually, there's some news in that department. I got a call from the very same Barney whose cabin you're staying in. He called me on his way into Seattle to pick up his nephew, who was catching a bus back from Pullman. Apparently, the kid's quite a basketball player and WSU has their eyes on him."

"So how does this relate to Erin?"

"Patience, Little Grasshopper. I'm getting to it."

"It really gets me hot when you refer to me as a bug."

"Actually, bugs are in an entirely different order of insects."

113

"Wow, my very own science guy and up to now, I thought it was your body that attracted me."

"Blame it on a sixth-grade daddy/daughter project. So anyway . . . Barney suggested we all meet for dinner at a place up near Green Lake. Kind of a hippy hang-out called The Sunlight Café."

"I've been there. Love their soup, salad and bread combo. How'd Erin and Joey get along?"

"You mean before or after they gobbled down their meals and left to take a walk around Green Lake."

"Really. Sounds like love—"

"At first bite. I know." Barney and I talked non-stop until they got back. Barney grew up with Paul and had some great stories. Felt like we'd known each other all our lives."

"I know the feeling. I wish we were down here together now, but for a different reason."

"Yeah. Any new developments?"

"No, nothing really. We're just minimizing the opportunity for Sal to try something, as well as making him aware of the problems he'll have if he does."

"Not much fun in that . . . for you or any of our Saint Croix friends."

"Exactly. Speaking of which, I should head over to the great house for dinner. It's quite a place they have here."

"Sounds like it. Give them all my best. Oh, and next weekend, Erin and I are staying up at Barney and his girlfriend Claire's. I haven't seen Erin so happy since she got her driver's license."

"Well, keep your eyes open. The last thing we need is the patter of tiny little feet in our lives."

"What? Oh, I don't think that's—"

"I love you, Wyatt, but I think you may know more about insects than your 17-year-old daughter's hormones."

18

"Does Sal know I'm here?" Sylvie asked Francis, as they turned off the airport access road onto the Melvin Evans Highway.

"No, and I'm pretty nervous about all this, Mrs. Boitano. He's gonna be real pissed I didn't tell him."

"Don't worry, Francis. Just drop me off outside the villa and leave. He'll have plenty to deal with from me."

"You don't know him like I do, Mrs. Boitano."

You're probably right, but I'm learning fast.

Arriving at the villa, Francis's nervousness escalated as he spotted the heavily dented Dodge Durango parked in the driveway. "I don't think we should go in there now."

"Who's in there with him?" When Francis didn't answer, Sylvie stepped out of the car muttering, "Well, I don't give one hill of beans what's going on in there. The old fool has plenty to answer for already."

Francis left the engine running as he pulled her bag from the SUV. Shrugging his shoulders, he fell in behind her as she approached the villa.

"You can drop that here, if you're so worried." Sylvie said, opening the unlocked front door.

Francis quickly did as suggested and returned to the idling car at a jog. He dropped the engine into gear just as Vincent appeared in boxer shorts on the porch. "Hey Francis, stay put!"

Minutes later Vincent and Anthony appeared with two of the three disheveled *masseuses* Sal had Francis hire. The third girl was jettisoned topless through the front door by a screaming Sylvia as the boys climbed into the back seat.

Francis was prepared for Anthony's sharp smack to the back of his head as he pulled out of the drive. "Looks like you really stepped in it this time, Shit For Brains."

"Even considerin' how stupid you are, that was one dumb-ass move," Vincent seethed. "Surprising the boss with his wife, right in the middle of our little party that you lined up. What the fuck were you thinking?"

"She told me she wanted to surprise him and I didn't think the girls were showing up 'til tomorrow."

"Well she was right about that. The boss was surprised," Anthony chuckled. "Wish I could've seen the look on his face when she walked in the bedroom. Too bad, too. Old Sal doesn't do blow or pussy anymore, but with the nose-full he got earlier, I think he was up to bangin' that broad."

Francis didn't anticipate the next smack, this time followed by ringing ears and shooting stars. "Take us back to that black bitch's restaurant, Dipshit," Vincent ordered. "Boss'll appreciate we're still on the job and with all the trouble you caused, me and Anthony got some serious drinkin' to do."

******

After throwing Sal's *masseuse* outside, Sylvie collapsed into a plush sofa, her head spinning.

117

"Sylvie, what are you doing here?" Sal descended the stairs wrapped in a white robe. "The boys must have drugged me. I don't know how she got in my room."

"Or how your worthless little dick got in her mouth?" Sylvie replied calmly. "Maybe you got roofied? Is that it, Sal? I thought you were through with all this," she added pointing to the razor blade and lines of white powder on the mirror in front of her.

"Honest to God, that must be it. I remember Vincent sort of smiling as he handed me a drink. Maybe he—"

"You know what I think, Sal? I think you're incapable of salvation."

"Here we go," Sal's face now shifting into a smirk. "More of your Pastor Eddie crap. Look, maybe I didn't get roofied. Maybe I'm just bored to death with all this religious bullshit. Maybe, if a little coke helps me get it up—"

"Stop!" Sylvie commanded. "This isn't about your drugs or what or who you have sex with. God forgive me for ever letting you between my legs."

"Oh nice one." Sal sneered.

"I flew down next to the nicest young lady who told me about a mafia chief hunting her family." Sylvie watched as Sal's face shifted from surprise to rage, as he approached her.

"If you . . .What'd you tell her?" He pulled his arm back.

******

"To the best damn family ever. We're gay, straight, black, white, young, old . . . whatever, wherever. We're always bound together by respect, humor and love."

Though new to the group, Connie found herself joyfully cheering the last of Andy's well lubricated toasts. Sienna's determination to enjoy every moment, despite the specter cast by Salvador Boitano, had caught hold. Connie had limited herself to a single rum punch, but the others had consumed several more to bolster their homecoming celebration.

Exhausted by the day, all but Andy and Sienna called it an early evening. The lone survivors spoke quietly. A single hurricane candle lantern cast an amber glow through the half-empty bottle of Patron in front of them.

"You know what I think?"

"Haven't the slightest idea, Andy." Sienna refilled their shot glasses.

"I think this is the first time we've really drank together."

"Probably should do it more often," she replied, slamming her empty shot glass on the table.

"We've been on a long road together, you and I. Gone through plenty of tough times. I'm still amazed that you found it in your heart to forgive me, after the way I treated you and Aaron."

"Let it go, Andy. What's done is done. You've been a wonderful grandfather to AJ and a second father to Paul and me."

"Thanks Honey, I just wish this had all happened before Aaron—"

"One more?" Sienna asked, holding the bottle above their glasses.

"Sure, why not?"

"Besides, I think Aaron knows all you've done for us."

"I don't think it's nearly enough. As for Aaron looking down on us, I'm not sure I believe in that afterlife stuff. Seems a bit farfetched to me."

"If you're talking about harps and angels, I'd agree with you. But, would an afterlife be any more miraculous than the miracle of life itself?"

"Wow, you sure don't lose your wits when you drink. Maybe it's the booze or that I'm just a dumb old cowboy, but I've got no idea what you're talking about. I will say this; I'll be goddamned if I'm going to sit here much longer and watch you and Paul worry about this Salvador character. I'm serious, Sienna, I'll take the dirt bag out myself before letting this go on." He drained his glass. "I've done it before."

Sienna's reply was cut off by her cell's chime. "It's the restaurant."

Andy left to use the bathroom. When he returned, Sienna had a puzzled look on her face. That was Gigi. She went in to close-up. The two big guys who were with Sal the other night are drinking at the bar."

Andy's face clouded. "Anything you think we should do about it?"

"Well, I've been thinking along some similar lines as you about Salvador Boitano. Maybe you and I should take a drive over to his villa."

"What? You mean now?"

"Probably good to do it when his bodyguards aren't there. Connie let slip where he's staying. I just need to grab something before we go. What do you think?"

"Sienna, I'd follow you through the fires of hell if there was such a place. Meet you back here in ten minutes."

******

120

"What's that?" Andy asked, as Sienna dropped the yard-long tube into the back of her Jeep Liberty.

"Climb in, Andy. We can talk on the way."

She turned on her headlights once they were through the gate, but waited until after bumping through the quarter-mile gravel drive, before answering his question.

"It's the pole spear that I used to hunt fish, when I was a kid."

"Oh? And what are we hunting tonight?"

"Look, Andy, I don't really plan on shooting Boitano with it. I just want to impress on him that I'm capable of doing it. It might give him something to think about."

"Well, if that doesn't work, maybe this'll help," Andy said, pulling the handgun out of his knapsack. "This here Colt Frontier Six Shooter has been dissuading bad guys since the late 1800's. Let's see how our big man likes this pressed to his forehead. Don't plan on pulling the trigger, but you never know."

"Andy, we don't really want to kill him," Sienna said nervously. "I think scaring him is the best we can do."

"I'm not sure of that. Scaring him might just piss him off and make him come after all of you. Look, I've lived a long time and had a full life. If the last thing I do is get this murdering scumbag off your tail, then whatever the consequences, it'll be worth it."

"I don't know, Andy, I think I'm sobering up. What the hell are we doing?"

Startled by flashing lights and a blaring siren, Sienna pulled over, as the fully illuminated ambulance sped by, almost leaving the road as it braked hard into a sharp turn.

"Jeez, that scared me, with you showing off your pistol like that. I thought it might be the cops." Sienna pulled back on the road.

"We haven't done anything yet to be worried about," Andy replied, with a snort. "Now back to what you were say—"

"That's where Boitano's staying!" Sienna pointed at the ambulance pulling alongside a police cruiser, already parked in the villa's driveway.

"You sure that's the right place?"

"Positive. I've catered a half-dozen dinners there."

Sienna parked across from the gated driveway entrance. Two EMT's pulled a gurney from the back of the ambulance and rolled it past a police officer posted at the front door.

"I wonder if it's for Boitano?"

"We can only hope."

Fifteen minutes later, the EMT's reappeared. The empty stretcher was lifted into the vehicle. Headlights washed over them as the ambulance pulled slowly out of the driveway.

"What was that all about?" Andy wondered.

"I have no idea. Maybe he'll tell us something," she replied, as the police officer left his post at the front door and headed up the driveway toward them.

Before reaching the entry gate, however, he stopped. A dark blue van turned into the driveway. "Coroner," Andy read off its side.

Another gurney was soon rolled through the front door and after a few minutes, reappeared with a sheet covered body strapped on top. The officer pulled the front door shut behind him and joined a second officer, who'd stepped from the cruiser to help the attendants lift the gurney into the back of the van. After the van departed, the police cruiser swung alongside Sienna and Andy. Lowering his window, the officer motioned for Sienna to do the same.

"What are you two doing here?"

"Oh, we were passed on the road by the ambulance that was here earlier and were curious. What happened? Who died?"

"Some tourist," the officer replied curtly. "You're so interested, you can read about it in the Avis. Have a nice evening." The cruiser shot off before Sienna could form another question.

"Well, that was informative. Now what?"

"Nothing more to do here," Andy replied. "I'd say we go home and get some sleep. Hank can find out tomorrow who's dead."

"OK, I don't think I've slept in two days."

Trembling, blue veined hands parted the front room's window curtains as Sienna wheeled through a U turn and drove away.

19

Wake up, damn it! This is a dream! Reeking of decaying flesh and putrid breath, three hooded figures formed a tight ring around him. As in similar dreams, heavy concrete cylinders strapped to his wrists and ankles made escape futile. The tallest of the three pulled back its hood. Worms crawled from an empty eye socket. "Your good looks won't save you now, Pretty Boy." The other two dragged him to the edge of a cliff. Far below, massive waves crashed against giant boulders. He was lifted into the air. A gigantic bald eagle sank its talons into his skull and pulled him out over the abyss. "This is what nice gets you." The great bird had an Italian accent. His fall was synced to the ending of, "A Day in the Life" from The Beatles' *Sergeant Peppers* album. As always, he awakened, just before being smashed on the rocks.

Paul knew it was hopeless to try and fall back to sleep, but waited until his breathing and pulse slowed. He grabbed shorts, sandals and a T-shirt and quietly left their bedroom. The eastern sky was beginning to lighten. He set his laptop and a cup of coffee on the porch table and sat down. Waiting for his computer to warm up, he chuckled, thinking about the dream. The Italian bird and musical accompaniment were new embellishments to the reoccurring dream. It was the first reappearance of the three hooded figures in several months. There was nothing funny about them, nor was it hard to guess why they were back.

Opening his Gmail, he discarded a half-dozen advertisements and travel company posts before reaching a previous evening's email from Anita, his former office manager who had retired in Los Cabos, Mexico with her husband, Lew.

Hola Pablo,
Not much to report down here. Lew's marshalling at a local golf course in exchange for free green fees. Chuy has just run in his "last" Mexico marathon. He said the heat this year was too much, but that's what he said last year. So, we'll see.
I've been busy in my garden and volunteering at Remy's. By the way, Smokey says you give better shoulder rubs than I do???
Anyway, stay in touch and when do I get to meet Sienna and AJ? Seriously, you are missed and long overdue for a visit down here.
Love always,
Anita

Paul toyed briefly with the idea of a quick exit to Mexico, but Sienna was feeling the financial pressure of the island's economic downturn on her restaurant. Also, AJ was starting second grade in a week. Still, the idea of leaving the island didn't seem worse than any of the other ideas he'd been entertaining. Maybe Connie's precautions would provide a sufficient deterrent to Boitano, but Paul wasn't convinced.

Alerted by soft footfalls coming up from the beach, he jumped off his chair and moved quickly to the rail.

"Well, well, what are you doing up so early?" Aunt Charlotte asked, a bit out of breath from the steep climb.

"You're up early. I couldn't sleep. Beautiful morning, isn't it?"

"Me neither. Yes, it is. I love watching the sun come up over the ocean. Would you mind some company or are you working?"

"I'd love some company. I was just catching up on emails. Want some coffee?"

"Absolutely, but stay put. I'll get it. You ready for a refill?" Grabbing his cup, she walked into the kitchen. "What time did Sienna come to bed last night? Those two must have had quite a party. I didn't hear Andy, but it must have been well after midnight."

"I have no idea. I slept like a rock until about a half-hour ago."

"I can't remember the last time you and I had a few minutes alone." Aunt Charlotte joined him at the table.

"Yeah, it's been too long."

Aunt Charlotte set her cup down and took hold of Paul's hands. "You know Dear, there's always something to worry about in life. I know you must feel like, *Again? When will this end?* I'm not suggesting that we should take this threat lightly. We all need to be extra alert. But, just keep in mind that you have something going for you that people like Salvador Boitano can't fathom."

"And that would be . . ."

"You are surrounded by loving friends who would risk their lives to protect you. Several of whom are very capable of more than matching anything that this creep can bring to the dance."

"The dance?"

"Andy's influence, I'm afraid. Too many old westerns, not enough literature."

126

Paul smiled as he looked into her loving, but determined eyes. "You know, sometimes I've wondered about my birth parents. What happened that caused them to give me up?"

"From what I remember, there was no father involved in the decision. You could always look into it."

"I think the reason I haven't has a lot to do with you and Uncle Ernie. Even after Mom and Dad died, I've always felt your love and support. I'd imagine the people who try to find their birth parents must feel like something's missing in their life. But with you two, and now Andy, I've never felt that way."

Tears welled in her eyes, "Oh Paul, you know—"

"Good morning," Connie called out, suddenly appearing around the corner of the cabin. "I hate to butt in here, but I just got a text from Agent Harper. There's been a development with Boitano and I need to meet him at the medical examiner's office, ASAP."

"I'll drive you." Paul headed into the kitchen to grab his keys.

"Would you like some coffee to go?" Aunt Charlotte asked.

"Sounds perfect." Connie followed them into the kitchen.

"How about some peanut butter on toast? No telling when you'll be able to eat something."

"With sliced bananas," Paul suggested.

"I practically grew up on peanut butter and sliced bananas. It's still my favorite sandwich," Connie said, as they headed for Paul's truck.

******

127

Agent Harper met them in the parking lot.

"Brad, this is Paul Armstrong. Paul, Agent Brad Harper."

The two men shook hands.

"So what's up?" Connie asked, as they followed him down a long hallway.

"Well, it looks to me like your worries might be over, Mr. Armstrong." He held the door open into a small room. "I had them move the body here so we could have some privacy."

Paul looked down on the diminutive, pale corpse. In life, Salvadore Boitano's small stature fueled his need for power. Now, it was difficult for Paul to imagine why he'd ever feared the man.

"The Saint Croix police brought his wife in for questioning," Harper explained. "Riga mortis had already set in by the time the ambulance arrived. Best guess is that her 911 call came in at least two hours after he'd croaked."

"Cause of death?" Connie asked.

"Massive heart attack. Possibly chemically induced. The wife told the officers that she'd surprised her husband and a prostitute in the shower, after he'd bolstered his libido with cocaine."

"Any signs of violence?"

"Nothing on him, but she had quite a shiner."

"You've seen her?"

"Yeah, got a call early this morning, and went down to the station for the questioning. I don't think anyone in that room wants to make things tough on her. She says she must have been knocked out and when she came to, he was gone."

"What do you think?"

128

"I think she waited two hours before calling to make sure he couldn't be revived. Can't blame her."

"Anything going on with his boys? There were three, I believe."

"Yeah. After the interview, Agent Wilson and I brought her back to the villa. The two big guys were playing some video game and didn't seem all that broken up. The smaller guy, Francis, seemed giddy. Kept saying how it was nobody's fault. That Sal'd had a long and productive life and wouldn't want anyone moping around."

"Wow, that's a positive spin," Paul said.

"Well, considering who gave that little eulogy, I'm not surprised," Connie replied. "It amazes me how these creeps can delude themselves into thinking they're somehow good guys, forced to play out a bad hand."

"I know she was married to a mafia boss for 50 years, but I still felt sorry for her," Agent Wilson added. "She looked old, sore and tired. Said that she'd be expected to put on a good funeral and it was the last thing she would ever have to do for the guy. They're all flying out tomorrow with the body on Sal's private jet."

Back outside, they thanked Agent Harper for his help. Realizing that after over two years, the troubles he inherited from Alan Sherman's venture into the dark side might be over, Paul brushed aside Harper's offered hand and hugged the startled agent.

Connie disconnected after a lengthy call as Paul drove back to Windsol. "That was our contact in New Jersey. It seems that Sal's death's been mostly met with relief by his lieutenants. Saved them having to unseat him is what our contact thinks. Since this entire stunt was brought on by Sal wanting to prove he's still top dog, I don't expect there'll be any interest in you from whomever takes over for him."

"But I thought it was all about an eye for an eye with those people? Wouldn't Buddy's murder still require some kind of retribution?"

"Probably not in Buddy's case. Buddy and his boys don't seem to be missed by anyone. I guess that can happen when you perfect the art of being a raging asshole. I don't think even his Uncle Sal missed him."

"I can't thank you enough, Connie. This thing has been hanging over us for so long. I'm having a hard time realizing it may be over. Maybe this will help shake it loose. Yeeeehaw!" he yelled. pounding the steering wheel.

Startled by the outburst, Connie laughed. "Well, that probably didn't surprise me as much as your bromantic embrace surprised Agent Harper."

"I hope he doesn't get the wrong impression and ask me out to a movie or something."

"Don't think he swings that way."

"You know, this entire thing with the mob was caused by something completely unexpected and outside my control. I guess, it makes sense that it would end the same way."

"Yeah, I guess all we can do, sometime, is just hang on and hope for the best."

"You're like that, too."

"What do you mean?"

"Completely unexpected. Sienna told me that you're quitting the FBI because you didn't want to bring me in. What made you think that was a good idea?"

Connie laughed, "I have no idea. Maybe I thought it was time for a career change . . . I've done a lot of thinking about that very question over the last year, and I still can't figure it out. Granted, if anybody deserved to be disappeared, those three did. But, I've brought in people before whose motives I empathized with. Maybe it was an emotional reaction to Adam's death. You know . . . that you two almost look like twins?"

"Good looking, was he?"

"Oh yeah, but not nearly as conceited about it," she replied sharply.

"I was kidding."

"So was I," she laughed, punching his shoulder. A few miles later she asked, "I think I read somewhere that you were adopted."

"Somewhere, like in an FBI file? So much for personal privacy. You probably know my blood type too."

"You really do sound like my brother. No, I don't know your blood type but there's better than a sixty percent chance it's either A positive or O positive."

"Nope. AB negative. I am in an exclusive minority. Less than one percent I'm told. Potentially a universal donor to all."

"Can we find a hat big enough to fit on that head?" Connie laughed. "Your parents, they're the ones that caused it. Mine too. I'm AB negative and so was Adam."

"So we have that going for us as well. Anyway, back to your question. My birth-mother gave me up in the hospital. My Mom and Dad lived just outside of Tacoma, a little town called Puyallup."

"The Puyallup Fair. I try and go every year. Is that where you grew up?"

"No, eventually we moved to the Leshi district in Seattle, a couple blocks off Lake Washington."

"Let me guess. You went to Franklin. Played quarterback and your girlfriend was a cheerleader."

"So you do have a file on me."

"No, it's just kind of predictable . . . You just give off this *All-American Boy* persona. You know, wouldn't say *shit if you had a mouthful*. No wonder Buddy didn't see you coming . . . You ever regret murdering them?"

"You ever regret **your** murders?"

"I'm an agent. It's called killing, not murder," she replied defensively, locking eyes with him.

"So, what is it you're asking? Do I lay awake at night feeling guilty? Am I sorry I did it? Does it affect my sex life?"

"Easy, Paul. My mistake, we're just making conversation. I didn't think that'd upset—"

"No. Connie, I don't regret killing them. Falco had attacked my wife, killed our baby, almost killed my best friend and threatened AJ. The police were powerless to stop them. I know it's called murder and I would like the opportunity to have proven it was self-defense. But since that option seems to bring with it the potential for more reprisals to my family, then I'll gladly accept being a murderer. I'm a murderer who's thankful that his wife, child and family were spared more harm."

After a brief silence, Connie chuckled. "I have to say, that for barely knowing each other, we can get into it pretty quick."

Paul dropped his shoulders and let out a long breath. "I guess that's a good thing. Right?"

"Seemed to have worked pretty well for me and Adam," Connie replied as they pulled into Windsol.

******

Invasion of privacy wasn't even a yellow light. She made the call as soon as she returned to the cabin and quickly breezed through the required authorizations, protocols and safeguards. Using resources only available to a handful of people in the intelligence community, it took her less than an hour. Blinking through tears, she stared at the pdf file open on her Blackberry. It all made sense . . . Flying to Dallas . . . Not bringing charges against him . . . Giving up a career for him and flying all over hell and gone to protect him.

20

The dogs sprang from the porch to greet Wyatt and Erin, who cautiously remained in the car. "Give it a rest boys and girls," Barney shouted. "We don't want to scare away our new city friends, before they even come inside."

Hearing the commotion, Joey appeared from the barn and jogged over to greet Erin who, seeing him approach, had fearlessly stepped from the car.

"Hey you."

"Hey *you*," she replied, with a giggle.

"Wanna see the herd?"

"You bet. Dad, will you take my bag inside? Joey's going to show me around."

"A . . . sure, Honey. I'll be inside . . . er . . . with Barney."

"A . . . er . . . Whatever," she laughed, as the two practically skipped away, hand in hand.

"Don't worry, Dad. They're good kids," Barney assured him, as the two men watched the young couple disappear into the barn.

"I have to say, since meeting Joey, she's been a different person." Wyatt took a seat at the kitchen table after dropping their bags in the guest bedrooms. "Happy, like she was before the divorce."

"Yeah, divorce's tough on kids, but as Joey once wisely told Paul, marriage can be tough on kids, too. You want cream in your coffee, or something a little more fun?" Barney asked, holding up a bottle of Baileys Irish Cream.

"Smart kid, Joey," Wyatt replied, nodding at the Baileys. "Pretty common scenario in some ways. Got married in our early 20's. Had Erin five years later, about the time we started wearing each other down. You know, her resenting the time I spent away from her and me feeling hemmed in."

"You try counseling?" Barney asked, joining Wyatt at the kitchen table.

"Not right away and not for the usual reasons. Erin was the center of our lives, so I didn't pick up on the signs."

"Signs?"

"Gretchen was having an affair with Roger, a house-husband who lived near us. Nice guy, actually."

"So, that's what caused the divorce?"

"No. It just helped me realize how dissatisfied I was in the marriage. She wanted us to stay together for Erin and talked me into seeing a counselor, who'd help us develop some guidelines for an open marriage."

"This is getting interesting." Barney stood and walked over to the cupboard. "You want something without coffee in it?" Barney placed a bottle of Cuervo, a salt shaker and a bowl of limes on the table.

Two shots later, Wyatt politely refused the joint that Barney had lit up.

"You know there's a state law now preventing random drug testing."

"Yeah, but I really never liked the stuff anyway. Makes me tired and withdrawn."

"That's because you never tried my primo weed. But, no problem. I'm all for every man making up his—"

"Dad? Are you smoking weed?"

Barney and Wyatt hadn't heard Erin and Joey's footsteps on the porch. Now, standing in the open doorway, Erin's disbelieving look left Wyatt speechless.

"Christ, Uncle Barney," Joey scolded, following Erin inside. "This is not what we talked about when we discussed making a good impression."

"You're right. Sorry Chief." Turning to Erin somberly he added, "But I promise you that your dad *just said no.*"

Rapidly nodding in agreement, Wyatt reminded Erin of a bobblehead. "You guys are fourteen. Come on Joey, let's leave these kids to their party."

"We're going into town. Mom texted me. The ferry broke down and we're on our own for dinner. We'll bring back some pizza. You guys need anything for the munchies?"

"Some ice cream and berries would be nice," Barney replied, sweetly. But Joey had already closed the door hard behind him.

"I thought that went well," Barney said, after the antique grandfather clock had ticked through several minutes of silence.

"I've got to say, I like your nephew. Seems really mature."

"Oh, he is that. He told me the other day that one reason he isn't keen on going away to college is because he's not sure I can stay out of trouble on my own."

"He might be right . . . So, is that the primo weed you were telling me about?"

136

******

Not able to wait any longer, Paul entered their bedroom and kissed Sienna awake. "Salvador Boitano has expired. Ding dong, the Don is dead, gone, kaput. Connie thinks that the mafia will no longer be interested in us."

"I thought that might have happened." she replied sleepily, pulling him down to her.

"Huh? What do you—"

AJ and Rose, Windsol's 130-pound, rescue dog, suddenly appeared in the doorway. "Hank and Roxanne are cooking breakfast at the big house and Hank said I was supposed to give you a message, but I'm not sure I should."

"What's the message?" Paul asked.

"Get your lazy asses out of bed." AJ giggled, then continued, "Aunt Charlotte's already there. Red's waking up Andy and you're supposed to bring Aunt Connie with you. So, come on!" he shouted, charging back outside.

"Lazy asses?" Sienna repeated.

"Blame Hank. I'm sure it's a direct quote."

"Aunt Connie?"

"The woman does grow on you."

Sienna stopped Paul as he started to rise. "Andy and I left last night to . . . speak with Boitano."

Paul rolled back in bed. "What?"

"Gigi called from work. She said that Boitano's men were at the restaurant, without Boitano."

"So . . . what? You thought you'd go over and keep him company?"

"Well, Andy and I thought we might be able to convince him that coming after you wasn't a good idea."

137

Paul looked at her, unable to form a cohesive sentence.

"There was tequila involved," she added. "But I'd pretty much given up on the idea by the time we got to the villa."

"OK, so let me see if I have this . . . You two were going to knock on Salvador Boitano's door, or did you plan on kicking it in and surprising him?"

"We hadn't really thought that far. When I saw Andy's pistol and the ambulance passed us, I realized—"

"Andy's pistol? Holy shit! What about you? What'd you bring?" Paul's eyes fell on the black tube leaning against the wall by the door. Smiling broadly, he pulled her close. "You were gonna spear him?"

"No, I couldn't have done it. But, Andy—"

"Not much doubt about that."

Sienna dressed quickly. They stepped out into a bright morning. The nightmare behind them, for a moment they felt giddy. A teary-eyed and puffy faced Constance Hunter waiting on the porch, stopped both in their tracks.

"What's wrong, Connie?" Sienna asked, fearing the worst.

A broad smile broke onto the agent's face as she wiped her eyes with the back of her hands. "Absolutely nothing's wrong, but I've got some news that's gonna come as a big shock."

Thinking she had put her FBI hat back on, Paul asked, "What's up, Agent Hunter?"

"That sounds a bit formal, don't you think . . . after all we've been through?"

"OK . . . What's up, Connie?"

"You know how easy it was for us to get under each other's skin when we were in the car, coming back from the hospital?"

"Yeah."

"Kind of like how siblings are with each other."

Hearing Sienna gasp, Paul shot her a bewildered look. Confused by the tears filling Sienna's eyes, Paul took the Blackberry from Connie's outstretched hand.

State of Washington
Certificate and Record of Birth
February 8, 1971
Caucasian male, 9 lbs. 7 oz.
Mother's name: Jeanette Louise Hunter

Paul looked up slowly. "It's my birthdate, but a lot of—"

"It's you, Paul. Your adoption by the Armstrongs was completed before you left the hospital. I'm surprised our mother had the awareness to spare you the childhood Adam and I suffered through."

"But how? Wouldn't you have known?"

"You and I are three-years apart. When I was two, our folks split up and I was shipped off to my grandmother. I guess our mom realized, since she was unable to care for herself and a two-year-old, there was no way she could deal with a new baby. She left me, and went to stay with a friend. That way, no one would ever know she was pregnant and she could give the baby . . . **you**, up for adoption."

"What about Adam?"

"About a year after you were born, Dad returned and I was sent back to live with them. When I was five, Adam was

139

born. Of course, Dad took off soon after and we never saw him again."

"So, it was just the three of you?"

"More like the two of us. Mom was a mess as far back as I can remember. You were lucky she gave you up."

"I never had a desire to find my biological family, but now I wish I'd searched. I don't know why it never crossed my mind that I might have siblings."

"You would have loved Adam."

"I wish I'd met him."

A wave of emotion swept over Paul. He stood and pulled Connie from her chair. "I didn't realize how much I've missed you, until now."

Overjoyed, Sienna joined them in the hug-fest, until an impatient AJ darted up the stairs, two at a time. "What are you guys doing? The eggs are getting cold. Come on, move it." Rose led the group back to the great house with AJ chattering continuously, alongside Connie. "I have six people who aren't my *real* aunt that I get to call aunt. There's Aunt Katie, Aunt Carmen, Aunt Sally, Aunt Roxanne and Aunt Charlotte. Actually, Aunt Charlotte would be my *real* great aunt if Papa Andy ever talks her into marrying him."

"You're a lucky boy to have so many people that love you."

"I know that. So, can I call you Aunt Connie?"

Connie was too choked up to reply, so Paul answered for her, "Yes you can, AJ, and it's for real."

******

Despite Boitano's passing, Sienna continued to check her rear-view mirror as she drove along the island's coastal road

140

to her restaurant. *Stop looking back,* she chided herself. *It's over.* Relaxing, she turned off the air conditioner, opened the window, and filled her lungs with warm salt air. But, her moment of Zen was short-lived. A dark SUV with heavily tinted windows closed in quickly. Thinking the vehicle was signaling to pass, she pulled on to the shoulder. The SUV pulled over and stopped in front of her. On high alert, Sienna dropped the transmission into reverse. Anxiety swept over her as the passenger door opened, but she instantly relaxed when the elderly woman appeared from the car proffering a friendly wave.

"Sylvie!" Sienna shouted, stepping out of her car.

"I wanted to see you before I left island. You deserve a full introduction, Sienna. I'm Sylvia Boitano."

Seeing Sienna's obvious shock, Sylvie continued, "My husband is dead. I wanted you to know."

"I heard. I'm sorry for your loss, but—"

"Don't be sorry, Sienna. It was his time to go." She raised her sunglasses to the top of her head, displaying a purple welt under her right eye.

"You're hurt."

"He wasn't very happy before he died. But, that's all in the past now. . . Or it will be after the funeral on Thursday." Sylvie looked out over the ocean. "It's beautiful here. What a wonderful part of the world." Turning to Sienna, she reached out and took her hand. "You don't have to worry anymore. The nightmare for your family is over."

"Thank you, Sylvie. Paul and I wish you all the best."

"You don't know how much that means to me." She pulled down her sunglasses and held out her hand. A large diamond ring sparkled in Sylvie's open palm. "He gave me this on our twentieth anniversary. Please take it, Sienna. My hope is

141

that you can get enough money from it to save some of the poor homeless animals I've seen on the island." She placed the ring in Sienna's hand, folded her fingers closed over it and walked back toward her car. She stopped and turned. "I hope you won't think too badly of me for all the grief my husband has caused. God bless you, Dear." She stepped into the car and was gone.

21

The black and white photo of a cowboy lassoing a cowgirl was the front of the announcement. Inside, the hand-written scrawl simply read, *She said yes!*

Andy had finally worn Aunt Charlotte down and offered to fly all the Washington residents to Saint Croix for their wedding. In addition to the original cast of Windsol's characters, the continental participants now included Wyatt, Connie and Erin. Also, Joey accompanied Barney and Claire, while Brooke celebrated Christmas with her parents in Arizona.

Andy had rented a passenger van, which Paul and Sienna used to pick up the first arrivals. Sally, Tex, baby Katie and aunts Kate and Carmen arrived exhausted after 12 hours in the air. On the ride back to Windsol, Kate shared another announcement.

"We're staying until June. We've become snowbirds."

"What? Who's going to take care of the ranch?" Paul asked.

"A rancher friend of ours is going to look after things through the winter. Name's Frank Wilkens. He's actually our sperm donor—"

"—who struts around town referring to himself as *Super Stud,*" Carmen added. "Frankly, I think he deserves the title. He agreed to the job, even after we explained his duties wouldn't include sex."

"Great news! Does Andy know?" Sienna asked.

"Nobody knows except those present," Carmen replied, furtively.

"Why?"

Kate winked at Sally. "You want to tell them?"

"They beat the odds. Carmen and Kate are both three months pregnant."

Letting out a whoop, Paul high fived the two expectant mothers.

"Hey keep your eyes on the road," a sleep deprived Tex grumbled from the back seat. "Driving on the left side of the road from the left side of the cab is nuts enough as it is."

"Yes sir, officer, sir," Paul replied, grabbing the wheel with both hands.

"That's wonderful, you guys," Sienna gushed. "When did you find out?"

"Well, we've known for some time, but didn't want to say anything until we got through the first trimester."

"It was my idea to stay here until the babies are born. I told Kate that if I'm going to be putting my body through the travails of bladder compression, stretched abdomen and morning sickness, I didn't think it too much to ask that it be done in 85-degree weather. It was twenty-fucking-four degrees when we flew out of Wenatchee this morning."

"In fact, if we can make it work, Carmen and I want Windsol to be our children's second home. So, after the trail rides next summer, we'll come back for another six months."

"We'll need to look at adding a room onto your cabin."

144

"Sounds good, Mr. Architect." Kate replied. "So, anything new with you two?"

"Oh, a few changes are about to happen with work and things." Sienna's glance at Paul wasn't missed by Carmen. "I have to go back to the restaurant for a few hours, but we'll fill you in tonight when we're all together."

******

Returning home from the restaurant exhausted, Sienna took a shower before joining the group on the great house porch.

Roxanne and Hank had just heard the news from Kate and Carmen. "That's so exciting. Hank, can you imagine, by next fall we'll have two new babies at Windsol to love."

"Good luck getting them back when Roxanne babysits," Hank warned.

"What a load of crap that is. Excuse my French but my Hanky-Bear goes absolutely, over-the-moon, nuts with anything that has to do with babies."

Hank waved-off Roxanne. "Seriously, we're elated for both of you. Actually, for all of us." Tears welled in his eyes.

"Oh god, there goes Hanky-Bear." Tex chuckled.

"He speaks," Sally observed, "but, can he also change a diaper?"

"So, you guys mentioned on the ride back from the airport that you have some changes coming up." Carmen prodded Sienna, as Tex shuffled inside, holding baby Katie at arm's length.

"Sure, Carmen. But, let me relax for a minute," Sienna said, collapsing in a chair. Paul served her iced tea with a concerned expression, then gave her a kiss. She took a sip. "Thanks, Honey."

"Sienna hasn't felt like booze since her night of overindulgence with Andy," Paul explained.

Carmen studied the blissful couple, suspiciously. "No one really asked. They've got something up their sleeve," she whispered to Kate.

Paul served the rest of the group icy Titos Martinis.

"Hey, where's *my* kiss, Honey?"

"Maybe next batch."

"Promises, promises." Hank laughed, and raised his drink. "To Kate and Carmen bringing two new lives to our Windsol Family and, of course, to Andy, Char and marital bliss."

"Sorry Hank," Sienna corrected. "That would be four new lives."

"What? Are Sally and Tex moving down here next fall?"

"We'd like to, but Sheriff Tex has eight more years before we can retire," Sally replied. "Anyway, that would've only made three little people."

"Dumbass." Tex returned with his freshly swaddled daughter. Seeing Sally's reproachful glare, he apologized. "Sorry Hank. I'm a little off my game, what with no sleep and all."

"I've slept less than you," Sally reprimanded him. "And you don't see me being mean."

"Relax. All is forgiven." Roxanne counseled. Hank was still turning over Sienna's comment and hadn't even noticed Tex's return.

"Four babies?" Hank repeated for the third time . . ."You guys are each having twins?"

146

"Oh my god!" Carmen jumped up from her chair, ran over to Sienna and smothered her in a hug. Soon, Roxanne and Sally joined in the mix, screaming, laughing and crying.

Not prone to such grandiose displays of emotion, Kate and Tex approached Paul. "Wow, twins, eh?"

"Yep."

When it finally sunk in, it was nearly too much for the already overly-emotional Hanky-Bear. Shaking his head in disbelief, he remained seated, muttering quietly to himself. "Holy Shit. Paul and Sienna . . . Twins."

Hearing the screams, Red and AJ dropped their baseball gloves and ran in from the field.

"Is everything OK?" AJ asked.

"Is Hank drinking too much rum?" Red probed.

"Everything's fine, AJ," Sienna explained. "We just told everybody about the twins coming."

"Oh, is that all," AJ groaned, disappointedly. "I thought it was a snake or something really cool."

22

"I'm trying to remember the last time we had a full house at Windsol," Andy said, sitting in the packed restaurant.

"It's the first time, Andy," the bride replied.

"No wonder I don't remember the last time."

"You two have on your dancin' shoes?" Paul asked the newly married couple from the stage.

"Yee haw!" Andy stood and pulled Aunt Charlotte to her feet.

Glancing over at Jon Jon Marley, who nodded his readiness, Paul and Music D'em, Jon Jon's three-piece reggae band, launched into a full hour of uninterrupted country western and reggae. Aunt Charlotte made it through the first quarter of the set before turning over her husband to fulfill his promise of dancing with "every woman in the joint."

It had been a simple wedding ceremony, held at sunset on the beach in front of The Green Flash. The conga line snaked out the restaurant and onto the two-lane coastal road. From the bar, she watched Andy, with 20 revelers in tow, reach the beach.

"What can I get you?" Arlo, the broad-faced bartender inquired.

Aunt Charlotte sighed and shook her head. Circling a red bandana above his head; she watched her husband dance barefoot across the sand into the ocean. He made a sharp U-turn when the surf reached his cummerbund and led the serpentine merrymakers back toward shore, without missing a beat.

"I think it's time for a Martini."

"You're the bride, right?"

"Guilty."

"Well . . . Congratulations. Looks like you've got yourself a live-wire there."

"You have no idea."

"Mind if I join you?" Paul took the seat next to her. "Our favorite cowpoke really knows how to have fun, doesn't he?"

"Sometimes I worry that I don't have enough energy for a younger man."

"I thought he was older than you."

"I'm referring to maturity."

"Looks like our fearless leader is making this a night to remember," Barney pulled up a stool. "I'll have what she's having, Arlo."

Barney's drink came as Andy turned for home. "Man, that little guy has more piss in him than . . . Ah, sorry about that, Aunt Charlotte."

"Nothing to apologize for, Barney. Paul and I were just saying the same thing. I'm surprised you're not out there with him."

"I'd say Claire seems to be doing just fine filling-in for both of them," Paul observed. Second in the line, a laughing Claire pranced enthusiastically, throwing up high-kicks and serious booty shakes.

"Truth is, I'm a bit jet-lagged." Barney explained. "Don't know where she gets her energy."

"We really do appreciate you all coming down." Charlotte reached over and patted Barney's hand. "I know how busy you are back home."

"No place we'd rather be. Gotta say though, I'm a little concerned with the pregnancy epidemic goin' on. Hope it's not something in the water. *Twins?* I thought you had slow swimmers, Ace."

"Yeah, well, maybe with all the ocean swimming I've been doing—"

"Yeah, right. Aunt Charlotte, do you think it's wise for a man of Paul's advancing years and fragile temperament to sire such a brood?"

"Without question. So, when are you and Claire going to tie the knot?"

Barney choked on his drink. Aunt Charlotte pounded the big man on his back. "OK, OK, I'm OK. Just caught me by surprise."

"Don't know why. You two were made for each other. I truly can't understand what you're waiting for. But, I'm not saying any more."

"Cha cha cha cha cha, Uh! Cha cha cha cha cha, Uh!" Disengaging himself from the Conga line, Andy twirled towards them. "The night is young. The air is filled with the sweet fragrance of jasmine. Care to dance, my most beloved?"

"I would, but I'm still a bit jet lagged."

"I'm up for it, if I can lead."

"Very funny, boys. How 'bout it, Char?"

"I haven't seen him so happy, since . . . ever," Barney noted, watching the newlyweds take the dance floor.

"That's what a good wife can do for you," Sienna said, slipping her arm around Paul's waist.

"Wow, I'm sensing a not so subtle message here." Barney scowled. Catching Arlo's attention, he pointed at his Martini glass.

"From the dance floor, Andy shouted over the music, "Well, it's about time," as Connie, Wyatt and Erin entered the restaurant.

Practically sprinting from the opposite side of the room, Joey lifted a giggling Erin off the floor and the two disappeared quickly down the stairs to the beach.

"Thank god," Barney whispered to Paul. "The kid's been like a caged tiger waiting for her. Guess they missed their connection in Dallas."

"It looks like things have been progressing rapidly." Paul observed.

Barney watched Wyatt crane his neck in a futile attempt to follow the young lovers, as they disappeared behind a row of palms. "I'm thinkin' at least third base, which is probably way too fast for Officer Howard."

"Do you think it's time to have *the talk* with your nephew?"

"You mean, the *take your time, there's a lot of fish in the ocean* talk or the *make sure you use a condom* talk?"

******

"Hey Sis," Connie placed her palm on Sienna's belly. "Hard to believe there's two in there. You look more beautiful than ever."

"Thanks, Con, I wish I felt as good as you say I look."

"Morning sickness?"

"Oh yeah. Afternoons and evenings, too. But, enough about me." She led them over to the bar. "It sounds like you guys had quite a time getting down here."

"We were delayed out of Dallas and missed our connection in Miami."

"So, I bet you guys could use a drink," Barney said.

"Thanks Barn, but my stomach isn't handling booze very well right now," Wyatt explained.

"Which is his way of asking Barney if he'd share some more of his primo weed," Connie clarified.

"Absolutely, my friend. Step out to my clinic in the parking lot and Dr. Barney will fix you up."

"Sorry about that," Paul said, watching Barney and Wyatt head for the stairs.

"Which part? Turning my police officer, fiancé into a pot- head or introducing him to Barney? Is that a Martini you're drinking?"

"Both, I guess." Paul caught Arlo's attention and signaled the order. "We're so glad you could come down. We have a lot a time to make up for." Paul gave his sister a welcoming hug and kiss.

"Speaking of separated at birth, do you think . . .?" Sienna quipped, watching the two plus-sized men lumber down the stairs to the parking lot.

"Could be." Connie thanked Arlo for her drink. "There's definitely a connection there. When he's not obsessing about his concern over how fast things have progressed with Erin and Joey, it's all about Barney this and Barney that. 'You should see Barney's cattle. What a great flower business he's started with Brooke.' And his primo weed . . ." She took a sip from her drink and continued, "apparently doesn't make him drowsy or impact his IBS."

"T.M.I.," Sienna laughed.

"Yeah, tell me about it. I know more about the ins and outs of my man's bowels than—"

"Stop, please," Sienna pleaded. "Look, I'll leave you two to catch up. It's close to 9:00 and I'm exhausted. It looks like AJ's still going strong," she observed, as AJ and Claire tirelessly danced and spun through Jon Jon's reggae version of the Dixie Cup's Chapel of Love.

"I've got AJ," Paul replied. "It'll give me an excuse not to have to close the place down with Andy and the boys."

After Sienna left, Paul and Connie walked down to the beach. "So what's with Claire?"

"Yeah, she's cutting loose tonight," Paul replied.

"Doesn't she have a history of bipolar behavior?"

"Cut her some slack. She's just having fun."

"Easy brother, I was just making an observation. She seems a bit over the top compared to the last time I saw her up at the farm."

Paul thought for a minute before replying. "Sorry, I just feel bad about how scrutinized she is by all of us. Barney doesn't complain about it, but I know it bugs him. He knows the signs and I trust him to keep her on track."

"I get that. Sorry I mentioned it."

They sat on the sand and watched the half-moon break above a cloud bank, illuminating the beach. "It's beautiful down here, Paul. Wyatt can retire in three years and we're talking about making this our second home."

"Andy already agreed that if you two are interested, we'll build another cabin for you. The original master plan allowed for three more."

"I'm not sure yet, what my job status will be at the FBI. I'm getting closer to the end of my furlough and still haven't made up my mind."

"How would that affect your coming down here more often?"

"I don't think you realize what a wheel your big sister is at the agency. My superiors wouldn't look favorably at my disappearing to the tropics each year for a few months."

"You want me to talk with them? Tell them you need some quality family time?"

"Oh sure, that would do it. Maybe you could negotiate a midday siesta for me, as well."

Paul spotted the vague forms of Erin and Joey approaching and greeted them. "Hey Kids, you might want to head back up to the restaurant before your uncle and dad polish off what's left of the cake."

Joey looked at Erin, "Maybe now's a good time."

"OK," she replied.

"A good time for what?"

23

Connie and Paul realized that given the foray into Barney's weed, the kids wouldn't receive a cogent response from Wyatt and Barney to the bombshell they'd dropped. Erin's recent eighteenth birthday had apparently triggered the announcement of a plan they'd been hatching for some time. Counselling patience to the young lovers, they suggested that it might be best if Connie and Paul broach the announcement first. This weighed heavily on Connie, as she lay awake beside her snoring boyfriend for most of the night. Thankful for daybreak, she dressed and left the great house bedroom for the community kitchen, to start the coffee. Surprised, she found the coffee already brewed by Claire, who greeted her from the porch table.

"You couldn't sleep either?" Connie asked, joining her outside.

"I tried, but couldn't shake some ideas I had bumping around in my head. I thought I might be able to sleep after writing them down." She stretched and yawned, then stood up. "I think I'll give it another try. Barney's such a sound sleeper; he won't have even missed me. It's great having you all down here, Connie. I'll see you a little later."

Connie sipped her coffee and watched as Claire disappeared down the path. She heard her give a distant greeting and Sienna appeared shortly afterwards, looking blanched and miserable.

"Rough night?" Connie asked.

"Not the pregnancy I was hoping for," Sienna slumped into a chair.

"Not drinking coffee, I'd imagine," Connie said, standing. "What can I get you?"

"Thanks Connie, there's some peppermint tea in the cupboard to the left of the sink that seems to help."

"Coming right up." Connie filled the teapot and set it on the stove. "Can I make you something else?"

"No thanks, I think that's about all I can keep down right now. So, Paul told me about your discussion with Joey and Erin. I don't suppose you've mentioned anything to Wyatt yet."

"No, he and Barney had quite the time last night. Reality's gonna hit them both hard this morning."

"What's hard in the morning?" Appearing suddenly, Barney laughed at his joke and lumbered into the kitchen for coffee.

"You know for a big man, you move pretty quietly," Connie observed.

"Like a big cat," Barney boasted. "Claire went back to bed. I guess she had a bit of insomnia last night. Happens sometimes with the meds she's taking. So, where's my cohort this morning? Kinda late for him to still be in the sack, isn't it?"

"Haven't any of you heard of island time?" Wyatt shouted, from the bedroom. "Christ, it's barely daylight."

"Well good morning bright eyes," Barney greeted Wyatt, as his disheveled partner-in-crime joined them.

The informal community breakfast lasted until mid-morning, when Andy arrived, appearing a little green around the gills. Sienna had already left with Kate, Carmen and Aunt Charlotte to meet with the Animal Shelter board, regarding the disposition of the $85,000 received at the charity auction from Sylvie Boitano's diamond ring. Claire, Joey and Erin had gone with Hank and Roxanne, who took the boys to the beach at Cane Bay.

Connie and Paul had waited for this opportunity to speak with Wyatt and Barney alone. Connie looked at Paul to get his read, if Andy's appearance should delay their discussion. Paul shrugged and started, "So, Erin and Joey asked us to discuss an idea with you two."

"Would you like me to take my breakfast back to the cabin to give you adults some privacy?" Andy asked.

"What idea?" A look of concern had appeared on Wyatt's face.

"That's not necessary, Andy," Connie replied. "You might have some insight we could use."

"Well, it's about time somebody recognizes it. I knew I liked you."

"She pregnant?" Barney asked, putting down the paper, prepared for the worse.

"No, they want to move in together down here, after Erin graduates." Paul replied.

"What about Joey?" Barney asked.

"Joey said he has enough credits to graduate and doesn't want to go back to school just to play ball. He wants to stay here with you and Claire and help with the boat charter business. Then this summer, after Erin graduates, she'll come down and join him and they'll run the operation through the summer.

"This is awful," Wyatt moaned. "I mean, I can't think of another guy I'd rather see Erin with, but they're too young to be making this kind of commitment."

"I agree 150%," Barney seconded. "You got to talk to him, Ace. Joey listens to you."

"Ah, excuse me," Andy said, clearing his throat. "May I add a thought here?"

"Sure, go ahead," Connie replied.

"When Erin and Joey came over to Winthrop last summer, I got a chance to really know them. They're hard working, straight thinking kids. I wouldn't worry too much about their age. You know, to this day I regret cutting Aaron out of my life when he married Sienna. 'Course that was a long time ago and for different reasons, I'm still embarrassed to say. These kids are a lot older than their years, so I'd say to give 'em your blessing."

"What do **you** think, Connie?" Wyatt asked.

"While I can appreciate what Andy's saying, Paul and I discussed it last night and we both think that it would be better if they held off for a while. They're young and in love, but as we all know, there are a lot of changes people go through in their late teens and twenties. If it's real, it will still be there for them. What's the rush?"

"Exactly my point," Barney agreed. "So will you talk to Joey, Paul?"

"Sure."

"OK," Wyatt said. "I'll talk to Erin. Connie, will you help out on this?"

"Sure, but you should probably let Gretchen know what's going on."

"Gretchen's Erin's mom?" Andy asked.

"Yes," Wyatt replied. "I might wait until after we talk with Erin, because the woman's gonna go through the roof."

"Well I won't be sayin' *I told you so* if this doesn't pan out the way you're hoping," Andy said. "Just remember, there are few things stronger and purer in this world than young people in love. I know from experience what can happen if you try and block it."

******

That evening, Paul stumbled on the young couple at the lookout, holding hands and admiring the crimson sky.

"Did you see the green flash?" Erin asked Paul, excitedly. "I thought it was all in people's imaginations."

"Sienna and I saw it the first time we looked at this property."

Looking at Joey, who nodded back at her, Erin stood, brushed off her shorts and started back to the cottages. "I think I'll go see what my dad and Connie are up to."

Paul sat down next to Joey. "So, how did the conversation with Barney and Wyatt go?" Joey asked, still looking out over the water.

"About like you probably expected," Paul replied.

"They're too young? Why hurry? The boy needs to go to college?"

"Something like that. Look, I know you don't agree with him, but college is really important to Barney, partly, I'm sure because he never went, but also—"

"He wants me to do something with my mind and college will open doors for me. I've heard it all, Uncle Paul. The thing is, I wouldn't mind it if I turned out just like him. He's a good man. He's smart, kind, and happy. He did just fine without college. I think it'd be a waste for me to go."

Paul scrambled for another line of reasoning. "I know working down here on a boat sounds ideal, but honestly, it can get old. I think that's what Barney's trying to tell you. College gives you the opportunity to explore new areas, new possibilities, find something you can really sink your teeth into, that never gets old."

"No offense, Uncle Paul, but I could never do the same job all my life. I mean, I know that you love architecture, but I'm more the entrepreneur type. You know . . . always looking for the next thing to get into and develop. If I have any questions about something, I can find the answer on the web. Really, it's a new game out there. Way different then it was back when you went to college. Had the incandescent light bulb even been invented yet?"

"Very funny. OK, I'm less concerned about your immediate college plans. If you change your mind, you can always go later."

"Exactly."

"But this thing with Erin."

"You mean, The Wife?"

"What?!!"

Joey smiled sheepishly and held up his hand to display the simple gold wedding band. "We knew what everyone would think of our plan. So, we decided to take matters into our own hands."

Paul was speechless, so Joey continued, "It was on the beach at Carambola, where you and Sienna were married. We thought that'd be good luck. Reverend Jimmy presided and his wife, Anastasia, was our witness."

"Did you know last night that you were going to do this?"

"Yeah, we did. I'm sorry Uncle Paul, but we figured that you telling Barney and Wyatt that we wanted to move in together would soften the real blow. We didn't lie. We just didn't tell you guys everything."

Paul chuckled, anticipating Uncle Barney's reaction to the news. He didn't know Wyatt that well, but the Uncle Barney eruption would probably register on the island's seismograph. "Well, it's done then. By the way, not everyone was against the idea of you two moving in together."

"Sienna?"

"No, Andy. Said that he thought you two were older than your years and we shouldn't try and stop it. Can I ask you one question though?"

"Sure."

"Why now?"

"Why wait? In your life, how many times have you met a woman you want to spend the rest of your life with?"

"Once," Paul confessed.

"Exactly. I just met mine earlier. You and Sienna have what we have and it's a beautiful thing."

"Yes, it is," Paul agreed, smiling. Walking back to the great house, he added, "Anything Sienna and I can do for you two, just—"

"Well, actually there is something."

24

"You know, things have been so busy, I never really thanked you for talking to Joey the other night."

Seated on the airport bench next to Barney, Paul knew what was coming. Locking his fingers behind his head, he leaned back against the wall and waited.

"Of course, after you agreed to try and convince Joey that he should go to college and not move in with Erin, I was *a little surprised* by the outcome. Must have been quite a talk for him to run off the very next morning and tie the knot. Even got your blessing, he told me. I'm not blaming you for any of this, of course."

"No, of course you're not."

"OK, then . . . well, good talk."

"It's all going to be fine, Barney. They're good kids." Paul wrapped his arm as far around Barney's shoulders as he could reach. "You needed a crew that you can trust to run the charter business in the summer. They'll work hard for you. Sienna and I are happy to have them stay on our boat this summer until they get a place. Andy even suggested we put in permits for building a cabin for them at Windsol next fall."

"Yeah, I guess, and it'll be nice having him here with me on the boat through the busy season. Especially now that Claire's decided to head back to the farm."

"What about that, by the way? I thought she was all excited about being *The Last Hurrah's* captain. You were going to be the cook and bottle washer."

"Yeah, well, it looks like I got a promotion. It's OK though. She's been writing short stories and poetry. Seems like a good outlet for her. She's joined a women's group in Port Townsend. Had them all down to the farm for lunch a few weeks back." Barney chuckled derisively.

"What's so funny?"

"Not really funny . . . just kind of ironic. It was my idea. I'd heard about the woman's group from one of my clients. It sounded like a good way for her to make some new friends, so I suggested she go check it out. You know, have a wider support system up there."

"Sure."

"I walk in to say 'Hi' and it was like I was tracking in cow shit or something. 'You must be Barney,' this tall skinny woman says to me. Barb, I think was her name. 'Yes I am, and you are?' I replied, real polite-like. 'Not interested in men anymore,' she answers. This cracked them all up. Thought it was the funniest thing they'd ever heard. Felt like a stranger in my own home. After they left, I said to Claire, that I was glad they wouldn't be back again, thinking she'd agree with me. She got all huffy and said that they were great gals and the group was important to her. Gave her a sense of validation-whatever the fuck that means."

"So, is there trouble between you two?"

"No, nothing serious. It's just that for some time now, I've been her support and closest friend. It seems like now she doesn't need me as much."

"That's probably a good thing, Barn. It'll give you both some breathing room."

"Yeah, I guess. It's just, with her bipolar business, I don't want to get too far away from her."

Joey followed Claire, pulling her carry-on, as they returned from the American Airline's ticket counter. "You boys look out for my guy for me. Watch that he doesn't go all postal over some litterbug or something."

"Will do, Claire." Joey promised.

"Don't worry. We'll call if we need reinforcements," Paul said, hugging her warmly.

Motioning for Barney to lean over, she stood on her tip-toes, took his face in her hands and gave him a brief kiss. Taking her bag from Joey, she turned and disappeared quickly through the *Departures Only* door, without looking back.

They watched the door close behind her. Barney sighed and shook his head. "Well, come on Joey. Daylight's burning and we've got to run through a maintenance check on *The Last Hurrah*. See you back at the ranch for dinner tonight, Amigo."

"Sounds good. Sienna thought we'd eat early, say around 5:30? Hank and Roxanne are joining us. Andy and Aunt Charlotte are taking the boys out for pizza and a movie."

Paul watched the $2.00 he'd given the disembodied hand with long curly-cue green nails disappear back into the parking attendant's hut. He wheeled his Dodge dual cab onto the roadway fronting the southern edge of the island's airport. Fifteen minutes later he carried a beer and icy lemonade from the bar over to Sienna, who sat waiting for him at Sand Castles Beach Club.

164

"Thanks, Honey. Did she get off OK?"

"Yeah, but something's going on between them. She didn't seem all that sad about leaving him for two months."

"Well, she did mention to me earlier that sometimes she feels a bit suffocated by Barney. Maybe he just needs to let go and trust it'll all work out."

"Is that what you'd do with me . . . just let go and hope for the best?"

"Well, I did that once. I don't see doing it ever again. I'm not letting you out of my sight." She leaned over and kissed him softly.

"Oh my God!" The waitress gushed approaching them with menus. "How sweet is true love?"

"Hello, Sharleen," Sienna said, as the tall, tan and augmented, bleached blonde threw a come-hither smile at Paul.

"Well, well, I thought it was you. If it isn't my old boss. Got yourself knocked up it appears. Is this the guilty party?" She set her hand on Paul's shoulder.

"Paul, this is Sharleen Gifford."

Paul shrugged off her hand as he turned to face her. "Nice to meet you. You used to work at The Green Flash?"

"That's right, Sweetie. I just got back on island a few weeks ago. What can I get you guys?"

"Oh, I think we're just having drinks," Sienna said, watching relief spread over Paul's face.

"Well, if you change your mind, just holler. Nice meeting you, Paul. You got yourself a real live wire there." Sharleen brushed Paul's shoulder with her breast, as she picked the menus off the table. Swinging her hips, she strutted back into the kitchen.

"That was uncomfortable," Paul said.

"Sorry about not ordering lunch, but I figured it wouldn't get any better. I'll grab a bite at the restaurant and there's some leftover chicken in the fridge from last night."

"So what's the story with Sharleen?"

"I found out that she'd been stealing from the till. We gave her the option of returning the money and quitting or we'd call the cops. She found a third option and left island. It must have been eight years ago, just before Aaron was killed."

"Think you'll get the money back now?"

"I'm not even gonna try. She's bad news. I'm just sorry I ran into her. She was always sticking her booty in every man's face, especially Aaron's. I think she stole around $300, which was a small price to pay to get her out of my hair."

"Well she'd better not go sticking her booty in my face."

"Or what, Mister . . . more discomfort? Remember, Paul, you can always **just say no**." Sienna laughed.

"Exactly, Missy. And then, there's the fact that there ain't nuttin 'bout that big ol' booty of hers that I like."

"Oh really? So much observation in so little time. What kind do you like?"

"Stand up and turn around."

"Very sweet, but that would take way too much energy. Seriously, Honey, I'm struggling to just keep it together."

Paul took her hand. "How can I help?"

"No, you've done all you can and more. I think we need to make a change, and I heard from the agent for that couple in Boulder again. They're really serious about wanting to buy the restaurant."

"I think it's the right thing to do."

"So, you're about to become the sole bread winner . . . At least until I start feeling better?"

166

"Sounds good, even long afterward. We'll figure out what makes the most sense. Right now, selling The Green Flash is the right move."

"I never thought I'd be able to let it go."

25

Paul placed his guitar back in its case as Hank, Roxanne, Barney and Joey arrived at the great house porch.

"Don't stop, on our account," Barney boomed.

"Yeah, play something, Paul," Roxanne coaxed.

"How about after dinner? Sienna called from the restaurant and I have instructions to follow." He stood and walked over to the stove and looked inside the oven. "Barney, how about a hand with the drinks?"

"No problemo, Amigo. What can I get you, Roxanne?"

"White wine's fine."

"Rum and apple juice for me," Hank requested.

"What the hell kind of pussy drink is that?" Barney laughed. "You want a little parasol in it?"

"That'd be nice, if you got one."

"Everything ship shape?" Paul asked Joey, who'd grabbed a Red Stripe out of the fridge.

"Some problem with the bilge pump and he's been complaining about a clunking sound in the transmission. All in all though, everything seems pretty good. He thinks we'll be ready for a shakedown cruise this weekend and our first booking's Tuesday."

"I tell you, Amigo", Barney said, overhearing their conversation, "I've got the best first mate ever. That deck's so clean, you could eat off it. Not sure what's going on with the transmission, though. I've got a mechanic coming by tomorrow to take a look."

"Why don't you ask me?" Hank asked. "I've torn my engine and drive train down so many times, I could do it in the dark. Great drink by the way. Next one though, a little less juice, please." He took another sip. "I work cheap too."

"Tearing it down has never been my problem," Barney replied. "It's putting the damn thing back together that I'm not so good at."

"You know me, Barney," Roxanne interjected. "I don't often toot my husband's horn, but he's a very good mechanic."

"Well, OK then." Barney conceded. "I'd be grateful for your help, Hank. Maybe, while we're working on things, we can also figure out a way to get Roxanne to toot your horn more often."

"I shouldn't have opened my mouth." Roxanne grumbled.

"Maybe that's the problem." Barney laughed, elbowing Hank in the ribs.

"Hey, Uncle Barney . . ." Joey mimed, zipping his mouth shut.

"Huh? Too much? OK, got it, Little Nephew. Sorry about all that, Roxanne. You know I don't mean any disrespect. Maybe I'm a little off with Claire busting out of here so fast."

"That's OK, Barn," Roxanne patted his arm. "I'm sure she already misses you."

"Yeah? Thanks, I hope so."

Roxanne turned to Paul, "Sienna looks real tired lately. I'm getting a little concerned."

169

"She is tired, Roxanne. But, hopefully that's going to change quickly. She's decided to sell the restaurant. It's just too much with the pregnancy."

"She's selling the restaurant? That's probably a smart move. Bet it's hard on her though," Barney said.

Paul heard Sienna's car drive through the gate and went out to greet her.

"Did you start the potatoes?"

"I did and the London Broil has about 10 minutes more." He helped her out of the car. Wrapping her in his arms, he kissed her deeply.

"Wow. My day just took a turn for the better," she sighed.

"So, how'd it go?"

"OK, I guess. I told them. Everybody was sad, but they understood. I explained that no one was being let go, but I'm not sure they believed it."

"It's tough." Paul took her purse and slipped his arm around her thickening waist, as they walked toward the porch. "They're like family to you, after all these years."

"Exactly . . . but, it's done. I held it together pretty well until I drove home. I was crying so hard I had to pull over." She stopped. "There's Kleenex in my purse . . . Thanks." She took a deep breath after wiping away more tears. "But, I don't want this to be a sad evening. We have so much to look forward to."

"Hey Good Lookin'", Barney greeted her with a gentle hug when she reached the porch.

"Thanks for that, Barney, but isn't that an expression usually said to a man?"

"Probably. I've had my foot danglin' from my mouth since I got here."

170

"No problem, Sweetie, I appreciate the sentiment. So, what's going on?"

"Paul told us about selling the restaurant," Roxanne said. "We're sad, but we think it's definitely the right thing to do."

"Who's taking it over?" Hank asked.

"A couple moving down from Boulder. They just sold a pub they'd started ten years ago in Denver. I checked it out online. Looks like a similar menu and has lots of very good reviews."

"They sound perfect," Roxanne replied. "Oh, before I forget, Kate and Carmen are planning on joining us a little later. We left them at the Carambola beach, so it probably won't be for a bit."

"Now those two know how to lay low," Barney interjected, "just toasting those brown bellies in the sun. Looks like you'll be joining them soon, Handsome."

"Very funny, Beautiful. But it does sound wonderful." Sienna retorted. "Also, I'm looking forward to doing more volunteer work for the animal shelter. I just hope it doesn't put too much pressure on Paul." She reached over and took his hand.

"I wouldn't worry about that," Barney laughed. "The boy's had a free ride for over three years now, workin' and playin' whenever he wants. It's about time old Ace stepped back up to the plate."

"Gee thanks, Barney. I hadn't realized I'd been such an oaf."

"Nothing personal, Amigo. Just sayin' between your golf, music, bartending and architecture, you've had things goin' pretty much your way for some time."

"And the problem with that is?" Hank rejoined.

"Uncle Barney, why don't we just listen to people for a while. No talk, just listen," Joey advised.

"Oh . . . went off track again. Man, this Claire thing has me bugged. Sorry, Amigo. You know there isn't anything about your life that I don't respect."

"I know that Barney, but, you can't take Claire's decision to head back to the states so negatively. She's been dependent on you for some time now. Having a life outside of your relationship's probably a good thing for both of you."

"Yeah, it was bound to happen someday. Fly, baby bird, fly." Barney rubbed his eyes, then slapped the table determinedly. "OK, enough of my goddamn whinin'. I'm surrounded by great friends and truth be told, since buying *The Last Hurrah*, I've dreamed that one day I'd be workin' the boat with Joey. 'Course, I thought it would be during his breaks from college, but, the kid thinks he's smarter than—"

"I propose a toast." Joey stood and held out his beer. "To Barney and Claire. To Sienna, Paul and The Green Flash. To Erin and me. To all of us and all whom we love," he added, looking at Roxanne and Hank. "May we embrace the inevitable changes in our lives with grace, optimism, love and dignity."

"That was beautiful, Joey," Roxanne said, barely able to compose herself.

"It's hard to believe that you two are related," Hank said, reaching over and shaking Joey's hand, while Barney finally sat silent, like a giant Buddha, bursting with pride.

26

"Lines are clear, Captain."

"Come up here then and take the helm," Barney shouted, over the twin diesels rumbling under the deck.

Joey guided *The Last Hurrah* out of the Christiansted Harbor, through the narrow channel into the open water, just as he and Erin had done most working days during the past month.

Sienna, now past her estimated due date, had gotten the approval from her OB for a short day-cruise to take her mind off things, provided she could return to shore within 30 minutes, if necessary. She signaled Paul to sit back down and relax as she carefully climbed the ship ladder to join Joey. Barney and Paul lounged comfortably in the rear deck chairs.

"Not a bad life, if you don't weaken, eh Ace?"

"Not bad at all." Paul cast a glance at Sienna. "She looks good, don't you think?

"I'd say for lugging around all that precious cargo, she's doing fantastic. Does she miss The Green Flash?"

"Sure, but she doesn't miss the work and stress associated with it. We'll take you and Joey there tonight. The new owners kept the same menu."

"Great, I'm thinkin' sweet potato fries, pot stickers and fresh grilled wahoo."

"We just ate a half-hour ago. You'd better slow down Chuckwagon, or you'll be as wide as you are tall."

"Nice to know you still care."

"Always will, Barn. You want one?" Paul asked, reaching in the cooler.

"You read my mind, Amigo."

Paul handed Barney a Red Stripe. "So how's things in Quilcene?"

"Busy. Brook's flower business has really blossomed." When Paul didn't react, he shrugged and continued. "Of course, my *Bad--Ass Barney Strain's* put me at numero uno for high quality Washington weed."

"That's great."

"Yeah, 'cept I've been busting my ass. I kid you not. Don't really like working so hard, but when the sun shines—"

"You've got to make hay." Paul pulled a water bottle from the cooler. "So how are you and Claire? She emailed Sienna that she's publishing a book of poetry?"

"Yeah, it's an anthology. She's using some of her poems, but mostly poems written by the ladies in her man-hater group. It's called 'Love Lies'. Actually, most of the poems are written by Barb, one of the group members. She's the one that set me straight when we were first introduced."

"I remember."

"I guess she's all right, though. Claire's asked me to cut her some slack. She's been knocked around pretty good, first her dad then later by two different husbands."

"What are Claire's poems about? I don't remember her ever having being abused by anyone."

174

"Well, she doesn't have a clear memory of anything specific, but sort of remembers her mom getting punched by her dad. Barb has her convinced that this might have caused a post-traumatic stress disorder that contributed to her bipolar condition."

"How's that all going?"

"She was feeling pretty dull about a month ago, so her doctor took her off lithium and put her on Depapoke, or something like that. Anyway, it seems to have helped. She has more energy and feels a whole lot better. Still, I just hate her having to be on all these drugs."

"Yeah, but until they figure out a cure, it's definitely the best alternative."

"You guys see that?" Joey shouted from the bridge, pointing off the starboard bow. Paul and Barney stood and watched a single dolphin leap out of the water. Joey altered their course and they soon found themselves in the middle of a small pod, sailing through the air and stirring-up the water around them.

Joey pulled off his T-shirt and joined Paul who'd already dove in the water, as soon as Joey cut the engine. Sienna snapped pictures from the bridge as the dolphins encircled the two swimmers, several times brushing up against their legs. Paul caught the attention of two large dolphins that fell in on either side of him as he dolphin kicked a respectable butterfly stroke away from the boat. A curious, young dolphin surfaced next to Joey who laid his arm across the creature's back, each staring benevolently into the other's eyes.

Barney grabbed another beer and joined Sienna on the bridge while she continued shooting pictures of the unexpected close encounter. "Spectacular, isn't it," Barney observed.

"There's something to be said about humans not being the most evolved inhabitants of the planet."

"I agree. If we're so smart, why do we have wars? Why are we polluting our planet, decimating entire species for their ivory or fur and still judging people by their color, or sexual preference?"

"Exactly. Although, I'd like to think that it's not people like you and me that are causing this shit. We're probably seriously outnumbered though."

"Yeah, but it's too beautiful out here to be talking about being outnumbered." She set her camera down and leaning back, took in a deep breath. "Thanks for asking us out, Barney. It's just what the doctor ordered. How are Joey and Erin doing running the charter business?"

"Well, when I bought the boat, I figured I'd leave her in dry- dock through the summer. Not enough tourists to make it worthwhile. But these kids are getting quite a reputation with the locals and hotels. It's all word of mouth, but we're booked solid through fall. Plus, they're making a good side business supplying the restaurants with fresh fish. When Erin had to run up to Seattle, I was happy to come down and cover for her. I tell you, now that I'm here, even if it's just for the week, I'm glad I came."

"It's great to see you."

"So . . . How's Erin's mom doing?"

"She's doing fine now, and I know she appreciated Erin coming back to help out. Appendicitis is no fun."

"I can imagine . . . Paul talked to Connie last night. She's coming back with Erin next week."

"I forgot, when are you due?"

"I forgot too," she laughed. "Tomorrow, I hope."

"And Kate and Carmen . . . they're due anytime, too. Windsol's never gonna be the same . . . Of course, I mean that in a good way."

"Of course you do, Uncle Barney."

"I'll probably be back here soon with Claire. I can't see her staying away very long, what with all the babies to gush over."

"I think you're more of a gusher than Claire."

"Me? Nah. I don't have much use for 'em until they're out of diapers."

"Great, we might be ready to ship them to you by then."

Barney stood and hollered, as Paul and Joey swam toward the boat. "Say, if you boys aren't too pooped-out from playin' with your pals, I say we head over to Buck Island for some snorkeling."

******

Kate and Carmen were sipping lemonades and fanning themselves with menus when Paul and Sienna appeared at the top of the restaurant's entry stairs. Barney and Joey'll be along soon," Paul said, helping Sienna ease into her chair.

"Such a gentleman," Carmen sighed. "It's that kind of thing I miss."

"Here we go," Kate murmured.

"You know, like having a man throw his jacket over a mud puddle. That kind of thing."

"You're missing nothing, Carmen," Kate shot back. "Walk around the damn puddle. Better than ruinin' a good jacket."

"Tiresome Pragmatist."

177

"Impractical Romantic."

"So are we ready to be over with this or what?" Paul interjected, attempting to lighten the mood.

"I'll tell you what I'm missin' . . ." Kate pressed both heels of her hands into the small of her back, "feeling comfortable. I can't find one damn position standing, sitting or lying down where I don't feel just about ready to burst."

"And what's with all the veins popping out all over my legs and other places," Carmen said, glaring at Paul, almost daring him to reply.

"I can't remember the last time I had a decent night's sleep," Sienna added. "This was supposed to all be over a week ago. Doctor's and due dates. Pffft."

"You guys are all doing great," Paul replied weakly, wishing he *had* stayed quiet or maybe in the car.

"Joey had to run into town, so it'll just be me joinin' you," Barney announced loudly, as he tromped in and took a chair at their table. "Say, you girls look miserable. Let's get the proprietor to put on some shit-kicken', country music. A couple swings around the dance floor heel-toeing it with Ol' Barn, and I'll have you ladies popping out those little creatures in no time."

Paul cringed. *Little creatures? Jesus.*

But before the mother's-to-be could respond, Barney stumbled his way into another morass. "Actually, it would be better for me if you guys held off another few days."

"Oh? Why is that?" Carmen asked.

Realizing his blunder, Barney pretended not to hear the question. He craned his neck, combing the dining room. "I could use a cold one. Anybody seen our waiter?"

Kate pressed on. "I'm sure the waitress will be here shortly. Why would it be better for you, Barney?"

Barney looked sheepishly at Paul, who glared back at him.

"Paul?" Sienna asked. "What's he talking about?"

Cursing Barney under his breath, Paul explained how Hank, Barney and Tex had come up with the idea of a baby pool. Fifty bucks entry for each mom. "The closest date guessed for each delivery wins."

"Are you in this pool?" Sienna asked Paul, much too quietly.

"You're damn right he is. We gave him first pick and he took the delivery dates the doctors gave you. He didn't want to be rooting for any kind of delays," Barney answered, attempting to put a positive spin on the admission.

"But not you, it would seem," Carmen replied. "You took the smart bet, hoping' that things would drag out and we'd be imprisoned by these bloated, stuffed bodies for what, ten days, two weeks, a month?"

"Well, no, see, ah . . ." Barney stammered.

Sienna folded her arms across her stomach. "I can't believe that you'd go along with making a game out of the birth of our children, Paul."

"This is the part I don't miss." Carmen quipped. "Men can be such oafs."

The waitress's sudden appearance brought a timely shift in conversation. "So, who's the big guy?"

Barney eyed the busty, bleached blonde waitress and smiled. "Name's Barney, but I have to tell you, I'm spoken for."

"That's never stopped me before. Anybody want something from the bar? Sienna, aren't you gonna introduce me to your entourage?"

"Guys, this is Sharleen Gifford and Barney, she speaks the truth."

"I'll have a Red Stripe," Paul ordered.

"Barney thought of several questions he shouldn't ask Sharleen, and instead shrugged and ordered the same.

"I'll be back in a flash with your drinks, Guys. By then Sienna can tell you all about me." She blew Barney a kiss and headed for the bar.

"Sharleen used to work for me and Aaron," Sienna explained.

"Until Sienna caught her with her hand in the till," Paul added. "Great, so now she's back working at The Green Flash. This might be our last dinner here until they fire her."

"Well, let's make it memorable then." Barney smiled at Carmen and nodded towards the dance floor.

"No, Paul," Sienna replied, easing slowly from her chair. "I'm not going to let her drive me away from here. We're going to have a little chat and see if we can put the past behind us." They watched as Sienna approached Sharleen and after a few moments of discussion, the two walked out toward the parking lot.

"Well, you gotta give the girl credit," Carmen said, shifting uncomfortably in her chair. "Sharleen clearly doesn't give a shit about first impressions."

The comment caught Barney in mid-swallow. His initial laugh turned into a choking cough. Eyes bulging, his hands flew to his throat.

Paul stood and slapped hard between Barney's shoulder blades, as the aspirated beer prevented air from filling his lungs. Pulling him to his feet, Paul braced himself behind the giant and attempted to clear his passage with the Heimlich maneuver. But, there was nothing stuck in his throat to dislodge. Barney toppled forward, crashing through and splintering his chair onto the floor.

"Paul, treat him like he's drowning. Clear his airway, then give him mouth to mouth," Kate shouted, as a ring of worried friends and restaurant patrons encircled them. But, Paul was unable to blow hard enough to fill Barney's lungs.

"His throat's closed down. Someone get a ball point pen," Kate ordered.

A Bic suddenly appeared. Pulling out the ink cartridge, Kate quickly handed it to Paul. She pointed to a spot on her lower neck. "Just below the Adam's apple. Stab it there, hard."

Fearful of inflicting serious injury, Paul hesitated. Sienna's panicked voice broke through, "Do it Paul! He's turning white."

He lined the pen up, took a deep breath and counted, *one, two thr*—

Barney gasped. His eyes flew open. His right hand shot out to block the piercing. Misjudging the distance, however, his massive paw landed with a loud thwack on the side of Paul's head, knocking him spread-eagled under the table.

Sienna's worried voice was barely audible over the ringing in Paul's ears, as he rolled from his back to a sitting position, beside the miraculously revived Barney. He'd heard descriptions of the room spinning from concussion victims. He'd experienced something similar brought on by copious amounts of alcohol, during his former run-and-hide days. This, however, was eerily different. He had the sensation of spinning, but could only see blackness.

Sienna's voice sounded like it was coming from a mile away. "Paul! Are you OK? Say something."

He tried to respond, but couldn't make his lips move. *Fuckin' Barney cold cocked me.* The thought made him laugh. His

181

vision began to return; blurry at first, but soon he could make out Barney's big worried face, inches from his.

"Ace, you in there? Jeez, I'm sorry. I just freaked out when I saw you about to stab me in the throat. Didn't mean to hit you. Gotta believe me, man. I know you were just tryin' to help."

"Just help me up, Asshole."

The two men found their seats. Barney described his near-death experience to everyone within twenty feet, as Paul's head continued to clear. "I swear, it was my dead grandmother. She looked like I'd seen her in those brownish pictures we have of her at home. She's all lit up-like, sayin' that she misses me, but it's not my time. Jeez I'm starved. Let's get that Sharleen over here and put her to work."

"I think Paul should head over to the ER," Sienna said.

"Concussion protocol, they call it in the NFL," Carmen added, as she switched off her iPhone's flashlight. "His pupils are responding."

"I'd rather just sit here for a while," Paul replied. "I'm feeling better by the minute. Let's order."

"That's my Ace," Barney laughed, opting for a gentle pat on Paul's back rather than his typical slap. "I've had my bell rung a few times. Not much to worry about, if there's no bleeding goin' on in there." He pointed at Paul's head.

Paul was feeling much better by the end of the meal. "I'm glad we had our little talk," Sharleen said to Sienna, placing their bill on the table. "Quite a show you guys put on tonight." Looking seductively at Barney, she added, "Maybe you don't bring the entire circus with you next time?"

27

The security guard's kind eyes brightened, as he held open the door. "Good afternoon, Miss Sienna. How are the girls today?"

"Good afternoon, Aldrick. We're a little on the cranky side. Is he with the contractor?" she asked, nodding at the closed door across the mahogany paneled lobby.

"Mr. McGowan left 'bout 15 minutes ago. Think you'll find Mr. Paul's alone."

In early November, Armstrong Architects, AIA was commissioned to bring an aging harbor side Christiansted hotel back to life. The steel and concrete structure was opened in the 60's and had survived the handful of major hurricanes since Hugo in 1989. More recently, however, it had fallen into disrepair. Paul had hired a local surveying company to provide the as-builds. Even so, there had been so many previous remodels and additions, all demonstrating varying degrees of true and plumb, that Paul found it was easier to produce the construction documents on site.

The developers were hopeful that the project would start an avalanche of needed repairs, renovations and upgrades to the venerable Caribbean town. With so many eyes on the project, extensive presentations had been required of Paul, as well as frequent and excessively long meetings. Those were the two things he'd hoped to have left behind from his glory days with T Squared Development. Additional complications had arisen upon the discovery of severe damage to the structural steel framework. The necessary remediation was extensive and required that the owners step up to a much larger project budget than originally estimated. Paul was gratified by the managing partner's response to the discovery. "Do whatever it takes, Paul. We're too far into this thing to try and do it half-assed."

Sienna had been a good sport regarding his absence. After having worked full-time for so many years, she relished the time she was having at home with AJ and the girls.

She pulled the double tram carefully through the door. Paul crossed the room quickly to greet her. "Ready for lunch?" she asked.

"Where do you propose the Armstrongs should dine?" Sienna laughed at the question, as Paul bent down and kissed Reed and Phoebe's foreheads, just under their sun bonnets. Since the girls had discovered the stone crabs at Rum Runners, their twice a week lunch date never varied.

******

A bevy of small gray creatures stretched their pinchers upwards as the giggling twins pushed cubes of bread off their trays. The crabs clicked sideways over the concrete, retrieving the food, then disappeared back into the rocks, edging the open-aired restaurant.

Sienna used the distraction to bring Paul up to speed. "This came in the mail today." She handed him a large pink envelope.

He pulled a red hearted, white laced Valentine's Day card from the envelope. "Valentine's Day in May? You gotta love the postal service down here. Is it from an old boyfriend?" he asked, feigning suspicion.

"It was postmarked three days ago. Read what's inside."

Sensing her discomfort, Paul opened the card. The script was shaky and childlike.

Dear Sienna,
Your husband's a fraud. He's screwing around on you.
I know because he's banging my wife.
The stupid bitch just bends over and takes it up
her ass.
Not much you can do about it now, I suppose. By the
time you get the twins down, you're probably too
pooped to screw anyway. (LOL)
Actually, Paul's given it to both of you in the ass, but
don't worry. Be happy. Judgement day is
coming.
Sincerely,
Butch Jugs

He'd seen this before. Paul looked up from the letter. "Butch Jugs has to be Claire."

"I thought so too, when I first read it. But, it's just too close to the email she sent me before . . . Maybe someone's trying to make us think it's Claire . . . Didn't Barney say she was doing well, when you talked to him on Monday?"

"Yeah, but Barney's evaluation might be biased. He mentioned that she's spending more and more time working on her anthologies. Still, I know how he worries about her."

"It's a big worry for both of them. Barney told me it's like waiting for the other shoe to fall. Maybe they don't want to see the signs, so they avoid looking . . . I guess it could be Claire."

"Who else?"

"Maybe Sharleen? You've seen how she acts around Barney."

"Any man, actually."

"True, but I really think she has a thing for Barn. Think about it. It's not a bad plan. She takes Claire out of the picture with a phony Valentine's Day card, something Claire could deny, but not disprove. The doubt would always be there."

"Yeah, but how would she have heard about Claire's manic emails. She wasn't even on island then."

Sienna thought for a moment. "No, but several waiters at The Green Flash were. You know how word gets around on this rock. Someone could have easily told her."

"Yeah, I suppose, but I still think it's Claire. They'll be here tomorrow and I don't want her around the girls, or any of us, if she's turning back into *Manic Claire*."

"I agree 100 percent. What about her friend, Barbara, sending the card?"

"I didn't think she and Claire see each other anymore."

"They don't, but it's because Barbara wanted Claire to leave Barney and live with her. Claire said no and Barbara went postal, from what Claire told me."

"So, why the Valentine's Day card?"

"Revenge maybe. Or maybe Barbara might be trying to create trouble between Claire and Barney, so that she could swoop in and rescue Claire from a partner who doesn't trust her."

"Wow, you should be a writer. This is good stuff. I just wish it were fiction."

Their conversation was derailed by a loud burst of wails following Reed knocking the pacifier off her sister's tray. Paul got up quickly and scrambled over the rocks to retrieve Phoebe's beloved binky.

"Hey Paul and Sienna. Hi girls." Lanky and darkly tanned, Erin stood on the boardwalk in a pink bikini.

"Hey Erin," Sienna replied, receiving Paul's hand-off and plugging the pacifier into Phoebe's gaping cake hole. "What's up?"

"Heading out. It's this older dude who's here on vacation for a week. This is the fifth day in a row. We've told him that the wahoo aren't running, but he doesn't seem to mind. Joey's opening up the boat and I just ran to get ice." She held up a plastic bag. "Are you guys going to Jump-Up tonight?"

"I think so," Sienna answered. "But I haven't talked to Paul about it yet."

"Well, I hope you do. We'll buy you a drink, er . . . of lemonade or something," having momentarily forgotten that Sienna was still nursing. Waving good bye to the girls, Erin turned and walked through the security gate onto the mooring pier.

"Did you like the front or the back view better?" Sienna asked.

"You mean Erin? I hardly even noticed. Both I guess."

"I guess is right," Sienna said, laughing. "I guess I know why the kids are doing so well with the charter business. I bet their afternoon charter doesn't even like to fish."

"I'd rent a boat to look at you in a bikini."

187

"Nice try. I still won't wear half of my clothes because of my muffin top. These love handles didn't stay after delivering AJ."

Standing, Paul pulled her into his arms. "You are, without exception, the most beautiful woman I've ever seen."

"Even with my muffin top?"

"Especially with your muffin top. I love your muffins."

"And they love you." Shouldering her purse, she asked, "Can you keep the girls for a bit? I want to run up to Danna's shop. She said that she's gotten in some new blouses that I might like."

"Sure, I'll take the girls out to the boat to see Joey."

Smiling, she shook her head. "Joey . . . Right."

28

Heading to Jump-Up, Roxanne turned in her seat, "Well, this is a first in a long time. When's the last time the four of us went out?"

"Probably our trip to Washington," Sienna replied. "I'm glad you asked us to join you."

"It was Hank's idea. He can be such a macho John-Wayne at times, but he really misses you guys."

"And we miss Hanky-Bear." Paul reached forward and squeezed his friend on the shoulder. "So, Sienna told you about the Valentine. What do you think?"

"A little to the left, Sweetheart."

"Hank, this isn't the time for your weird humor," Roxanne scolded. "Answer your friend. They're worried."

"Sorry." Hank turned his head slightly, keeping an eye on the road. "It's probably Claire."

"Barney said that she's doing fine." Paul fell back in his seat.

"Look, none of us want it to be Claire," Hank said, easing into the parking stall, "but they'll be here tomorrow and we can all see for ourselves."

189

"Until we figure this out, we need to watch out for the kids." Sienna added. "Whoever sent the card is either batting for the dark side or mentally ill."

They left the car at the downtown floatplane terminal and strolled along the boardwalk. Jump-Up, Christiansted's Friday night street party is held quarterly. Traffic is routed around the town. Galleries, shops, restaurants and bars are filled, some operating inside centuries old stone and concrete buildings. Island music spills through the warm evening streets. Stilted Mocho Jumbies loom above throngs of Crucians and tourists, shopping and enjoying the island cuisine.

The conversation during the car ride had caused a darkened mood, but it didn't last long. Sienna and Roxanne chatted with a jewelry vendor, while Hank, holding a Cuba Libre in one hand and a pizza slice in the other, waited in line for barbequed chicken.

Paul moved slowly through the crowds along Queen Cross Street.

"Hey Handsome. She should know better than to let you out of her sight."

A large breast pinned Paul's arm against his side as she pressed into him. Stumbling unsteadily on her ridiculously high heels, he caught her arm and cautioned, "Steady there, Sharleen."

"And so strong, too," she purred. Giggling at his tongue-tied response, she kissed his cheek. "Relax Handsome. She's a good woman. But, don't tell her I said so."

He watched her disappear into the crowd. A tap on the shoulder turned him around.

"Well, if it isn't Mr. Paul Armstrong."

Paul, long past holding any grudge, managed something resembling a smile, as he extended his hand. "Attorney Joseph."

Casey Joseph looked suspiciously at the offered hand. Their last contact had ended with Casey on the receiving end of a kick in the nuts. But, Paul determinedly kept his hand out, "No hard feelings?"

Casey scowled, as he pondered the offer, then suddenly threw a fake punch stopping an inch from Paul's nose. Laughing at Paul's startled reaction, Casey broke into a wide grin. "I still owe you one, man."

"Yeah, I'm sorry about that, Casey. I was pretty messed up for a while."

"To tell you the truth, I never got that one. What'd you have to be drinking about? Sienna was the one got kicked and lost the baby. You had it all. I just figured you were weak."

Starting to simmer, Paul took a deep breath before replying. "Well, maybe you could come out to Windsol sometime. I know AJ would really like to see you."

"AJ? Yeah? OK, I just might do that. Maybe I'll bring a friend, a woman friend."

"Sounds good. Glad we talked, Casey." Paul turned to leave, but was turned back by the strong grip on his shoulder. "She OK?"

There was still an unmistakable longing in the attorney's face. "She's good."

"You take good care of her, Armstrong. I'm still watching."

Paul found Sienna, Hank and Roxanne at You Are Here, a popular pub, less than a block off the boardwalk in King's Alley. They finished their evening at From The Gecko,

Sienna and Roxanne's favorite boutique, while Paul and Hank stood outside listening to a Cuban jazz band across the street.

"So you and the attorney, bff's?" Hank queried on the ride home.

"Don't see that happening, but seriously, he still has it for her. I don't know if I could muster up that much good will if the shoe were on the other foot."

"Well, **her** still holds out hope that he'll give up the ghost so he can return as a friend. AJ misses him," Sienna added.

"Sounds like Mr. Gandhi-here, invited him to dinner. I'd like to be a fly on the wall for that meal."

"You are so insensitive sometimes," Roxanne scolded. "I think it was very sweet of Paul to try and smooth things over. Good job, Paul."

"Yeah, good job, Paul," Hank mimicked, then winced from Roxanne's punch to his shoulder. "OK, OK, Paul's a saint. I admit it. I'd never be able to do that. The guy showed up at your house before the toilet water'd quit circling from your final flush."

******

Paul spotted only one figure large enough to be Barney, as passengers from Seaborne's Puerto Rico to Saint Croix flight disembarked into the outdoor terminal. Although it had only been a few months, Barney'd been transformed from an overstuffed Caribbean cowboy into a full-blown hipster. Sporting black jeans, an art deco T-shirt, Maui Jim titanium sunglasses, and a close shave, this new look had Paul wondering if his best friend and ex-wife had missed their connection.

"Hey Paul," Claire greeted him with a warm hug and kiss. "You look confused. Doesn't he look great?"

"Yeah . . . great," Paul echoed, wondering what had caused his giant friend to enlist in the witness protection program.

"It took me some time to get used to the new look," Barney admitted, taking off his sunglasses. "Claire had the idea that it would make me look younger—"

"And definitely more handsome," Claire added, enthusiastically.

"I know. I tell you, it was hard for me to believe it was possible, but . . . Voila." Barney struck a pose, pursed his lips Zoolander-like and turned around slowly.

"Yeah, who'd have thought it," Paul replied, recalling Rod Sterling's words, *You've just crossed over into the Twilight Zone.* "It's so great to see you two. Is this all you brought?" Paul grabbed their carry-ons and escorted them out to his truck.

"Paul, if you're not in too big of a hurry, do you think we could swing out to Gallow's Bay? I'd like drop off my latest anthology at Undercover Books. I spoke with the owner and worked out a consignment arrangement. I think *Love Juiced* will sell great down here. Don't you, Honey?"

"It's her third collection of poems," Barney boasted, "just in case you've lost count. The first two haven't made the best sellers list yet, but this one . . ."

"Barn came up with the title." She held up the flaming red paperback. "Not all the writings are by women, which is surprising, given your species regard for foreplay as a down payment, rather than blissful enjoyment."

"That's from one of the poems in the book," Barney explained, a little too quickly.

"Sure, no problem." Paul turned east on the Melvin Evans Highway.

"So, how are things at the day care center?" Barney asked.

"Nothing like it will be in a few days when Kate and Carmen arrive with their little bunchkins."

"Well, I can hardly wait to see the twins . . . and Sienna of course." Claire took Barney's huge arm and wrapped it over her shoulder. "It's so great to be back."

They drove in silence for the remainder of the ride. "Come on, I'll buy you a beer," Barney offered, as they watched Claire stride confidently into the bookstore, a dozen copies under her arm.

"You go on in. I'll call Sienna and give her an update."

Sienna sounded worried when she picked up. "Where **are** you guys?"

Paul gave her the rundown on Barney's new look and their detour to the book store.

"Couldn't she have waited until later? We're all here, looking forward to seeing them."

"Guess not. You know, there's something a bit strange going on. I think that Barney's new look's more about appeasing Claire than a style epiphany."

"You think he senses something?"

"No. I think he's trying hard *not* to sense something." He thought briefly before adding, "I think it's her, Sienna. She seems spun up."

"Oh God . . . now what?"

"I'm not sure." He rubbed his temple. "Maybe she's just excited about her books, but we definitely need to keep our eyes open."

Paul found a contemplative Barney sitting at the bar inside Maria's Mexican Cantina.

"Anything you want to ask me, Ace?"

"What do you mean?"

"My new duds. My new look. You don't like anything about it."

Paul hesitated, as Cass, the bartender, placed a 16oz UFO in front of him. "It was a surprise, but that's not it."

"What the fuck is it, then?" Barney asked, growing irritated.

"What the fuck is what?" Claire's entrance had been missed by Barney and Paul. She glided into the chair between them. "But before you tell me, don't you want to know how it went?"

"You got them in?"

"She took all twelve. I was so excited, when I signed the copies, my signature was a mess."

Cass set a basket of chips and salsa in front of them. "Can I get you something to drink, Claire?"

"I haven't had anything in ages. Barney, do you think a single margarita would be OK for a celebration?"

"You bet. I'll join you." Barney finished his beer. "What about you, Ace?"

Paul hadn't had a mid-afternoon drink in over a year, but was so relieved the *what the fuck* question had been temporarily shelved, he decided to take one for the team. "Sure, make it three, Cass."

"To My Lady's success."

"I think that one day, *Love Juiced* will make a real difference with women's relationships to men . . . and to themselves too." Claire said, finishing her drink with a burp and a giggle, before Paul had taken two sips.

195

"We're all proud of you, Claire," Paul said, pushing a fifty toward Cass.

"Hey, Fella. This one was on me." Barney complained.

"Great. Thanks. Now let's get outta here. Andy's been working on a welcome home meal and you know how he gets."

"That little bugger's got more piss in him at 84 than most people have at 83." Barney quipped, as they headed back to the truck."

"Have Connie and Wyatt arrived yet?" Claire asked.

"They're due in tomorrow afternoon. It looks like Connie's officially retiring from the F.B.I. and Wyatt's taking an early retirement from the SPD. They're coming down to scope out becoming our next full-time Windsol residents."

"I think Connie would really like my book. I knew I should have brought some extras."

"She's probably into e-books and can buy it on Amazon," Barney assured.

"You don't know that," Claire snapped. "I shouldn't have listened to you. I wanted to bring 20."

Barney looked out the window and didn't reply.

Paul had grown increasingly uncomfortable with their interaction. Little else was said during the half-hour drive to Windsol. Paul told Sienna later that evening that it seemed to take hours.

29

At six foot six, there was no question who should occupy the aisle seat, but it was Wyatt's face that filled the porthole window. The 737 American flight from Miami swept in from the northwest and lined up with the 7,000-foot runway. He leaned back to give Connie a glimpse as they crossed over the western shore of the island, just north of Sandy Point.

"It's so green. I thought they were in a big drought."

"I just hope it's not too small for you, if we decide to make this our primary home. It's only 26 miles long and 6 miles wide."

"Yeah, but it seems a lot bigger, since the roads are for crap. I remember it taking forever to get from one end to the other."

"And that's a good thing?"

"It may be a good *ting* and it may be a bad *ting*. It's de islands, Mon."

"Honey, please don't talk like that again, at least not around anybody else. Promise me."

"Sure . . . OK, but I don't see what's wrong with a little island slang."

She shook her head and took his hand as the jet's wheels skidded onto the tarmac.

The Jeep they'd reserved was waiting for them, but seeing Paul and Sienna was a complete surprise.

"What are you guys doing here?" Connie asked, exchanging hugs and kisses with her brother and sister-in-law. "And where are the twins?"

"Home with everybody," Sienna replied. "Another advantage of communal living. We thought we'd fill you in on a few things before going back to Windsol. How 'bout following us to a beach bar just north of Frederiksted for a drink?"

"That's a jambin'-good idea, Mon," Wyatt singsonged.

Connie glared at him. "You'll have to excuse Calypso Joe here. He's a bit overwhelmed."

"Never lived anywhere 'cept Seattle," he explained. "I can't believe I be movin' here."

"Well, all right then." Paul started his truck. "Jump in your Jeep and stay close."

"We be drivin' on the left side of de road?" Wyatt yelled out the open window as he started the Jeep.

"Cheese an' bread Mon . . . Will you ever stop?" Connie laughed, as they left the airport.

******

"It sounds as if Barney doesn't want to acknowledge the cues, which doesn't surprise me, given the severity of her earlier bout with mania." Connie had slipped her sandals off as Sienna went to get drinks from the beach bar.

"You know, she's seeing a psychiatrist," Paul said. "You'd think he'd pick up on it if she were spinning out of control."

"She told me about him. He's given her a lot of hope that she can control her disorder with exercise, meditation and diet. He might have too much invested in his methods to spot the signs. Also, you and Sienna haven't seen her for a few months. If the onset has been gradual, Barney may have gotten used to the changes."

"Yeah, I hear what you're saying Sis. But, I just hope—"

"Look Paul, I really do understand you and Sienna giving Claire the benefit of the doubt, but this is serious stuff."

Wyatt pulled his face out of the water. "Hey Con, it's super clear and I've never seen colors like this. There's a long, skinny silver fish chasing a school of tiny fish." A gray cloud of chum leapt in the air then splashed back into the sea. Putting in his snorkel, he gave a *thumbs up* and returned to his adventure.

"Wyatt reminds me of how I was when I first got here. I couldn't wait to jump in the Caribbean," Paul recalled.

"Ever since we started planning this trip, he's been saying the first thing he'd do is head for the beach."

"Well, he got his wish."

Carrying a tray of rum punches, Sienna returned from the outdoor bar, as Wyatt waded toward shore.

"Did you get the tiny umbrellas?"

"I got you two, Wyatt. And I'll give you mine as well."

"Could he be high?" Paul asked Connie.

"I don't see how. Honey, Paul wants to know if you're high?"

Wyatt stumbled up the sandy bank and took the offered drink from Sienna.

"Thanks, Sienna . . . Who wouldn't be high?" He raised his drink to eye level. "I've got rum. It's almost dark out and still at least 85-degrees. Also, you may not have noticed, but that's the most beautiful sunset I think I've ever seen."

"So I guess you like our island?"

"Sienna, this is the place I be seein' myself doin' some major chillin'."

"If he's not high, it could be island fever," Paul suggested.

"No fever Mon, just diggin' my new crib."

"Crib? Really? You seem to be mixing your slang."

"So, what'd we miss?" Sienna asked.

"Connie was saying that she thinks the card's from Claire."

"I think we're all in agreement on that. Right? . . .Paul?"

"Yeah, I was just thinking about Barney. It seems like he's doing everything he can to keep from rocking the boat; keeping things on an even keel. It's not like him at all."

Wyatt took a long draw on his island punch. "So, what now?"

"If it were just us, we could wait it out and see what happens next, but we've got the kids to worry about," Sienna cautioned.

Paul stood and stretched. "Honey, she's hardly even noticed the kids. I don't think they're even on her radar."

"I agree, so far, it hasn't been a problem. She's been holed up in their cabin working on her Facebook marketing since they got here. But can we trust her around them?"

"I think you need to talk with Barney about it. I'll join you, if you'd like," Connie suggested.

"Me too," Wyatt volunteered.

"No, he might feel like we're ganging up on him. I'll talk with Barney when we get home." Paul glanced at Sienna, who nodded her agreement.

******

Standing over the barbecue on the great house porch, Hank spotted Wyatt and Connie's Jeep, following Paul's truck through the entry gate. Heavy into a game of cribbage, Barney and Andy dropped the cards to welcome the new arrivals.

"Well, well, if it ain't J. Edgar Hoover's former associate. Who's that guy following you?" Andy kidded.

"Hey Andy," Wyatt laughed. "I'm the guy who took you down at horse shoes last spring in Winthrop."

"So, you say. I might need a rematch to refresh my memory." Andy held out his arms. "Come here, former agent Hunter, and give an old man a kiss."

"I'd watch it with him, Connie. He'll slip you the tongue if you're not careful. Done it to me a couple times."

Andy scowled. "Don't mind him, Connie, that's just Barney mistakin' indecorum for humor. If he was a kid . . . and much smaller, I'd time him out."

"Wow, you've really been hitting the Scrabble board. Indecorum . . . good one." Connie threw her arms around his wiry frame.

AJ and Red came onto the porch, a twin in each of their arms. "Look, Reed and Phoebe, it's Mommy and Daddy." AJ's announcement triggered a burst of reproachful tears, lurching, flopping and cries of "Mama, Dada" by the girls, as payback for their three-hour abandonment. Aunt Charlotte and Roxanne greeted Connie and Wyatt, after setting bowls of potato salad and coleslaw on the table.

When you guys are done huggin" and kissin," Hank announced, "the burgers are ready."

Barney grabbed a beer from the bar fridge and headed down the stairs. "I'll go get Claire. She needs a break. She's been pushing hard on her last book. Got book signings lined up all over Washington when we get back."

But fifteen minutes later, a furious Claire stomped onto the porch alone. "You should all know that Barney is not the kind-hearted, big goof-of-a-man you think he is." Reading the confused looks on Paul and Sienna's faces, she exploded. "Of course, you think it's all me! He's got you all so wrapped around his finger. I'm sick of it."

Turning abruptly, she moved quickly toward her rental car. Everyone but Connie was paralyzed by the outburst. She caught up with Claire as she pulled open the car door. "So what's going on?"

"Nothing that's any of your business, Agent Hunter . . . But, since you're the only one concerned enough to ask, I'll tell you something you can pass on to the rest of the idiots living in this bullshit hippy compound. This entire fucked-up charade will be documented in an article I'm writing for the New York Times." Claire dropped into the front seat and pulled the door shut.

Connie considered standing behind the car to block her exit, but wasn't confident that the risk of running her down would be a deterrent to Claire. She shielded her face from the rocks thrown up by the spinning tires, as Claire wheeled toward the entry gate. Paul and Wyatt ran out to Connie.

"Shit." Connie moaned. "I should have grabbed her keys. She's definitely manic."

"It all happened so fast," Paul said. "At least you—"

The sound of an approaching car engine stopped him. At first, they thought Claire was returning, but instead, a shaken Erin pulled through the gate in her Jeep. "What's up with Aunt Claire? She practically ran me off the road."

"This isn't good," Wyatt muttered.

"I'll go check on Barney."

"Hey Paul, want me to come with you?" Hank shouted from the porch.

"No, but thanks. He's probably not in the mood for many visitors."

Barney and Claire's cabin door hung open. Paul stuck his head inside, but there was no sign of Barney. He jogged toward the lookout and spotted the hulking figure standing at the guardrail, facing the sea. "She's gone?"

"Connie tried to talk with her, but . . .yeah, she left."

"I should have been the one to stop her. I saw it coming. Just didn't want to believe it."

"I'm sorry, Barney . . . This really sucks."

"Well, at least she can't get very far. It's a small island and she left her purse."

30

By two o'clock the following afternoon, Claire's whereabouts were still unknown. They'd searched the island all morning before Barney finally reported her missing at the Frederiksted police station.

Regrouping at Windsol, Andy *rustled up some grub* and advice as he served the roast beef sandwiches. "Maybe this time you let it run its course. There ain't much trouble she can get into without you hearing about it on this dinky little atoll."

"By then, it might be too late, Andy. She's been gone for hours without cash or credit cards and we still have no idea where she is. It's not good." Connie wiped a smear of mayonnaise from Wyatt's chin.

Barney, who'd spoken little all morning, weighed in, "A while back, she got pretty depressed. I didn't think too much about it at the time. Now looking back, I should have seen this coming. I told myself that it was just because her books weren't selling."

"I thought they were going like hotcakes." Andy took a seat at the table.

"That's what Claire was telling me. But she left her email open one day and I saw a royalty notice. Her total sales after seven months were less than seventy-five paperbacks and 100 e-books."

"Wow. She told me Oprah wanted to plug her books on her TV show . . . and I believed her."

"Oprah's not even on TV, Paul. She just maintains a cable presence," Andy corrected.

Aunt Charlotte joined them on the porch. "Once AJ showed Andy how to use his iPhone to access the internet, he's become quite the authority on a variety of subjects."

"No reason that age should stop a person from learning. Got myself enrolled in an online Spanish program, too," Andy boasted.

"Well, Bueno, Dear. I'm sure everyone here is quite impressed. But we're drifting away from Claire."

"No, no." Barney straightened. "A change of subject would be just super. It's only the second day for you guys, but I've been dealing with this bullshit, seems like, forever. Fuckin' tip-toin' around, tryin' to keep things calm."

"Has she been tested for schizophrenia?"

"I don't know, Connie," Barney sighed. "But here we are talking about her mental health again. She wants to get away from me and go for a walk-about? I say let her go." He stood abruptly. "Sorry for the language, Aunt Charlotte, but I need a fuckin' time-out from all this crap."

"Uncle Paul, Don McGowen's on the phone. He says it's important." Joey emerged from inside and handed him the receiver.

"Don's the contractor who's built this place," Andy explained to Wyatt and Connie, as Paul took the phone.

"What's up, Don? . . . Right. Is she OK? . . . Should we meet you at the hospital? . . . OK, great. See you in a few." He turned to the group. "Don's bringing Claire home. She was in

205

some kind of altercation at Plaza East and has a few bruises and scratches, but he doesn't think it's anything serious."

******

"How is she?" Barney'd been pacing outside their bedroom door.

Sienna rested her hand on Barney's forearm. "She's pretty shook up, Barn, but won't tell us what happened."

Connie followed Sienna from the room and shut the door behind her. "She has some scratches and some facial bruises. I checked her out carefully. There were also some bruises on her back and both legs. There doesn't appear to be anything else. She's not lucid, but breathing more evenly than when Don dropped her off."

"She seemed to calm down a bit when Aunt Charlotte came in. She'll stay with her for a while, then Connie and I will take turns watching her through the night."

"Thanks." Barney stared at the door. "I got her an appointment at Doctor Brusseau's, first thing in the morning."

"I just hope she'll be receptive to taking medication," Connie said. "You would think that whatever happened at the grocery store scared her. On some level she's got to know that she's not safe like this."

Andy appeared, carrying a tray of tea and homemade cookies. "Think the patient might be receptive to a little snack?"

"Give it a go, Andy." Connie took hold of the door knob.

"Wait. Don't you think Barney should deliver this?"

"Thanks Andy, but no. I think right now, she needs to relax. She's still pretty much off her rocker and I'm afraid that having my big ass in there would just stir things up."

"OK, suit yourself." Andy passed inside, as Connie opened the door for him.

Moments later he reappeared with Aunt Charlotte behind him. "Well, good luck son, but she's asking for your big ass."

******

Spotting Don McGowen heading for his truck, Paul walked over to the porch rail. "Hey Don, where you goin'?"

"Figured you all had enough to deal with. Don't want to intrude."

"No way you're getting out of here that fast," Hank called-out, standing next to Paul. "Come join us."

Paul greeted Don with a handshake. "We can't thank you enough."

"Nothing any one of you wouldn't have done." He looked over at Hank reaching into the refrigerator. "I can't stay long, but I do have time for a beer."

"Of course, of course," Hank replied. "Maybe something stronger?"

"A beer's fine."

"Any idea what happened?" Paul asked.

"It was strange. I'd seen her inside the grocery store. Said hello to her, but she seemed not to notice. Thought she might not have recognized me. Then I noticed she was talking to herself . . . Well, I do that all the time, so I just didn't think too much about it. About fifteen minutes later, I walked outside and heard a bunch of yelling and screaming coming from over by my truck. I looked across the lot and saw Claire standing over this twenty-something, heavy-set woman, shouting at her like crazy . . . Something like, 'How'd that feel?' I think she may have called her a bitch, but frankly, I'm not sure, because everything happened so fast. Two young punks got a hold of Claire and threw her on the ground. Before I could get there, they started kicking and punching her. I screamed '**Stop**'; which they did. . . probably just to see what was comin' at 'em. Then I'm on 'em yellin' 'Out of the way. Get the fuck back' . . . Like I'm a cop or something. I dropped my bag of groceries, grabbed Claire and got her in the cab of my truck . . . Locked the doors, drove off and called you."

"Wow, it sounds like you saved her from a serious beating. I wonder what started it." Hank looked over at Paul.

Paul pulled several twenties from his wallet. "Who knows, with Manic Claire. How much damage for the groceries, Don?"

"Probably less damage then when I shove those bills up your ass, if you try to give 'em to me."

Hank laughed as Paul replied sheepishly, "I didn't mean to offend you, Don. I just wanted to—"

"Yeah, yeah, I know, but that's just what we do on this island. You should know that by now. We help each other out."

"Well . . . thanks then, Don. You were a bigger help than you could ever imagine."

"And of course, there's the other thing."

"What's that?"

Don drained his beer. "You do have some pretty fine looking women around this place. Doesn't hurt that they're probably thinkin' pretty highly of me, should any of you guys ever fuck up."

"Yep, there is that," Hank acknowledged, handing the hero a second beer.

31

She sat up, looking wild and frightened. "Quick! Shut the door."

Barney took a deep breath, steeling himself as he approached her. "How are you feeling, Claire?"

She put her index finger over her mouth and patted the bed. "They're listening. We have to be quiet."

Barney sighed and sat beside her.

"We have to get me out of here. That FBI agent said she was just making sure I didn't have any broken bones, but what does she think? That I'm a fool?" Claire leaned closer to Barney and whispered, "I see what's going on . . . Andy came in. He's wired-up, for sure. They're listening."

"Andy's not wired-up and nobody's listening, Claire. You're having a manic episode. It's affecting your judgement and making you paranoid."

"No! You're all just keeping me from where I need to be." Her face softened. "I know you aren't on their side. It's a conspiracy, Barney. You've been fooled by the others. They're trying to distract you from the problem. Children are being abused by their parents! It's my job to save them."

"What happened at the grocery store, Claire? Why were those people so mad at you?"

"The woman was trying to break her child's arm. She pulled her out of the car onto the cement." Claire chuckled, softly. "I punched her in her fat face. Then the others were going to stone me, just like Joan of Arc. But that little guy, Don, saved me." She leaned forward and rested her head against Barney's shoulder. "I wished you'd been there. I always feel so safe with you."

"Damn it, Claire. There's no fuckin' conspiracy. You're sick and it's not safe for you to be running around the island punching people in the face."

Frightened, Claire pulled away. "Don't hurt me! Please, don't hurt me." She burst into tears.

"Jesus, Claire, I'd never hurt you. Look at me. Remember? I love you. You're safe here. Tomorrow we'll go see Doctor Brusseau."

The name seemed to calm her. "He'll give me pills."

"Yes, he will, and you'll take them. Do you want to be safe?"

Her face, now a reflection of sad resignation. She let out a long breath. "Yes." Her voice, that of a little girl. "Will you stay with me?"

"Forever, Claire."

"You're nice." Her eyes fluttered shut.

He kissed her forehead. *Fuckin bipolar bullshit. I won't let it take us down.* Barney carefully slid his arm from under her and quietly left the room. With great effort, he pushed the entertainment cabinet in front of the bedroom door. Maybe that might be paranoid, but he wasn't taking a chance, as he headed to the great house.

"How is she?" Joey asked, as Barney trudged up the porched steps and fell into the chair, completely rung out.

"About as good as can be expected."

211

Hank brought Barney over a beer. "She tell you what happened in the parking lot?"

"Thanks, Hank. Yeah, a woman reached in a car and grabbed her little girl by her arm and yanked her out onto the concrete. Claire popped her in the face."

Sienna'd gone to check on the twins and caught the last of the conversation. "I've wanted to do that a few times myself."

"Listen Sienna, I'd understand if you and Paul want us to move off the property until Doctor Brusseau has her stabilized."

Sienna looked over at Paul, as she answered, "There's really no place on the island for you to go, Barney. My only real concern with her mania is that our kids are safe. We can all keep an eye on things. I think it'll be fine. You shouldn't have to leave your home. She'll recover faster here than alone with you in some hotel room."

Barney's head dropped. Andy walked over and set his hand on his shoulder. "We're a family, Barn. Families are messy. We'll get through this. She'll get better and we'll all be better at keeping this from happening again."

"It's not on you guys to do that. I should have seen it coming. There were signs, but I just didn't want to see them."

"I think we all ignored them, except for Connie. She thought Claire seemed spun up at the wedding. I wouldn't listen to her. Sorry about that, Connie." Paul nodded over at his sister.

"No need to apologize. There's no right or wrong here. In hindsight, we all might have acted differently, but I'm sure she's had other hypomanic phases that didn't develop into full blown mania. I think we all were hoping this would reverse itself. Fortunately, no one was badly hurt."

Don stood up. "This bipolar business is really the shits, isn't it? All right if I grab another?"

"Of course. Grab me one, while you're at it. I've decided to cut back on booze and just drink beer. It's better for my digestion." Roxanne rolled her eyes, as Hank patted his belly.

"Come on, Andy. I'm pooped."

"Well, looks like the missus' and I are gonna call it quits for the evening. I'll have coffee, eggs, bacon and toast ready for anybody that wants it at 6:30."

"Think I'll take this beer as a traveler and head home. Got a dog to feed. Was nice meeting you, Wyatt." Smiling warmly at Connie, Don added, "from where I sit, you're one lucky man."

"He is so very lucky," Connie agreed, straight faced. Then smiling she added, "Thanks for saving the day, Don."

"We can't thank you enough." Paul said, walking him to his truck.

"See you in the morning, Mr. Architect," Don hollered out his cab window, as he pulled down the drive.

"You ready for bed, Mr. Architect?" Sienna asked, following a big yawn.

"I might come back out here for a while after we put the kids down for the night. Feel like a Martini?"

"Not tonight, Sweetheart. It's been a very long day and I think I'm going to call it good. I'll put the kids down and you can wake me up when you come to bed," she smiled and kissed him goodnight.

32

"Been a while since you came to bed that late. You plan on sleeping all day?"

Paul's eyes strained, adjusting to the daylight as Sienna rolled up the black-out shades and laid down beside him.

"There wouldn't be any coffee nearby would there?"

"Yes Sir, right away Sir." Saluting him flippantly, Sienna hopped out of bed and reappeared shortly with two steaming mugs.

"So, what gives?" she asked, blowing over her coffee.

"Connie, Hank and I had a few Martinis."

"I'm actually glad. It's good to see you cut loose. Although, I didn't actually see it. Because if I'd stayed up drinking, I would have been a basket case at 6:00 when the twins woke me up . . .but it's good to hear about it anyway."

Although groggy, he would have needed to be unconscious to miss the sarcasm. "Yeah, about that . . . I know I haven't been much help with the twins lately."

"That's not what bothers me, Paul. I have more help than I know what to do with." She took his hand. Her amber eyes misted over. "You just haven't been here, even when you're here. There's always something you're worried about at work. I know the pressure is on you to make the money, but I worry about you."

"I'm fine. You know us Norsky's are known for our longevity."

"I thought you were British."

"Same thing...northern European."

Sienna shook her head, "I'm not worried about your health, Lars. . . . I'm worried about what you're missing. Time passes too quickly. AJ and the girls will be gone sooner than you think and if you keep on this pace, you'll regret how much of their childhood you missed."

The urge to defend himself passed quickly. "You're right, Sienna. It's been a pretty hectic few months and with all the steel repair, Don says we're not going to be done with the hotel remodel for at least five more months."

"Have you told the developers that?"

"No, not yet. But I will Monday morning, when I tell them that I'll be off island for ten days."

"Oh? Where you goin'?"

"We. Where are **we** going?"

"OK, where are we going?"

"You know how we've talked about taking AJ and the girls down island?"

"I think the twins are too young for that trip right now. It would be a lot of work and not much relaxation. At least here, we have plenty of support and—"

"I agree. That's why we leave the kids with Aunt Connie and Uncle Wyatt. Connie said last night that they'd love to do it. Andy and Charlotte will be here most of the time, not to mention Hank and Roxanne. Look, I do want to spend a lot more time with the kids, but you and I need some time together, one on one, to figure things out."

215

"One on one sounds pretty nice." She startled Paul by bursting into tears.

Paul put their cups on the bedside table and held her. "What? What is it?"

"I guess I just realized how much I've missed . . . us."

******

The ticket agent hadn't moved or spoken for so long that Paul wondered if she'd fallen asleep over her computer. Finally, she tilted her head and stared at the guitar case. "You got to check that." Paul set the instrument on the scale and waited . . . and waited . . . his frustration mounting. Sienna kicked him lightly on the side of his leg. He got the message. Finally, the other two bags were set on the scale and ten minutes later they were released to stand in the customs line.

"Sir, take off your sunglasses and remove your hat. What's your home address? Are you carrying any alcohol, fruits or vegetables? Where are you going? Why? You look upset. Something bothering you?"

Inside the terminal, Sienna returned from the small gift shop with two bottles of mango juice. "Take a couple swallows," Sienna said. Taking the bottles back, she poured two shots of Cruzan rum in each. "Good thing the customs guy didn't ask if we were carrying explosives. You've been like a time bomb since we got to the airport. Now drink this and let's not talk anymore about TSA employees or lazy ticket agents. In fact, let's not talk at all, for a while."

Paul shut his eyes and tried to relax. The booze was helping. He didn't know why he was so bugged by the customs agent. Probably had something to do with the 30 minutes it took to get through his line. Also, he'd been on-point seven

216

days a week for the hotel project and then there was Claire flipping out. No wonder he was drinking again.

"Paul. Honey, sorry I was cranky. It's just that for me our vacation started when we left the house and you seem . . . well, tense."

"That's probably too kind of a description. More like hostile, I'd say. But that customs officer could save time if he'd quit ogling the ladies. The guy barely listened to our answers, he was so busy checking you out. I thought he might ask for your bra size."

"He was a kid, Paul. I don't think he was over twenty-five."

"Yeah, well I don't think young Officer Horny was thinking about age disparity."

Sienna laughed. "Really? Frankly, I didn't even notice. So, you think I still look pretty good?"

"More beautiful than ever."

"Excuse me." Small in stature, the intelligent eyes of the brown-skinned girl looked frightened. "May I sit with you two?"

"Sure." Paul lifted their carry-on from the chair next to Sienna.

"Are you OK?" Sienna asked, after the girl settled next to her.

"I'm fine, but those two couples don't seem to be. My name's Sophia. I'm sorry to inconvenience you, but I'm worried they're trying to have me booted off the flight."

Paul guessed the two couples on the other side of the room to be in their early seventies. One couple was engaged in a heated exchange with Paul's favorite TSA officer, while the other couple stared over at the girl. Judging from the two men's lobster red arms and flowered shirts, they were probably tourists returning home.

Still a bit on edge, Paul returned their glare. "What's their problem?"

"They haven't said anything to me, but I'd imagine they're telling the officer that they think I might be a terrorist and want me booted off the flight to Miami. They can do that now. I read about a Palestinian who was thrown off a flight because a couple said he made them nervous. I thought if I sat next to you, and if we were talking, they might feel more comfortable."

"Sure, we can help. I'm Sienna and this is my husband, Paul."

"What brought you to Saint Croix?" Paul asked.

"I'm a teacher and came down for a final interview. I got the job and am headed back to Atlanta to organize my move down here."

"Is the school providing lodging?"

"Oh yes, Sienna. They're treating me very nicely. They'll provide a car and a small apartment that one of the directors rents out for school employees."

The boarding for Jet Blue's flight to San Juan, Puerto Rico was announced. Paul watched the two couples stand and walk toward the gate. "Those two couples aren't going to be a problem. Looks like they're on a different flight."

Sophia was visibly relieved, as she stood up. "I'm sorry to have burdened you two. I never imagined that I'd be so paranoid traveling in America."

Sienna took her hand. "The root of all prejudice is fear and it's always ugly. Sit down, Honey. Our flight won't be boarding for at least fifteen minutes."

******

The engines of the Dash 8 groaned as the commuter plane bumped down half the length of the runway before pulling into the late afternoon sky. Rubbing the painful knot on his head, Paul looked past Sienna through the porthole as they climbed east toward St. Maarten, the first touchdown on their island-hopping trip. "Why would they put the seats a step up from the aisle? I may be concussed."

"Poor baby," Sienna purred, kissing his forehead. "That overhead storage compartment just seemed to appear out of nowhere. Listen, I know what would make you feel better."

"What?"

"We have a five-hour layover in St. Maarten. Let's catch a cab and head out to Orient Beach. It's on the French side of the island."

"Isn't that a nude beach?" Paul asked, feigning disgust.

"There's a sign marking the section at the end that's nude, but I'm afraid a lot of the women are topless even on the bathing suit side. You gonna be OK with that?"

"Can I use my French?"

"Oh god."

33

The cab ride took a little over a half an hour. Gerrard, the middle-aged, rotund proprietor of the beach club, warmly greeted them.

"Bonjour, mes amis. My nephew, Etienne, will take you to the beach and set up your chaises and umbrella. He's recently arrived from the Cote d'Azur and is very shy about his English, but understands it sufficiently to take your orders. We have a full lunch menu and a well-stocked bar with 42 different brands of bottled beer."

"Thank you. We'll be fine, Gerrard. I speak a little French myself," Paul replied cheerfully, as Sienna rolled her eyes. They fell in behind Etienne, who led them along the sea-grape-lined path to the beach.

Although Paul tried to appear disinterested in the two bare-breasted women jogging past them, Sienna wasn't fooled. "No penalty for looking, Paul, but now that Gerrard's set us up, could you focus on your French for a minute and order your wife a margarita? Paul? Hello. Earth to Paul, do you think you can do that?"

"Huh? Of course, I can do that. I took three years of French." Turning toward Etienne, he hesitated briefly, and in a vain attempt to sound fluent, ordered. "Monsieur, ma femme et je voudrais deux margaritas."

"Avec du sel?" the attendant replied earnestly, playing for tips.

Sienna saw the blank expression on Paul's face, as he combed through his dusty high school memory bank. "I think he wants to know if we want salt on the rims."

Paul smacked his forehead. "Of course. Oui, garcon . . . du sel." The attendant bowed and left with the order.

"You can say what you want, but people really warm up to you when you communicate in their language."

"Paul, you're such a goof, I think they'd warm up to you, no matter what language you're using. Hey check out that guy. You're not the only one who gets to enjoy the eye-candy."

The subject of interest was no spring chicken. Naked except for a thick layer of grey hair that covered his entire body, his one visible protuberance appeared unusually adorned.

"What's that flashing down by his balls?"

"It looks like a watch fob strung from his penis to his testicles," Sienna replied, laughing.

"Wow, you don't see that every day. Think it hurts?"

"It doesn't look like he's in any pain, but you could ask him."

"Yeah, I could, but I'm really more comfortable watching from a distance."

"Chicken." Sienna leaned forward and untied her top. "When in Rome" . . . Standing, she smiled innocently and jogged into the ocean.

Paul watched her dive into the surf. Never had he known a woman like Sienna. She surprised him daily. A strange sadness came over him. Had they already been together for five years? It'd gone by too fast. He recalled his time away from her in Cabo. He vowed then, that if he ever won her back, he'd never take one minute of their time together for granted. Now, he knew what was important . . . Sienna, their kids, friends and their life together. Yet, he was still holding something back. *What am I afraid of?* He placed a bookmark in his thoughts as he jogged toward Sienna, who had been joined by two young men in the surf.

"Well, that didn't take you long," Sienna commented as they watched her new friends move on to their next target. "I don't know what I was thinking, pulling my top off."

"Well, it caught my attention." He pulled her into him and laughed. "Damn people, go away. Do you want me to bring it out to you?"

"No, I really didn't feel uncomfortable until those two dudes from Missouri appeared. Now that you're with me, I feel so free and relaxed. This is wonderful."

"Sienna, I . . ."

"What?"

"You know, it may be as natural as hell and all that, but seeing your breasts all sunlit and wet really turns me on."

"Well, I'm glad about that. Are you too distracted? Should I put my top back on?"

"No way. I say let the girls be free. We're on vacation. I'm gonna head back in. I don't want to miss out on our deux margaritas. Au revoir, mon amour."

******

Paul pulled his cargo shorts over his swimsuit and fished out his wallet. Sienna headed in when she saw Etienne reappear with their drinks.

222

Etienne greeted Paul, "Monsieur, voici votre command."

Command? Paul wondered if the attendant was ribbing him about his free-spirited wife, but took the offered drinks and complimentary chips and salsa. "Attendez, monsier." Paul started to reach into the front pocket of his cargo shorts. "Je voudrais vous donner la bitte."

Reaching the beach, Sienna watched the attendant turn abruptly and sprint back up the path.

"What was that all about?" she asked, drying herself off.

"Etienne seemed like he couldn't get away fast enough. I have no idea."

"What did you say, or should I say . . . try to say?"

"I told him to wait, because I wanted to give him a tip."

"I can't see why he'd run from that. What's the French word for tip?"

"Bitte. No, wait that's not right. Shit, now I remember. It's decharge."

"What's bitte mean? How do you spell it?"

"B-i-t-t-e, I think."

"We've got wifi from the bar." Sienna reached in their beach bag and took out her iPhone. Moments later, a playful smile spread over her face. "Bitte appears to mean cock or it can also mean dong as in long dong, or maybe as in your case, ding dong."

34

Sienna grabbed Paul's hand as the pilot misjudged the distance to the ground by five-feet and plowed into the runway with a bone-jarring thud, accompanied by the sound of screeching tires. Nevertheless, as with most Caribbean flights, the passengers, grateful to still be alive, broke into a cheerful round of applause.

It had been ages since Sienna felt like she could relax. She had dozed for most of the 40-minute flight to Antigua, their second stop on Liat's multi-island flight. Paul had reserved a room at The Trade Winds, a moderately priced, but well-maintained hotel, near the VC Bird Airport. On route to the hotel, Fabian, their cab driver, volunteered to take them on a tour of the island for another 20 USD.

"We're pretty tired," Paul explained, taking the offered business card, "but we'll look you up next time we're on island."

"Very well, Sir. But please allow me to return you to the airport for your morning flight."

Paul, still stirred-up by Sienna's earlier topless foray, convinced her to cancel their reservation at Sheer Rocks, a fine dining restaurant in St. Mary's, in exchange for a romantic evening and room service.

The following morning, the same charming young man who had delivered their dinner, knocked on the door with their breakfast order. "You have seen so little of our beautiful island, but the smile on your faces tells me it was a wise decision. Perhaps next time you will stay longer."

Paul signed the slip, adding a generous tip on top of the customary room service charge and handed it back to the affable youth. "Thank you so much. The food and your service has been outstanding. We hope to be back again soon." Closing the door, Paul took the breakfast tray off the stand and carried it to the table on the deck. "Well, this isn't bad, is it?"

"Just what the doctor ordered. I do feel a little guilty, though. I haven't even missed the kids. I must be a terrible mother."

"Yes, you are."

"Paul!"

He laughed. "No. It's a good thing. I'm sure they're not missing us. You know with everybody fighting over them, they're probably getting spoiled rotten. We really need to rest up on this vacation, because it'll take us a solid month to get them back in line once we're home."

"You're right."

"I say no guilt allowed for the next nine days. Deal?"

"OK, deal."

******

The island of Saint Lucia is a topographic marvel with two steeply sloped volcanic mountains called Pitons stretching over 700 meters into the Caribbean sky.

The Body Holiday LeSport Spa and Resort sounded perfect when Paul made the reservations. He knew that Sienna would love the resort. Snorkeling, scuba diving, yoga classes, spa treatments, fitness trails and fine dining were among the offerings. The fact that the resort was a ten-minute walk from The Saint Lucia Golf Club had sealed the deal for Paul.

However, even with all the available options, the two lovebirds only ventured outside their room for occasional meals during the first two days. "I guess we could have just stayed on Saint Croix and rented a room at Sand Castles," Sienna joked. "Let's go do something."

"How about you go have a spa treatment and I'll check out the golf course?"

"Yeah, maybe . . . Or, I could come with you and be your caddie and drive the cart."

"That's not what caddies do. They carry the clubs."

"Well that's not happening. I'll drive the cart. Maybe I'll even play. Then you and I could do the spa tomorrow. I'm kind of enjoying your company."

"Perfect."

Checking in, the golf pro gave them the option of taking a cart or hiring caddies. Paul thought his game would benefit from a caddie's local knowledge of the course and Sienna liked the exercise they would get walking the six miles.

Paul, rusty from lack of play, unexpectedly, striped his first drive down the middle of the fairway. "Well played, Sir." Ernesto, his caddie, took the driver from him.

"Thanks. Just call me, Paul. You play?"

The large, St. Lucian's white teeth gleamed as he smiled proudly. "Yessir. I play to a scratch. I'm the island champion."

"Wow." Paul eyed the big man's bow legs and tattered sandals. "A scratch? I guess you must play a lot. I bet you hit it a mile."

"Uh-huh. I show you later."

They walked toward the women's tee, where Sienna was taking practice swings under the watchful eye of her caddie, Frank. Paul watched Sienna as she stood over the ball. Although he expected her to whiff her shot, he had to admire how athletic her posture appeared. Instead, she took a powerful, full swing and met the ball solidly, sending it twenty yards past his own.

He stopped in his tracks, dumbfounded.

"A little surprise I've been waiting to spring on you." She bent over and picked up her tee. "Golf is easy. Golf is fun."

"She's pretty good and she is very beautiful," Ernesto called back to him. "You're a lucky man."

Paul caught up to her after she hit her next shot, a five iron, on the green.

"How long has this been going on?"

"I started taking lessons from Kenny about the time you started getting real busy. I made him promise not to tell you. I wanted to see the look on your face, which, by the way, was priceless."

"So, you plan on turning pro anytime soon?"

"I don't know. Kenny says I've got a lot of natural ability."

"That's great. By the way, remember that I loved you even before you got famous."

Sienna laughed. "Well, my short game's inconsistent, but Kenny thinks I could play competitively one day, when I have more time to practice. I really love the game, Paul."

"Well, this definitely lands third place in the big surprises category, right after your agreeing to marry me and the birth of the twins. How many strokes are you giving me?"

"I'm not sure what that means beyond the bedroom, but isn't it gorgeous out here?"

Later, Sienna walked alongside Paul, as they approached the 7th green. "I really like Frank. He lives in the little building by the clubhouse and works on the ground crew with Ernesto. Did you know that Ernesto's his younger brother?"

"No, I hadn't heard that."

"Frank says that Ernesto has a wife and two young kids and is a great golfer."

"He told me that he was the island champion and that he'd hit a few shots later. I bet he bombs it."

"From the size of him, I think you're probably right. He's almost as big as Barney."

"I wonder how they're doing. I hope the medication is working and she doesn't beat herself up too much. She needs to just move on."

"She's lucky to have Barney and all of us. Can you imagine how isolated a person would become without support?"

Three hours later, exhausted by the heat, they reached the seventeenth hole, a lengthy par five that returned toward the clubhouse. "Want to take a swipe at it?" Paul asked Ernesto.

"Sure." Ernesto took Paul's driver out of the bag and stuck a tee in the ground. With a beat-up ball, he pulled from his pocket and without a practice swing, he drilled it two hundred and eighty yards. "Caught it a little thin," he complained. The next one, however, he hit flush. Paul and Sienna watched in awe as the ball landed fifty yards beyond his first shot.

"I told you my brother's good." Frank boasted. "I think he beats Tiger Woods."

Paul and Sienna hit their shots and walked together, listening to the brothers squabble. "I've told you not to say that, Frank. Maybe now I could, but before his wife put a five iron through his car window, nobody could beat The Tiger."

"You're wrong, Little Bro. You could have beat him before that. You're too powerful to lose."

"Power's just one weapon. You need touch."

Paul smiled and shook his head. "Frank could be right. I've seen the pros play and I've never seen anyone hit the ball like that."

"Just think what he could do if he had a pair of decent golf shoes. Those sandals can't be much help."

Over Ernesto's objections, Paul miss-clubbed on the short par three 18th and dumped his tee shot in the lake. "I told you the wind was too mighty for an eight iron."

Paul hit onto the green from the drop area. "Next time, I promise I'll listen to you, Ernesto."

The expected caddie fee for carrying their bags through almost four hours of blistering heat was 15 USD. Sienna and Paul gave them each sixty, and thanked them profusely for their company.

After a beer at the clubhouse bar, they walked back to LeSport, "It's sad that with all of Ernesto's talent, he'll probably never get a chance to compete on a wider stage than his island tournaments."

"You know Paul, fame and fortune isn't for everybody. Ernesto loves his wife and kids and he is the island champion. Their life and needs are simple. Frank lives in a shack, but they both seem happier than most anybody I know. There's something for us to learn here."

Paul thought for a few minutes. "Do you think we'd be happy living in the bag room at the Buccaneer clubhouse?"

229

"I think you're taking me too literally. Don't get me wrong. I appreciate all your hard work, but how much money do we need? You've been pushing for almost a year now. Life's short. The kids miss you and I've missed our downtimes together."

"Yeah, finding the right balance has always been a challenge for me."

"That's just another reason you're lucky to have me. We'll figure it out together."

35

"They're done with me. I've ruined everything," Claire sobbed, sitting up in bed.

Barney wasn't surprised by the outburst. He sat up and turned on the bedside lamp. "Who's done with you? Paul? Sienna? Andy?"

"All of them, and you should be, too. I'm poison. I hate myself."

Claire's lucidity was returning rapidly with the ingestion of lithium, but so had her depression, as she began to deal with the impact of her mania.

"Claire, this disease sucks, but mostly it's tough on you. We're together for the long haul. Hell, you put up with all my farting."

A flicker of a smile turned up the corner of her mouth. "I guess we've already earned the 'in sickness' merit badge."

"Exactly, and do you think Paul or Sienna or any of them are judging you for this? This isn't your fault. No more than if you were to come down with . . . whooping cough."

Claire's brow furrowed. "Why whooping cough?"

"Christ, I don't know. The point is everyone's here for you. Dr. Brusseau warned you that you'd be feeling guilty as you came out of it. The thing is not to wallow in it."

"I'm just so disappointed in my—"

Barney held up his hand. "You'll get better faster if you quit blaming yourself."

"Look, I know you're trying to make me feel better, but I'd like to imagine for at least one fucking minute that I have some control, some responsibility in all this." Hearing her words tumble out faster and louder, she paused and took a deep breath before continuing softly. "I have to believe, Barney, that I have some responsibility in this thing otherwise, I'm like a sheet in the wind just waiting for the next big blow."

"I get that. I just don't see how beating yourself up is going to help."

"I'm just really sad. I didn't think this would happen again." She rolled over, her face pressed into the pillow.

"Yeah, well, it sucks, but we'll get through it." He gently engulfed her in his massive arms. Her muffled sobs filled the room.

"OK, I'm done feeling sorry for myself," she said, lifting her head onto his chest.

"So, what happened in the parking lot?"

"Oh, that. Honestly, I think I just went postal." She lifted his arm off her and sat up. "I woke up that morning on the living room floor of two gay guys that I met dancing in Christiansted. I felt like shit, I guess 'cause I'd been doing some weird stuff for quite a while."

"Like what?"

"This whole book thing. I'd turned it into an obsession. I can't believe you put up with it. Also, I sent a terrible card to Paul and Sienna. I knew it was wrong when I did it, but I wanted to hurt them." Her voice trailed off.

Barney couldn't respond.

"You still think I'm worth the effort, because I don't."

"Yes. Of course, you're worth it. What did the card say?"

"I pretended to be this guy whose wife Paul was having sex with. I think I threatened that I'd hurt him."

"Jesus."

Claire waited as Barney's frozen features gave no indication of what he was thinking. Finally, he asked, "Was it because you still love Paul and you want to break them up?"

"No, it's not that. I think I'm jealous of what Paul and Sienna have. You know, they're so perfect together and now with the beautiful twins . . . Plus they don't have to deal with all this crap."

Relieved by her explanation, he spoke without thinking. "Honestly, Claire, things are never as perfect as they appear. You can't even imagine the struggles they've faced."

She looked at him, quizzically.

Barney had promised Paul and Sienna that he would never share the secret of the murders with anyone, especially Claire, but Claire had his heart and keeping things from her felt wrong. Still, he had to honor the promise and tried to recover. "You know, losing their baby, then Paul going on that bender and them breaking up." Barney was relieved to see her curiosity vanish. "I think he's still holding himself in check; afraid to let go and enjoy life."

"Yeah, he's never seemed quite the same since coming back from Cabo." She leaned over and rested her head against his shoulder. "Of course, I love them both. I'd risk my life for them. It's just when I get the way I am when I'm manic, my bad ideas seem like good ideas."

Claire rolled into him, sobbing again. "I'm just a bad person, Barney. You should get as far away from me as you can."

"This is as far away from you as I want to be."

"You're an idiot."

"Probably true. Now try and get some sleep."

******

Sienna was pleased how quickly Paul had fallen into the rhythm of their vacation. He'd enjoyed the spa treatments and relaxation on the beach almost as much as their rounds on the golf course. The food was excellent and the Le Sport staff were friendly, yet respectful of their privacy.

Returning from the beach, the fourth afternoon of their stay, they entered their room. Housekeeping had pulled the shades to keep the room cool. The phone blinked through the darkness. Sienna picked up the receiver and listened to the message. "It's your sister. She says the kids are fine but you need to call her."

Paul couldn't imagine anything good that would cause Connie to contact them. His stomach was doing flip-flops by the time she picked up on the fourth ring.

"It's Claire, Paul. I didn't want to call, but I thought you and Sienna would want to know. She's had a heart attack."

Sienna read his expression. Her hand found his as she sat down on the bed. "Is it Andy?"

"It's Claire. She's had a heart attack." He put the phone on speaker. "How serious is it, Connie?"

"It's bad. She's on life support. She was alone in their cabin when it happened. Barney found her unconscious when he came home. The doctors aren't sure if she'll ever wake up, and if she does, they think there's significant brain damage."

Paul was too stunned to think of anything else to say. Sienna choked her thanks to Connie for calling and promised they'd be on the next flight home.

"Barney. How's he doing?" Paul asked, before hanging up.

"He's devastated and blames himself for leaving her alone."

******

The turbulent flight back to Saint Croix did little to lessen the anxiety they both felt. "We need to stay positive, Paul. Doctors aren't always right."

Any hopes for Claire's improved condition, however, were immediately lost in Andy's grief-stricken expression, as he met them at the airport.

"How is she?" Paul asked, expecting the worse.

"She passed a few hours ago, kids. The poor thing never regained consciousness. Barney stayed in her room the whole time, just praying she'd come to."

Paul felt like he'd been kicked in the gut, but managed to ask, "Where's Barney now? I should be with him."

Sienna couldn't hold back her tears.

Andy put his arm around her shoulders. "There, there. Yes sir, quite a shock, this one is. She was so young. Poor girl. Barney's down at his boat. He called from the hospital to let us know she was gone. You've known him all your life, but it sounded to me like he'd rather be alone."

They loaded the luggage into the back of the truck. Driving toward the attendant's shed, Paul caught site of a man jogging after them, waving and shouting. "Paul! Hold up!"

The man arrived beside the truck, breathing hard. He dropped down, his hands on his knees, to catch his breath. Paul thought he looked familiar, but Sienna recognized and greeted him immediately. "Hi Herbert. You're looking winded, but well."

"Hello Sienna, you're just as lovely as ever. You don't recognize me, do you, Paul?"

The straw-colored hair had turned a little grayer, but with Sienna identifying the first name, Paul got it. "Herbert Pascall, of course I remember you. This is our good friend, Andy." Andy reached across and shook Herbert's hand.

"Please to meet you, Son. You live on Saint Croix?"

"No. I'm here on business. I have a law practice on Saint Thomas." Herbert could see that Sienna'd been crying. "Look I won't keep you, but we do need to talk. I was going to call you tomorrow morning to set up a time. I spotted you pulling out in front of me and thought I'd save the call. I hope I didn't intrude." He looked worriedly at Sienna.

"Of course not, Herbert. We just found out that a close friend died."

"Oh, I'm so sorry. We can catch up next time I'm over. This is nothing urgent. Once again, I'm sorry for your loss."

"Seemed like a nice enough fellow," Andy observed. "Kind of odd, that he went to so much trouble to see you, then said it probably wasn't important. Any idea what it's about?"

Sienna looked at Paul, who nodded. "He was Andrew Sherman's attorney. Andrew left a considerable sum of money for AJ, if he goes to college. If not, then it goes to our next child . . . I guess it would go to the twins."

"Well, I'll be. Seems like the scoundrel was trying to make up for things toward the end. I guess there's some good in most everybody."

"I didn't think Herbert'd be contacting us again. It was left that we would let him know when AJ was ready to start college. Paul, you have any idea what this might be about?" Sienna seemed nervous, asking the question.

"We never felt totally comfortable taking the money," Paul explained to Andy, "since it had been taken from Buddy Falco and the mob. Herbert was placing the money in C.D.'s. It's probably nothing more than updating us on the account balance."

"I'd just as soon not even think about it," Sienna groaned, "but we should try and meet with him before he leaves island. Otherwise, I'll just be worrying about it."

"I'll give him a call tomorrow morning and set it up."

They rode in silence. Paul turned off Creque Dam Road onto the drive into Windsol.

Andy spotted Barney's Jeep in the parking lot. "Looks like he might rather be with friends, after all."

******

AJ and Red were outside throwing the ball for Rose. Red heaved the ball across the field and both boys ran over to the truck. "Hey, Mom. Hi Dad."

Sienna bent down and kissed AJ's cheek. Paul scooped him up in his arms, while Andy ruffled Red's hair and exclaimed, "Man, you threw that ball 50 yards. I think we might have a pitcher in the family."

"It's very sad here," Red replied, somberly, "because Aunt Claire died."

Phoebe and Reed burst into tears when Sienna walked into the great room. "Come on girls, Mommy will think that you didn't have fun while they were gone." Connie's words were barely heard over the twin's wailing.

Aunt Charlotte walked up to Paul and kissed him on the cheek. "Welcome home, Paul. What a tragedy." Her sad, loving eyes reflected the loss they all felt.

"Barney's down in his cabin," Connie volunteered, as Sienna and Aunt Charlotte left to put the twins down. "He got here right after dinner. Said he was turning in early. I don't know if he's eaten."

"Probably not hungry's my guess," Andy said.

"I should see how he's doing." Paul walked into the kitchen.

"There's a plate in the refrigerator that Aunt Charlotte made up for him. You want any company?"

"Thanks, Wyatt, but I think it'd be better if I went alone."

Barney and Claire's cabin was dark. Paul knocked on the frame of the open front door. "That you, Ace?" He followed his friend's voice out to the deck, where he found him sprawled in a leather recliner that he'd moved from the living room. A half empty bottle of Jack Daniels sat within fingertip reach of his dangling arm. "You want a glass?"

"No, the bottle's fine." Paul pulled up a canvas deck chair. Neither spoke as they passed the bottle back and forth.

"You heard I left her alone. She's coming off mania, and I leave to get her some guava-berry ice cream. If I'd been here, I could have given her CPR. Yelled for help. She might've lived."

"Jesus, Barney. I'm so sorry, but you can't blame yourself. Nobody would have thought she'd have a heart attack."

"I don't think the lithium had anything to do with it. Nobody ever said it could cause heart trouble. I know her parents died in a plane crash, so who knows if there was anything genetic that could've caused it. Maybe it was the stress from her mania." Barney took a swallow. "Who knows?"

"Yeah, who knows?"

"I mean, what's out there?" Barney pointed the neck of the bottle at the star-filled sky. "You think she's up there somewhere?"

"I don't know. Maybe in some other dimension or parallel universe."

"Yeah, we really don't know what happens, do we? I can tell you one thing for sure, though . . ."

"What's that?"

"We didn't have nearly enough time together. That's what. It's all fucked up . . .goddamn it." Barney threw the empty bottle over the guardrail. Paul thought he heard it crash, but it might have been a wave hitting the rocky beach, 200 feet below.

"I blamed myself when we lost our baby. It was my baggage that brought Buddy to the island."

"That's bullshit. You can't be serious. You didn't know that Sherman was mixed up with the mob."

"And you didn't know Claire would have a heart attack."

Paul heard a muffled sob. Barney's voice cracked. "I loved her. She'd always tell me when I was full of shit. She knew me. The whole bipolar thing never kept me from loving her. Even when she left me. I would have waited for her forever . . . Now, she's never coming back."

Paul reached over and softly gripped Barney's shoulder, as the muffled sobs turned into a loud roar of pain.

239

"Barney? Paul? Everything OK, in there?"

"Yeah Hank. We're OK," Paul shouted back.

"Well, all right then. Let me know if I can bring you guys anything."

"Sorry about that, Hank."

"No problem, Barney. Just holler if you need anything."

"What a fuck up. Screaming like that, with kids trying to sleep. I shouldn't even be here. Should have stayed down at the boat. I'm sorry, Ace. You go back to Sienna."

"I'm not going anywhere and this is exactly where you belong." Paul went inside and returned with another bottle.

"She knew what a pain she was. You knew about her manic bouts, but I kept a lot of her hypomania to myself. Didn't want to burden you. She told me about the Valentine's Day card she sent Sienna. Said that when she was manic her bad ideas seemed like good ideas."

"Yeah, we thought it was her, but didn't want to tell you, in case it wasn't."

"She was going to tell you and Sienna about it when you got back. Wanted to be the one to do it; to apologize . . . I tell you, Amigo, Claire knew how hard it was loving her. Even told me I should leave her. Of course, I never would have . . . But, when I came home and found her, for an instant there was a flash of relief. I'm so fucked up. I loved her more than I've ever loved anybody, but there were times, a lot of times when I felt like it was all too much."

"Don't torture yourself, Barney. She knew you loved her. You can't judge yourself for feelings you can't control."

"Jesus, I miss her so much already. I don't know if I can get over this. Do you think I'll ever feel normal again?"

"You never were normal."

Barney smiled sadly, "I don't mean normal, normal, Ace. I mean normal for me. I just don't see how this pain will ever end."

36

It was daylight before Paul left Barney dozing on the deck and climbed in bed beside Sienna.

"How is he?"

"Shoot, I didn't want to wake you up." He kissed her on the forehead, pulling the single sheet over him. "He's hurting, but I think he'll be OK. It's 5:30, go back to sleep."

"I wasn't asleep. How are you?" She propped herself up on her elbow.

Paul thought for a minute. "My life's been tied to hers for so long, I feel like there's a big whole in my chest."

"She was one of the most important people in your life. The fact that you two were able to have a friendship after your divorce shows how close you were."

"She knew that you and I were meant to be together, just like she was with Barney."

"When we're 110, let's jump out of a plane without parachutes, so neither one of us has to be without the other."

"I'm not really a fan of kersplat endings. Couldn't we do something with pharmaceuticals?"

Sienna leaned over, her face inches above his. "Take care of yourself, Mr. Armstrong. I need you around for a very long time. I can't imagine losing the love of my life." She kissed him and dropped back on her pillow. "Poor Barney."

******

It was Paul's first day back, and he'd already had site meetings in Christiansted with the contractor and hotel developers. Sienna had left a note reminding him to call Herbert Pascall.

It had been over two years since Paul and Sienna had been called to the attorney's office, after their honeymoon in the BVI's. He recalled the last time he'd seen Andrew. Their chance meeting had set in motion the events that eventually led to Buddy Falco's attack on Sienna; the loss of their unborn child, and Paul becoming a triple murderer. He shook his head, trying to clear the haunting memories, and called Pascall.

"This is Herbert."

"Paul Armstrong, Herbert. If you have the time, I'd like to meet while you're on island."

"I'm staying at The Buccaneer. I'd come to you, but I'm without a car."

During the forty-minute drive east he couldn't help wonder what Pascall wanted to discuss. Was Andrew's gift to AJ discovered by the mob? With all the publicity, had Pascall been tempted to tell the wrong somebody something about his notorious client's act of benevolence? Paul felt sick with the thought, especially knowing what the reemergence of the mafia into their lives would do to Sienna.

He pulled his truck into the half-filled parking lot of The Mermaid, The Buccaneer's beach bar restaurant. Walking in, he spotted Pascall talking with a waitress, who was just leaving the table.

Pascall stood as Paul approached. "I hope you don't mind, but I'm on a tight schedule, so I just ordered us both the lunch special and a couple Caribs."

"That's fine. Thanks."

"First, I'm really sorry about the loss of your friend."

"Thanks, Herbert. We're still in shock. She died of a heart attack and wasn't even forty-five."

"Jeez, that's rough. Well, we never know, do we? Gotta enjoy every minute we have, I guess."

Paul waited until their drinks were delivered before asking, "What was it you wanted to talk about?"

Pascall took a large manila envelope from his briefcase and pushed it across the table. Paul recognized the handwriting on the outside of the sealed envelope.

> *Herbert,*
> *As we've discussed, there are people who wish me harm. Should I meet with an untimely death, I ask that you deliver this envelope, in person, to Paul Armstrong. It is extremely important, however, that you wait a minimum of three years after my demise to carry out this request.*
> *Thank you,*
> *A.S.*

"I've had a few sleepless nights over my responsibilities carrying out various requests for my deceased client," Pascall confessed. "While I'm confident that I've broken no laws, Andrew Sherman apparently broke several. So, knowing that . . . I may, in fact, have some culpability here."

"OK . . . but I'm not sure I understand what you're saying."

"Sorry Paul, I'm not used to this kind of a thing. If I'd known who was after Andrew and why, I never would have taken him on as a client."

"Should Sienna and I be concerned about any of this?"

"No, no. That's all water under the bridge. Nothing will come of this, if we keep it between ourselves. We don't need anybody poking around in our business."

Paul's appetite was marginal before he arrived. Now, hearing Herbert's worries over possible illegalities or worse, mob intervention, he pushed his food away and considered whether he should even take the envelope.

"Look Paul, I'm probably being overly cautious and a bit paranoid. Maybe you should open the envelope and we can see if it's anything to worry about."

Paul weighed his options. Shrugging his shoulders, he took a Swiss army knife from his pocket and slit open the top. A folded cream-colored sheet was the envelope's only contents.

"That's parchment," Herbert exclaimed. "I've seen it used on several old land documents. Probably made from goat skin."

Paul unfolded the sheet and laid it on the table between them. The hand drawn map had an elaborate compass rose in its center. There were burn marks on the edges. Paul recognized the kidney bean shape of Saint Croix. He pointed at the shapes closest to Saint Croix and called them out, "Saint Thomas, Saint John."

Herbert studied the drawing. "Yes, and that one's a pretty good rendition of Tortola."

"But it gets a bit confusing to the north and east." Paul counted seven additional islands. "He's got the total number of British Virgin Islands but after Tortola, they're not the right shapes or in the correct locations."

245

He looked up at Herbert and laughed. Pointing to a small blotch of red ink on the western edge of one of the islands . . . "Good ol' Andrew . . . He always loved pirates."

"Judging from what I've read about him, he probably fancied himself one, too."

"Yeah, but too bad he wasn't into cartography. If he was trying to leave directions to a hidden treasure, this is unusable."

Finishing his beer, Herbert sat back, "I remember reading that there was still a significant sum of money he fleeced from the mafia that was never recovered. I guess a person could explore the shorelines of all the BVI's and—"

"What? Look for clues? This is such typical Andrew Sherman bullshit. He loved being either the center of attention or controlling the direction of attention. If this is a treasure map, then someone with a helluva lot more free-time than I've got, should look for it."

"Yeah, but I wonder if there's some clue here. Something that would resolve this pattern into the actual locations of the islands."

"Tell you what. . . Why don't you keep the map and if you find something. . . You can keep that, too. Sienna and I have had enough Andrew Sherman for a lifetime."

"No, no, no. It was left to you. I've done all that's required of me."

"OK, so nothing to worry about here, right?" Paul slipped the map back into the envelope. "Nothing to keep you awake at night? No laws broken?"

"Certainly seems that way."

"Great." Paul stood and extended his hand. "Thanks Herbert, I hope you have a wonderful life."

"Don't forget to contact me a couple months before AJ enters college. I'll need some time to pull out the funds, which, I might add are doing quite well. I'm sure that even with the cost of good colleges nowadays, you and Sienna will be pleased."

37

Paul had planned on just a brief stop at the hotel site on his way back to Windsol, but it was after 6:00 when Sienna handed him the twins. "I think we might need to discuss what each of us had in mind when we talked about slowing down."

"I know. I know."

"I'm heading over to the great house to help with dinner. Barney's agreed to have a meal with us. Could you give the girls a bath and dress them in their nighty-nights before bringing them over? I'll have AJ give you a hand."

"Not necessary. We've got it covered, Mommy. Don't we girls?"

"That's great. We'll see you there. Oh, I almost forgot, what was all that about with Pascall this afternoon?"

"Nothing important, we can talk about it tonight."

Paul enjoyed his time with the girls, as they giggled over bathtub bubbles, floating ducks, and his Disney character imitations. Barney hadn't appeared by the time Paul and the twins arrived at the great house. He set Phoebe on Hanks lap and Reed on Roxanne's, as he left to look for him.

"Take your time," Roxanne requested. "Andy just came out to announce that dinner's going to be awhile."

The door to Barney's cabin was open. Paul spotted the big man, shirtless in the bathroom, shaving. "Sit down Ace. I'll be right there. Thought I'd clean up a bit. Don't want to scare the girls, looking like Grizzly Adams."

"I'm not sure that shaving's enough."

"Very funny. Yeah this old face isn't lookin' so good. Seems like there's a lot more lines on it than before."

Paul saw his friend catch himself, holding back tears as he dropped the razor in the sink and gripped the wash basin with both hands.

"Hey Barney, if you'd rather eat alone tonight, I can bring you back some sandwiches. Andy's got a roast in the oven."

"No, no, I'll be fine. I have to be, don't I?"

"You know, eventually you'll get through this . . . Remember how it was when your brother was killed?"

"Yeah, I almost drank myself to death. Then your Uncle Ernie told me to quit feeling sorry for myself."

"Uncle Ernie was a great man."

"You here to tell me to quit feeling sorry for myself?"

"No. It's going to take some time."

Barney pulled on a T-shirt and headed for the door. "C'mon Ace, it's show time." They walked silently under a darkening sky toward the great house.

"'Bout time you two showed up. I was near ready to send out a posse after you." Andy stood at the top of the porch stairs wearing an apron Barney had given him for Christmas that read *Dude with the Food.*

"Heard you have a roast in the oven, Old Man."

"Old man! For the life of me, I don't know why I put up with all this abuse." He winked at Paul and returned to the kitchen.

"Well, we don't have to worry about Andy getting all sad and morose on us," Barney observed, as they climbed the porch steps.

"Wouldn't bet on it. The night's still young."

Fortunately, Sienna had realized just before Andy rang the dinner triangle that Aunt Charlotte had accidentally set one too many place settings. Horrified by her oversight and already fighting back tears over Claire's absence, Charlotte excused herself and ducked out the back door. Sienna followed and found her sobbing at the lookout.

"Aunt Charlotte, are you OK?"

"Oh, Sienna, I just can't stop crying. I feel so sorry for Claire. You know, my first husband, Ernie, would have loved you, but he adored Claire. Sometimes I think Paul married her because Ernie constantly told him how wonderful he thought she was. Honestly, I always thought back then that she was pretty much out for herself, but she did know how to capture a man's attention."

Sienna joined her at the guardrail. "I know what you mean about some women lighting up around men. I never felt that with Claire. Except when she was in a manic phase, I always thought she seemed really grounded in her relationship with Barney."

"She changed when they became a couple. They were good for each other. I think she felt totally content in their relationship. With Paul, I don't think she ever felt that."

"Poor Barney, I worry about him."

"First it was her mental illness, now this. Barney's devastated . . . it makes me sick. I can't stop crying."

The two women stood quietly looking out over the Caribbean, until Sienna spoke, "Do you remember when we stood here with Claire and she promised that she would always listen to us if she seemed to be revving up?"

"Yes. I was just thinking about that. She carried a great burden of guilt after this last episode. I don't think she could forgive herself. Maybe the heart-attack . . ."

"Well, Barney followed her wishes and had her cremated. I don't think there was an autopsy done, so we'll never know for sure what caused it. But she was also on powerful medications that have dangerous side effects and Paul told me that she knew little of her biological family's history, so there could have been a genetic predisposition."

"The cards seemed stacked against them. She was a courageous woman. Not just for how she saved Barney, but to face her challenges with such grace and humor. I'll miss that sense of humor and her fiery spirit."

"We're all going to miss her."

"I love you, Sienna. At my age, I expect to lose contemporaries, which is hard enough. You take care of yourself and Paul. I'm too old to go through this kind of heartache ever again." The two women hugged briefly, but were interrupted by the ringing of Andy's dinner triangle. They quickly returned to the great house where the venerable chef was shouting last minute orders to AJ and Red.

"Take the water pitchers out to the table, boys. See if anyone needs anything. I'm about ready to bring out the roast." Spotting Sienna and Charlotte, he smiled sadly. "You two OK?"

"As good as we can be, Sweetheart."

******

The night felt dark and thick with sorrow. Discussions centered around the great meal and the weather, until Barney cleared his throat and spoke. "I want to thank you all for being there for me. I don't quite know how I'm going to get through this, but . . . I will." Aunt Charlotte pulled a handkerchief from her pocket and gave it to Andy, whose face was now lined with tears. "Paul has spoken with the folks up in Washington and they're all coming down, day after tomorrow. So, I think we can have the memorial on Sunday. We'll take Claire's ashes out on *The Last Hurrah* . . . and say goodbye."

Paul and Connie watched him lumber down the path toward his cabin, as they walked to the lookout. Connie caught the look on her brother's face. "Don't worry Paul, he'll get through this."

"I don't think he ever will, completely. She was the love of his life. There are certain things you never recover from. Losing a child would be one, too."

"Losing a brother would be another. Even when you find another one that you never knew existed."

"I wish I'd known Adam."

"Yeah, me too." Connie picked up a rock and threw it over the cliff.

"Wow, you got quite an arm . . . for a girl."

"Pick up a rock and we'll see who can throw farther, Mr. Big Shot Quarterback."

Paul laughed, "No way. It's a lose-lose proposition for me. I'd throw my arm out trying to beat you . . . So, what do you think? Is there enough to keep you and Wyatt busy on this little island?"

"Good plan, change the subject. Yes, between the consulting I'll be doing with the agency and my island boy's dream of opening a dive shop, I think we'll stay as busy as we want to be."

"We need to start building your cabin then. We're just submitting a permit application for Joey and Erin's place and it'd be more efficient and less expensive if we built yours at the same time."

"Wow, and the cost for this?"

"The construction cost's on Andy. You guys will just pay a monthly charge for maintenance and utilities. Since we're off the grid, it won't be more than four or five hundred a month."

"Seems too good to be true. I'll talk to Wyatt. I'm sure he'll be thrilled." Connie shook her head and leaned back against the guardrail. "I can't believe how much my life has changed. Wyatt, you, Sienna and all the Windsol folks have become the most important people in my life and two years ago, I didn't know any of you existed."

"Yeah, it seems that every setback brings something good. I remember thinking after I lost my first marriage and business that I'd never be happy again. Now, apart from Claire's death . . . Anyway, you know what I mean."

Joey and Erin appeared shortly after Connie left to join Wyatt. "Hey, Uncle Paul. I know this seems like bad timing, but Erin and I want to make a change in our cottage plan. We don't want anybody to know, 'cause the focus should be on Aunt Claire's memorial, but we're pregnant and we need a room for the baby."

Lost in thought, Paul didn't respond.

Erin assumed that he was upset by the news. "I know that it must seem too sudden, as young as we are and all, but we feel absolutely wonderful about it and—"

"No, no, it *is* wonderful news." Paul hugged them both. "I was thinking about a conversation I just had with Connie . . . When one door closes another opens."

"Oh, and if we find out that it's a girl—"

"We're naming her Clarabelle," Joey explained.

"That'll mean a lot to Barney . . . To all of us."

Roxanne and Hank met Paul on his way back to the great house. "Good timing, Paul," Hank joked. "The clean-up's done. Sienna's still there with the twins. AJ's spending the night with Red. We're heading to bed."

"We love you guys, Paul. We're really sad about Claire," Roxanne added.

"I love you guys, too. We can't take anything for granted. It can all change so fast."

Hank could barely choke out the words, "I love you too, Buddy."

******

It took several tries before the twins went down for the night. Finally collapsing, exhausted in bed, Paul's eyes fluttered open, as Sienna asked, "So what happened with the attorney today?"

"There's a map. Andrew drew a map. It looks like it's of the BVI's, but it's all wonky and doesn't make sense. I think it's supposed to be a treasure map."

"Did you plan on showing it to me?"

"Crap, I left it in the office." Paul hadn't missed the undertone and rolled out of bed. He pulled on shorts and stepped into his flip flops.

Her voice trailed after him as he headed to the equipment shed, which also doubled as the home office for Armstrong Architects. "Thanks, Honey."

Returning five minutes later, he kicked off his sandals and unfolded the map, spreading it between them on the bed.

Sienna looked it over. "I see what you mean about the drawing being all wonky. It looks like the BVI's, but this red mark could be on any of the islands."

"Yeah, I told Pascall, that I thought it was just another attention grabber from Andrew."

Sienna read the instructions on the outside of the envelope. "Hmm, I don't know . . . It could be more than that."

"Who the hell knows? Do we really want to involve ourselves again with something that Andrew cooked up? We've already spent years untangling ourselves from his drama."

"You're right. I'll burn it."

Sienna had to wait only minutes before Paul was sound asleep. She pulled out the built-in dresser's bottom drawer and set the map on the floor. After replacing the drawer, she took the empty envelope outside and dropped it on the smoldering embers of the fire pit. *My fingers were crossed and maybe one day you'll be glad.* She watched the envelope curl into ash before returning to bed.

38

Kate and Carmen had arrived as expected on Saturday, but the group from Seattle; Sally, Tex, and Brooke were delayed out of Dallas until Sunday afternoon.

Paul sat on the hood of his truck. He'd parked outside the cyclone fence on the side of the runway, waiting to see the 737 swing into view. Swatting at a mosquito, he looked nervously at his watch. The others were already at the marina. Barney was anxious and Paul didn't want to show up later than the 2:00 they'd agreed on. A flash of reflected light caught his attention as he spotted the airplane in the distance.

He waited until the American jet touched down before jumping in the truck's cab. Security was lax, allowing him to park in direct line with the single door egress from the tarmac. Greeting his friends, Paul explained that they were going to have to head straight for the marina, after picking up their luggage.

"We all just brought carry-ons. We figured with all the transferring we'd be doing, our luggage wouldn't get here anyway," Sally explained.

Leaving the airport, Brooke shouted, "Paul! You're on the wrong side of the road!"

Paul laughed. "Sorry Brooke, I forgot you haven't been on our crazy island yet. That's the way we roll."

"Then why aren't your steering wheels on the right, like they are in England? How do you ever see to pass?"

"Very carefully."

"Well, that's reassuring . . . I guess."

"All good questions. A few days on this rock and I guarantee you'll have lots more." Paul pulled off the East Airport Road onto Melvin Evans Highway toward Sunny Isle.

"So how is he, really?"

Paul could see the concern on Brooke's face. "You know Barney. He puts on a good show, doesn't want to be a burden . . . but he's devastated."

"I know how much he loved her. Poor guy. He's always been there for everybody. I hope he'll let me be there for him."

Sally leaned forward between them. "We couldn't believe it when we heard. We were going to bring Katie with us, but Tex's mom offered to grandma-sit. We heard that Carmen and Kate were leaving Alexis and Brianna with the bio-dad. I think we all want to focus as much as we can on Barney."

"Sienna and I haven't seen their kids since right after they were born. It sounds like Kate and Carmen have their hands full."

"Don't we all?" Tex added.

"Amen," they replied in unison, as though prompted in a Sunday sermon.

******

Paul led them down the dock to *The Last Hurrah*, which sat idling in its slip. Captain Joey and Erin sat side-by-side on

257

the flying bridge. Andy and Charlotte greeted the new arrivals, as did the rest after they let loose the lines. AJ and Red sat on the bow, searching the clear water for tarpon.

Brooke pulled Barney to his feet and held him tightly, both bursting into tears. Sienna and Aunt Charlotte watched the two as Brooke softly promised, "We'll get through this Barney. Don't worry. We'll get through this. I'll make it feel like home again."

"Brooke and Barney?" Sienna whispered to Aunt Charlotte when they were alone in the galley.

"I've often wondered what would have happened if Claire hadn't arrived when she did. Brooke was too raw from her disastrous marriage to want anything to do with a man. Maybe by the time she started to have feelings for him, it was too late."

"Knowing Brooke, I'm sure if that were the case, she'd never have let him know."

"Wow, what self-control that must have taken. Working with him, all three of them under the same roof."

"And consider the opportunities she would have had when Claire went AWOL."

"What are you two talking about?" Hank's sudden entry startled them.

"Just girl stuff," Aunt Charlotte replied. "Nothing you'd be interested in."

"Don't be so sure. For such a manly-man I have a fairly developed feminine side as well. What gives?"

The inappropriateness of their discussion wasn't lost on either of the women. Sienna finally conceded, "Barney and Brooke."

"Really?"

"OK, no more about this." Aunt Charlotte shut down the conversation. "Let's go up and say goodbye to our dear Claire."

******

"Near as I can tell, this is about where it all went down. I was knocked overboard by a baseball bat to the head. I don't remember anything else. Sienna can tell you . . . Claire jumped in and found me. She kept me afloat under the swim step until they left. She sat by me in the hospital every day while my brains unscrambled."

Barney stood at the rear of the boat and signaled Joey, who put the craft in gear. They motored slowly, as Barney poured Claire's ashes from a silver urn into the wake. "Goodbye, My Love."

The urn was passed to Sienna. "Ashes to ashes, dust to dust, but your spirit will live with us forever."

Roxanne was only able to choke out, "I love you, Claire," as she poured from the urn, then handed it to Kate.

"You'll be missed."

Andy stood and took the urn. "I know some of you don't believe in heaven and hell. I personally don't put much stock in hell, but regarding the heaven part, I gotta believe you're wrong. The creator would never let something as beautiful and wonderful as the soul of our Claire perish. It would be like a great painter burning their masterpiece. Just wouldn't do it." He looked down at Charlotte, who was weeping openly. "One day, this woman will lay my tired old body to rest. When that time comes, I'm counting on Claire to greet me and show me around the farm." He tipped the urn, before handing it to Paul. "It's about empty, finish it, Son."

"She was my first wife. We were two kids in love with the idea of being in love when we met. Afterwards, when we each found the love of our lives, we became friends . . . real friends." Paul poured out the remaining ashes. "Goodbye, Claire."

Sienna took Paul's hand, "You OK?"

"Yeah, I guess."

Erin stood up. "I loved Claire, too. She was a kind and courageous woman. Joey and I have decided that if the child I'm carrying is a girl, we'll honor her by naming our daughter Clarabelle."

******

"Anybody see that one coming?" Sienna turned toward Hank and Roxanne, who sat on either side of Red in the back seat of the truck.

"I sure didn't, and I'm certain Wyatt had no clue, either," Hank chuckled.

"You love it when this kind of thing happens," Roxanne scolded.

"You're right. The problem is that this kind of thing doesn't happen all that often. So, when it does, I really savor it."

Sienna looked at Paul, suspiciously. "Did they say anything to Uncle Paul about this?"

"Well . . ."

"You knew?"

"Yeah, but they said they weren't going to say anything now. They wanted the focus to stay on Claire's memorial."

"Barney seemed OK with it. In fact, the look on Wyatt's face gave him the first laugh he'd had in a week."

260

"That's true," Roxanne admitted. "I think that Andy's 'Yee Haw' may have also helped. Well, all in all, it was quite an event. I think Claire would have appreciated that we didn't walk away so sad that we wanted to shoot ourselves."

"Why would anybody want to do that?" Red asked.

"Sorry Honey, I didn't mean it. It's just an expression."

"It's a very stupid expression."

Hank beamed and held out his fist. "You're right about that, Son. Come on, give me a bump."

39

The two friends filling bar stools at The Green Flash hadn't seen much of each other since Claire's memorial.

Barney sipped his beer, then held the cold bottle to his forehead. "Think I'll head back tomorrow with Brooke."

"Jeez, Barney, I feel bad I've been so busy . . . chasing my tail mostly. We're still replacing rotted steel columns and beams."

"Sounds like you're rebuilding it from the inside out. Don't worry about me, Ace. You got shit to do. Anyway, Brooke could use my help back in Washington with her flower business."

Barney and Brooke were the only stateside residents remaining at Windsol. Wyatt and Connie had gone back two days after the memorial with Tex, Sal, Kate and Carmen. Andy and Aunt Charlotte followed a few days later.

Brooke had tried to keep Barney busy showing her the island. Sienna'd told Paul of her suspicions regarding their potential blossoming romance, but Paul was hesitant to bring it up with Barney, so soon after Claire's passing. "How's Brooke liked Saint Croix? Do you see her spending more time down here?"

"What's not to like? You never know, but with her business going great guns, I can't see it happening very soon."

"How are you doing, Barn?"

"Better, I guess. Brooke's been a big help; keeping me busy. I know she misses Claire, too. They got to be good friends."

"I know. The three of you living together since Joey moved down here really seemed to work out well for all of you."

Barney looked over at Paul and chuckled. "You think maybe we had a ménage-a-three thing going on?"

"No, I wasn't saying that."

"Tell you the truth, Amigo, I'd thought about it a couple times. Not a three-way, but maybe something with Brooke, when Claire got all caught-up in her women's group. Never acted on it, though. Neither one of us would have done that to Claire. 'Course, Brooke probably didn't have any of those kinds of thoughts, with me being me and all."

"I wouldn't be so sure. I don't get it, but there's something women seem to find attractive about you, despite yourself."

"I'll tell you what it is." Barney leaned in closer. "It's my big—"

"Cock?"

"Jesus, no, Asshole. Don't you know anything about women? Heart. They think I have a big heart. Which I must." He tapped his chest. "It feels huge . . . and broken."

"You do have a big heart. That's what everybody loves about you. You know I was kidding about not getting why women find—"

Barney waved him off. "You think I'm such a sad sack that you can't flip me shit? That'd be a new low for us, Ace."

263

Killing the rest of his beer, he slapped a $20 on the bar. "Think I'll push off. See you back at the ranch." He stood up. "Oh, I almost forgot, can you give us a ride to the airport tomorrow? We need to be there around 2:00."

"Sure, no problem. Anything else you need, just name it."

"You and Sienna've got plenty of things to do besides nursemaidin' me. It'll be good for you not to have me around to worry about."

"OK, but promise me you won't sink into that big chair of yours and try riding this out with your miracle weed. Remember what Uncle Ernie said about making a life for yourself."

"Honestly, it's hard to imagine much of a life without Claire." Barney spotted Brooke pulling their rental car into the parking lot. "Brooke'll keep me plenty occupied. I think keeping me occupied has become one of her pet projects."

Paul always suspected that Brooke downplayed her good looks to avoid attracting another loser like her former husband. Reaching the top of the steps into the dining area she spotted them and waved. Her full red lips widened into a smile between dangling gold earrings as she moved toward them. Her tan, long legs continued up past the hem of a short white knit cover-up, a new red bikini clearly visible underneath. She took hold of Barney's hand, which he'd forgotten to lower after waving back at her.

"Hi Paul. If you boys are done bonding, I thought I'd see if the big guy would like to do a little snorkeling? The water looks perfect."

"Sure, but I don't have my—"

Brooke pulled the tent-sized trunks from her handbag.

"You brought a table cloth?" Paul joked.

Brooke glared at him, while Barney disappeared into the men's room.

"Sorry. Force of habit." Paul smiled sheepishly. "By the way, the island seems to be good for you. You look great."

Brooke smiled. "Thanks. It's a beautiful island. I wish, though, it had been under better circumstances. He's really hurting."

"You've been a big help to him, Brooke. Thanks."

She looked at Paul. "You aren't naïve, and even if you were, Sienna isn't. I've kept my feelings about Barney to myself for a very long time, and I intend to keep it that way for the foreseeable future." Spotting Barney's emergence, she kissed Paul on the cheek and whispered, "Thanks for being such a good friend to both of us . . . You ready, Barn?"

"I was born ready."

******

Paul walked into the great house to find Red and AJ on their computers.

"Hey Dad, Mom isn't here."

"Yeah, but my mom and Hank are watching the girls at our place. Hank said you're a lucky bastard."

"Thanks for the update, boys."

"We're inside," Hank announced, as he heard Paul climb their porch steps. Hank and Roxanne each had a twin in their lap. Hank greeted Paul with a knowing wink.

"So, what's with the Cheshire-cat look, Hank? You swallow a canary or something? Where's Sienna?" Paul asked, picking up both girls.

"We've been given instructions that, after cleaning up, you are to immediately proceed to The Salt River Marina where you are to board *Stargazer*, a forty-six foot, three berth, 2000 Beneteau."

"I remember the vessel. What's up?"

Hank stood and approached Paul. "That's all the information we're at liberty to provide, other than make sure you thoroughly scrub those pits of yours. Eww." Hank grimaced at Phoebe who giggled wildly, as he took her from Paul and set her on his foot for a horsey-ride.

Roxanne threw Hank a disgusted look, as she took Reed from Paul. "Why do you always have to embellish? That was not in the instructions."

"Just making sure our boy doesn't foul things up."

Paul shook his head, kissed Reed and Phoebe on the forehead and fifteen-minutes later reappeared shaved and showered, in board-shorts and a T-shirt. The girls were in their high-chairs. Roxanne was at the stove and Hank was flying the airplane spoonful of mashed broccoli into Reed's mouth. "Well, it looks like you have everything under control, so . . ."

Roxanne broke away from making the boys pizza, "Have fun. We've got everything covered. Don't worry about a thing."

"Well, thank you guys." He started to leave, but stopped at the door. "So, what do you guys think about Brooke and Barney?"

Hank looked up. "Life's short. They're not doing anything wrong."

"I'm just concerned that Barney hasn't had time to grieve; that Brooke is . . ."

"What? Trying to take Claire's place?" Roxanne asked.

"Yeah, maybe . . ."

"I don't see that being the case. Barney's grieving and Brooke is there for him. Simple as that. Who knows what might happen down the road."

Paul ran his hand through his hair, searching for the right words. "But Barney often said how perfect Claire was for him; that she was the one. Now, after only a few weeks—"

"Barney and Claire weren't you and Sienna, or Hank and I," Roxanne explained. "Who knows what binds people together? Claire saved Barney's life. She needed him. When things were good, they had fun together. Maybe that was enough."

Hank grabbed a beer out of the refrigerator. "You want a traveler for the road?"

Paul shook his head. "No thanks."

"We shouldn't be keepin' you any longer." Hank took Paul's arm and turned him toward the door. "Just remember, we're all doing the best we can, playin' the hands we're dealt."

Roxanne sighed, "Enough, Kenny Rogers, let the poor guy go."

"OK. Thanks, you guys. See you later tonight."

"Doubtful," the Cheshire-cat replied, smiling.

******

A flood of unpleasant memories washed over Paul as he walked the dirt path to the mooring dock. It had been nearly 2 years since he'd lived aboard Sienna's yacht in a drunken, self-imposed exile of self-loathing. He stopped and stared into the lagoon. *Sienna's got something special planned. Let's elevate our mood a bit here.*

"You lose something in the water, Sailor?"

Unable to hide his feelings, he turned to face her.

"You haven't been back here in a very long time. I was worried it might trigger some rough memories."

"Yeah, I didn't really see this coming. I'm not sure what's going on with me."

"Whatever it is, we'll figure it out together."

She took his hand. "Come on, let's go back to the boat."

Instead, he pulled her into his arms. "I love you so much, Sienna."

"As well you should." She led them through a narrow passage back to *Stargazer's* secluded mooring and stepped aboard. "I've got plans for you."

Paul uncorked the champagne she'd set in the ice bucket, while Sienna flicked on a dozen small LED candle lights.

They sat next to each other. He filled their glasses for her toast. "To the man I always hoped was out there. You're my best friend, lover and protector. I love you more each day, even when you're moody and pissy." They kissed and drained their flutes. "I don't know if I tell you that enough, Paul."

"That I'm moody and pissy?"

"Very funny. You know what I mean. We've seen each other in every kind of situation and mood and there's nobody I'd rather be going through life with."

Paul refilled their glasses. "You know when I was living here and you were with . . . and you weren't . . . I knew we belonged together, but I used the excuse that I couldn't tell you what I'd done, to stay away from you. The truth is, I felt guilty for the murders and losing you and AJ seemed right. It was the worst punishment I could imagine."

Sienna sighed and put her glass down. "Honestly, sometimes I can't believe you weren't raised Catholic." She took his hand. "Honey, you've come a long way from when you lived here last, but I still see it in you . . . the guilt. You remember when Barney said he wished he'd been the one to kill those three. He knows you as well as anybody and how important it is for you to do the right thing."

"I know I did the right thing."

She pointed to her temple. "You know up here, but the jury's still out right here." She placed an open palm over his heart. Then moving both hands up to the sides of his face, she looked him directly in the eyes. "Listen to me, Paul. You were right doing what you did to save your family and friends. You've suffered enough. I absolve you from your penance."

After their kiss, Paul chuckled. "You do a pretty good Pope."

"Bless you."

"You're my rock and my compass, Sienna. You've put up with lifetimes of troubles already because of me. How did I deserve you?"

She thought for a minute before replying. "Maybe you were a Saint in a previous life."

"OK, then what did you do to deserve me?"

"I won you in a poker game."

"They play poker up there?"

"Yes, and I'm very good."

"Oh yeah? Would you like to play a little game right now?"

"Well, Mr. Armstrong, I don't have any money on me. What *will* I do?"

"We can play for your clothes."

Sienna laughed. "My absolution seems to have worked. Anyway, hold that thought for later. Let's take the kayak over to the bioluminescent bay before dinner."

Paul's hand flew up.

"Yes, Paul, do you have something to share with the class?"

"I think we should head to the forward berth, first."

"Patience, Honey. It's been pretty hectic lately."

"I know. All my talk about slowing down with work and—"

"It's not just you. It's us, Paul. I'm just as jumbled-up each day as you are. I used to think that if we ever got through our problems with Buddy Falco, we'd have . . .well, a perfect life together."

"Maybe this is what a perfect life feels like."

Sienna looked at him and laughed, "Ya think?"

"Tonight feels pretty good."

She put her glass down and took his hand. "You come up with that on your own?"

"Sure. I'm deep."

"No, not yet." She smiled and stood. Still holding hands, he followed her into the cabin. She pulled her top over her head and stepped out of her skirt. "You gonna just stand there looking?"

"Maybe for a little while."

Her laughter floated outside, filling the moist night air. An iguana quietly slid off a mangrove branch into the lagoon. The ripples from its entry radiated outward meeting those from *Stargazer,* as it gently rocked the two lovers, under a brilliant blanket of stars.

Seven years later . . .

40

"Big day for the Armstrong clan, eh, Ace?"

"Big day for all of us, Barney."

"You've got egg all over your face." Brooke dipped her napkin in a water glass and went to work muttering, "You'd think with a mouth as big as yours, you'd get some of it inside."

Barney winked across the table at Hank. "If a woman fusses over you this much, it's gotta be love."

Hank raised his Bloody Mary. "To homely men and their beautiful wives. God only knows what they see in us."

"One of the greatest unsolved mysteries." Roxanne reached across Kate and Carmen's eight-year-old daughters, Alexis and Brianna, to clink her glass with Brooke.

Red poked his head out from the kitchen. "Anybody need another flapjack?" Barney, Wyatt, Tex and Hank's arms shot up. "Nobody? OK, then I guess I'll turn off the griddle." He spun around and darted back to the kitchen, laughing.

"That's what I get for teaching the kid how to kid," Hank moaned.

"Actually, I think he was looking out for all four of you." Connie sipped her coffee. "Doesn't look like any of you need another flapjack."

"Wyatt, I believe your woman just gave us plus-sizers a bit of a smack down," Barney kidded.

"I think you might be right."

"Think maybe you should . . . you know . . . teach her a little plus-sizer respect?"

"I would, but she can still kick my ass."

"Well, there is that."

Red appeared with a stack of pancakes. "I'm out of batter. Kitchen's closed."

Hank took the platter and helped himself. "Age before beauty, boys. You want any, Paul?"

"No thanks. Phoebe and Reed, why don't you show the girls your fort while we clean up."

"OK, Dad." Phoebe was out of her chair and down the porch steps like a shot. Even the year older Katie couldn't close the distance as the four other girls took off after her.

"That's one herd of healthy girls." Tex commented, taking the platter from Hank. "Might've evened things out a bit if one of us had had a boy sprinkled somewhere in that batch."

"Boy's feet smell," Carmen kidded.

Sienna excused herself. "Speaking of boys, I think I'll go see how AJ's coming with his speech."

"Erin called. They'll meet us there." Brooke hollered, after her.

******

"Welcome graduates, family, friends and honored guests. I give you your valedictorian and recipient of the Ned Washburn Excellence in Literature Scholarship, Aaron Armstrong."

273

Although less than four hundred people were in attendance, the enthusiastic applause could have filled a much larger venue. Heads spun around when a thin, elderly man stood up and, twirling a red scarf, shouted at the top of his lungs, "Yeehaw!" much to the embarrassment of the 8-year-old twins, sitting either side of him.

During the ovation, the charismatic student reached the podium. He adjusted the microphone 15 inches up from Principal Eggabrauten's 5 foot nothing height, and set the single index card in front of him, just in case. Smiling, he stepped away from the microphone, pointed back at the aging cowboy and mirrored the twirling motion above his head. A burst of laughter followed several additional "Yeehaws" from his classmates. Once things settled down, AJ stepped back up to the podium.

"Thank you, Principal Eggabrauten." He looked briefly at his note card. "We are blessed to have been taught in classrooms overlooking the Caribbean Sea. We have also been blessed by a dedicated faculty and administration that has demonstrated a deep commitment, not only to its students, but also to the health and vitality of our entire island community."

Pausing for the eruption of applause to die down, AJ continued, "Since Good Hope's reopening three years ago, we have been incentivized and led into providing valuable community service as a major portion of our high school curriculum. Saint Croix is a healthier, safer and happier place because of our schools' outreach programs . . . You all know the active role Good Hope took in redirecting the misappropriated funds back to the bike path project. Students and staff also provided volunteer labor, tools and supervision. Through this process, we've learned hard realities about members of our government, who'd placed their interests above the interest of the citizens they represent. With the help of Governor Green, Attorney's Babcock and Jamieson, and Right Pathways, we've also learned the power of perseverance."

Barney leaned toward Paul. "I swear, the kid's gonna be president one day."

AJ continued, "Channeling the curiosity, energy and optimism of young men and women has created an unstoppable force on our island. Fresh eyes and minds have seen around the roadblocks that have kept important change from happening.

For myself and other members of our class, that have been accepted into off-island colleges and universities, this graduation is bittersweet. Leaving the home that we love, even with the knowledge that one day we may return, is a hard pill to swallow. But, I know I speak for all my classmates, when I say that no matter how far from our island we may live, we will always be Crucians.

We come from all walks of life, yet we have learned on our small island how to live and work alongside each other. We not only respect our differences, we Crucians embrace our differences. As we go forward, let's become instruments of change for a more accepting and tolerant world. Fellow graduates . . . There is much to do and now is our time."

******

Apart from a single, late model, black SUV, all the cars, trucks and vans that had filled Windsol's drive and parking lot for the graduation party were gone. Governor Arthur Green and Paul sat across from each other, finishing their Cuban cigars and ruby port. From as far upwind as possible, Arthur's wife, Ingrid, and Sienna conversed in the porch swing.

"I never thought I'd be in politics, Paul. I still don't know how you and Sienna talked me into running."

Ingrid broke away from her conversation with Sienna. "You're forgetting that I had something to do with it, as well."

Arthur laughed. "How do they do that? I'm usually too occupied talking to listen."

"Basically, women are superior and the proof is how long we've kept you from knowing it," Sienna explained, matter-of-factly.

Arthur held his glass, suspended in front of his face. "My god, Paul, do you think she's right? We think we have volition and power, but we're actually just their minions?"

"Yep. And they pay us with sex, when they feel like it."

"Well then, it's worth it."

"Absolutely."

"What's worth it?" Sienna asked, as she and Ingrid joined them at the table.

"Do you want us to put out the cigars? We're almost done." Arthur asked.

"Do you want to put out the cigars?" Ingrid laughed.

"Actually, that's what we were just talking about. Do we?"

"I'm thinking, no," Paul guessed, "or they would have had us knowing it by now."

"Very astute of you, Mr. Armstrong." Sienna took the cigar from Paul. "They actually smell pretty good." She took a shallow puff and handed it back to him. "Yuck, they smell better than they taste."

"Arthur, we should be saying goodnight." Ingrid slipped her purse strap over her shoulder. "Remember, we have an early flight tomorrow."

"OK. Paul, we'll tee it up when I get back from DC. By the way, what's your handicap now?"

"He's a seven," Sienna volunteered, "and I'm a 3."

"A three? Wow. OK. Sienna, you and I can take on Paul and Ingrid. You all remember, I was a 6 before you guys talked me into this thankless job. Now, the last time I played, I couldn't break 90."

"Poor Baby." Ingrid tossed him the car keys. "It's too bad that saving this island from corruption and ruin has resulted in a negative impact on your golf game. Now get that big governor's ass a-movin'."

Arthur winked at Paul. "She wouldn't talk that way if I were the boss."

Paul and Sienna waved goodbye from the porch. Once the tail-lights disappeared, Sienna fell back in the porch swing. "Are you as tired as I am?"

"Not sure." Paul grabbed the half empty bottle of port and their two glasses off the table and collapsed next to her.

They sat quietly, enjoying the nighttime chirps and buzzes from the coqui and cicada. "So how's it going to feel when AJ heads off to Swarthmore?"

Paul handed Sienna a refilled glass. "Well, the twins will keep us jumping, so empty isn't the right word." He set the bottle down, his arm covered her shoulders.

She snuggled against him and sighed. "It's just gone so fast. I can't believe we're where we are so soon. I've got more grey in my hair now than black, for god's sake."

"You? What about me? Blonde is a distant memory."

"Yeah, but you're a guy. What do you really care?"

"True on both counts, and you shouldn't either. You're more beautiful than ever."

277

Sienna turned toward him, "Are you just trying to get into my pants?"

"Absolutely."

Sienna laughed, then sighed. "You're sweet."

"You OK?"

"Yeah, I suppose."

"What?"

"OK, don't think I'm crazy . . . but how about we push the pause button for a year? You'll be finished with the Peterson home and the Eco-Office Park this month. What would you say if we took off for a year and traveled? Let's just get off the treadmill for a while."

"I'd say, do we have to wait a month and where do you want to go?"

"Well, it'll take us that long to get everything buttoned up. As for where we should head . . . Since we sold *Stargazer* to help fund AJ's college tuition, a sail is out. I still don't understand why Pascall pulled the funds out of the CD's."

"I guess when he heard that the tuition cost would exceed the funds in the account, he took a gamble—"

"On a 'sure thing'. I remember. . . . But we'll still have enough to cover us. We could take an RV and head north to Alaska or south to Cape Horn. Maybe we'd stop for a time along the way and you could make a little cash with your guitar and golden voice."

Paul chuckled. "Yeah, that might pay for a few burritos . . . You know who'd want us to limit our route to Eastern Washington, don't you?"

"I can just hear him . . . 'I'm 92 years old. Do you really want to take the girls away from me for my final days?'"

"Andy's become a 92-year-old drama queen. He's sprier than most men twenty years younger."

"Aunt Charlotte will straighten him out, and we can certainly arrange to meet a few times during the year."

"We can do the same thing with the others, too."

They sat in silence for several minutes before Sienna added, "Maybe one day we can do a round the world sail?"

"Absolutely. How about when the girls graduate?"

"You'll be 64." An idea suddenly came to her. She stood up. "Wait here for a minute. I'll be right back."

41

Paul didn't have to wait long. Sienna returned, carrying a folded piece of parchment and sat down next to him. "I know that you thought I'd destroyed this, and you were so freaked back then about anything to do with Andrew Sherman, that I almost did." She unfolded the map and laid it on the table.

"Well, this is a surprise. I can't believe you kept it from me all these years. I thought we didn't have secrets."

"No, the deal is you don't have secrets from me, because I can read your mind."

"This map still doesn't make any sense."

"Maybe we're not seeing something. Your sister's *The Bloodhound*. Let's show it to her in the morning and see if she can make something out of it. I mean, what if it is a real treasure map?"

"Listen, you don't have to twist my arm, and I love seeing you so excited. If Connie can make something out of it, I know Captain Joey won't have a problem filling a crew for a treasure hunt in the BVI's."

******

"Just a waste of time, if you ask me. Seems like you've been knocked off track enough times by that Sherman character, that you'd know better."

Charlotte shook her head and sipped her coffee. "I swear, Andy, you're sounding crotchetier every day. This could be a wonderful adventure for the kids."

"Don't see what's wrong with adventuring closer around home. I'm not gonna be here forever you know. You heard 'em. This map turns out to be something, no tellin' where they'll be heading next."

Sienna opened the map on the kitchen table while Paul shut the blinds. Connie washed the UV pen-light over the parchment. "If this doesn't turn up anything, I'll bring it to Brad Harper at the agency to look over . . ." Under the light, 03.73724678.09281 appeared in the upper right corner. She studied the numbers. "This might be a scrambled latitude and longitude location."

"The latitude of the BVI's is around 18 north. Maybe it's inverted." Sienna guessed, excitedly.

Connie studied the number. "Can somebody tell me a longitude for the BVI's?"

Hank was perched over her shoulder scanning the numbers. "Inverted, eh? Try 64."

Moments later, after a couple false starts, Connie wrote out the number 18 29 0.87N, 64 27 37.30W.

Joey pulled his laptop from its carry case and plugged the coordinates into his google earth program. "It's on Great Dog Island in the BVI's."

"I've dove off the south side of that island," Hank recalled. "There's an Air BVI fuselage in about 50-feet that went down in the 90's, just off the main reef."

Joey turned on the topographic overlay. "The coordinates put the location just back from a steep face on the western coast."

AJ looked over Joey's shoulder. "We'll need to bring climbing gear along then."

"And scuba gear," Hank added. "I think I remember there being underwater caves along the west coast of Great Dog."

Joey counted noses. "Not sure there's enough room on *The Last Hurrah* for everybody."

"That's OK. We can bring *Caribe Daze*, too." Roxanne volunteered. "Hank and Red have been spending so much time working on the engine, it's about time we put her to use. There should be plenty of room for all of us."

"So's everybody in?" Barney asked, refilling Brooke's coffee.

"I'm not." Andy announced. "The whole thing sounds like a big waste of time."

"I think we'll keep the home fire's burning with Andy and the girls." Carmen turned to Kate, who nodded in agreement. "Us Eastern Washington landlubbers need to look out for each other."

"Clarabelle and I'll pass, as well." Erin looked over at Joey, who nodded in agreement. "I think she'll have more fun here with her cousins and I've got some studying to do for my real estate license."

"But you all go ahead with all this nonsense." Andy puffed his chest out. "I'll be here looking after the womenfolk."

"Womenfolk? Really, Andy? You're ninety-two, not nine-hundred and two." Aunt Charlotte stood to clear the table.

******

"Welcome aboard." Barney's meaty hand wrapped around Connie's, as he helped her onto *Caribe Daze's* deck. "I see you brought the necessary provisions."

"Very gallant of you, Sir." Connie set the two 1.75 liter bottles of Cruzan rum beside the ice cooler. "What would a treasure hunt be without rum? You know, as in *Yo, Ho, Ho and a bottle of* . . ."

"That's the spirit." Barney reached out to help Wyatt board, but Wyatt brushed Barney's hand away then grimaced as he stepped off the vessel's side wall onto the deck. Connie shook her head. "He's two weeks from a knee replacement and won't take an offered hand. Men."

"You can't live with 'em or without 'em." Brooke took the grocery bag from Wyatt and went below.

"Say, I don't remember hearing many complaints amidst all your orgasmic cries of joy and ecstasy." Barney winked at Erin as he waited for Brookes impending comeback which was returned in a flash.

"I should be nominated for an Oscar."

"Don't worry, Erin." Sienna stepped down onto the deck. "Uncle Barney was just as gross when he was Joey's age as he is now."

"No worries there, Sienna. I've always considered Joey a mature version of Barney." Erin ruffled Clarabelle's red hair, who stood on the dock beside her. "I just hope that whatever Uncle Barney has doesn't skip generations."

"You're enjoying this, aren't you?" Barney scowled at Joey, who'd been running through a supplies checklist.

"Sure, and as usual, you started it." Joey finished scanning the list, then looked down at Paul on the dock. "We're all aboard and ready to go. Let loose the lines."

"Letting loose the lines, Captain." Paul jumped aboard.

"Be safe." Erin hollered from the dock, waving.

"Be safe, Uncle Barney." Clarabelle shouted.

"I will Sweet-Potato," Barney shouted back and put his arm around his nephew. "Say what you want, Joey, but Uncle Barney has always been that kids' favorite."

Joey eased the vessel from its slip into the Christiansted harbor and out the narrow passage through the protective reef. Once clear, he eased the throttle to 15 knots and headed for the west side of Buck Island to rendezvous with Captain Hank, Roxanne, Red and AJ. *The Caribe Daze* had departed a half hour earlier from the more westerly Salt River Marina.

The two vessels arrived within ten-minutes of each other. Barney dropped down to the deck and helped Paul and Wyatt raft the boats together.

"Ahoy, Captain Joey," Hank bellowed from *The Caribe Daze* bridge. "How 'bout you join me for a little nip of rum and a toast before braving the elements and our voyage across the sea?"

"Is it good rum?"

"Single Barrel Cruzan, of course."

"Be right there. Barney, you've got the helm."

"Seems to drop the *uncle* when he's in his captain mode," Paul noted, as he reached the bridge.

"Yeah, I gave up on that a long time ago. I like him taking his captainship seriously." Barney looked north toward their route. "We all know, bad things can happen on the open sea, even when you're careful."

284

He knew that Barney was thinking of Eddie, still blaming himself for his brother's death in the Bering Sea.

Barney leaned forward, anxious to talk about something else. "So, you think there might be a treasure?"

"No idea."

"Still, you got to figure you've earned whatever we find."

"How do you figure?"

"Well, for starters, he bankrupted you. Probably caused your divorce, too." Barney held his hand up. "I know. I know. You and my dear Claire were not going to last much longer. Even still, it did lay a shit-storm at your doorstep. Forced you to come scratching on my door, like a homeless orphan."

Paul reminded himself, as he often did, that Barney's directness was the quality he admired most, even when his first instinct was to punch him in that big, pious, pumpkin face.

"Then you go and travel half-way 'round the world to put the past behind you . . . and he shows up out of nowhere. So, you're right back in it again. Plus, now you've got the mob after you. Incidentally, it should also be mentioned that when you killed those three scumbags, you probably killed whoever put the bullet through Andrew's brain. So, in a wild-west sort of way, you avenged Andrews death, to boot. You've earned the treasure. I rest my case."

Connie climbed the ship ladder and joined them. "You boys 'bout ready to head out? If it's a four-hour crossing, hadn't we'd better start?"

"I think you're right, Special Agent Hunter-Howard. I'll rally the troops." Barney stood and bellowed. "All hands-on deck." He looked at his watch. "We depart in fifteen minutes."

Paul dropped down into the galley, where he found Sienna on her cell phone. "He's just coming down now."

Sienna muted her cell. "Andy's sorry he was so negative. I think Aunt Charlotte worked him over pretty good."

Paul took the cell, but kissed Sienna first before talking.

"What's that for?"

Paul mouthed *I love you*. "Hey Andy, what's up?"

"Well, I figured I owe you all an apology. My darling wife has convinced me that I acted like an ass and what I should have said was good luck."

"Andy, you don't have to apologize. We know you love us and that's why you don't want us to leave for a year."

"Yeah, that's what I told Charlotte. She said it didn't matter and I was being selfish and a wet blanket."

"That sounds like Aunt Charlotte."

"I'll tell you Son, it's not easy to be married to a saint. Never have figured out how I got her to say yes."

"It was always a mystery to me," Paul laughed.

"Well, I appreciate your making light of the situation, but I do agree with her. You guys go find that treasure and if we get too lonely when you're away, we'll hop on a plane and come find you."

42

Caribe Daze led the way, with *The Last Hurrah* following two hundred yards back. Fifteen miles into the 40-mile crossing Hank cast a worried look to the east. "That doesn't look good."

"Oh shit." Roxanne brought Joey up on the VHF. "This is *Caribe Daze* calling *The Last Hurrah*. Come in, Joey. Over."

"Good afternoon, *Caribe Daze*." Joey's calm, resonant voice replied. "You noticed the black cloud too? Over."

Hank took Roxanne's hand. "Don't worry, Sweetie, *Caribe Daze* can handle this."

Joey continued broadcasting. "Make sure to secure all openings in the cabin. We'll need to prepare for strong winds and a good roll. My guess is, it'll hit us in about a half-hour. We'll get through this, but I still want everyone in life-vests."

******

The western sky was a brilliant orange by the time the exhausted crews motored into The Bite, a protected deep-water harbor off Norman Island. Loud music and the roar from a full crowd at Willie T's, drew both crews to the festivities at the venerable freighter-turned-restaurant. Arriving first, Red tied off the Zodiac and helped Hank and Roxanne step through rows of rocking dinghies, toward the dock.

Joey slipped in next to Hank's spot, with Barney complaining loudly, "We'd been front row, if it hadn't been for that squall. Where's the bar? This mariner needs a drink."

"I'm right there with you, Chief," Hank replied, finally reaching the floating dock.

Brooke almost knocked them over, as she bolted past. "I've got to pee."

Finally stepping onto the floating dock, Barney nearly catapulted Roxanne into the water, as it pitched under his 320-pound frame.

"Stay in the center Barn, and follow me. There's rum close by."

"Twist my arm, Captain."

Hank disappeared with Barney and Red into the crowd, while Roxanne waited on the dock for the others.

"Would my lady like some assistance?" Paul offered his hand, then lurched forward as he tripped over a gas can stepping into the first dinghy. Sienna grabbed the tail of his shirt, barely keeping him from falling overboard.

"Nice grab, Sienna." Wyatt chuckled. "Stay there a minute, Paul, I might need a hand, too."

Brooke broke through the crowd back onto the dock. "Wow, that was close. Fortunately, there was no line for the men's room."

"Men's room? Ick." Roxanne grimaced.

"The women's line was out the door. It was better than the alternative."

"You've got moxie, girl . . . I just think we're blessed to be here, at all." Although not Catholic, Roxanne embellished their good fortune with the sign of the cross. "I haven't seen a storm come up that fast. Hanky-Bear is a good captain, but I could tell how concerned he was. Especially when that one swell reached the bridge."

"Where's Captain Hanky-Bear now?" Paul asked, trailing behind Sienna and Connie in the dinghy shuffle.

"He and Red are at the bar with Barney. I think they're hoping for a topless high-dive off the second level."

"Sounds like that's where I'm headed," Joey said, following close behind Wyatt, in case his father-in-law's trick knee gave out. "That was one hell of a crossing."

"Cool it Joey. I was kidding with Paul. I'm perfectly capable of making it to the dock without help."

"Of course you can, Dad, but I promised your daughter that I'd look after you. She didn't even want you going, if you remember."

"I'm not real pleased myself," Connie muttered, as she stepped onto the dock.

Paul and Connie volunteered to secure a table on the dining deck while the others headed to the bar. Surprisingly, they were seated at the long picnic table almost instantly. "Think I should go get the others?" Connie asked.

"Naw, they probably just ordered their drinks. Why don't you and I catch up. It's been a while." They sat down opposite each other.

"No kidding. Between the consulting I've been doing with the agency, and running the dive shop with Wyatt, I'm beginning to miss those days when I only had 300 people to supervise."

"I know what you mean. Sienna and I have talked about slowing things down for years. Hopefully, taking off for a year on the road should make that happen."

"I can't believe you'll be gone a year. We have to figure out a way to see you guys a couple times."

"I agree. If Andrew's treasure's a bust, we'll probably spend most of our time traveling throughout the U.S. That should make it pretty easy to connect."

"Even if Sherman leads us to millions and you and Sienna take the girls on your round-the-world voyage . . . We'll find you. We've missed too much time already."

"I agree, Sis." He reached across the table and took her hand. "Sienna and I talked about staying around to help out with the dive shop, until Wyatt recovers from the knee replacement."

"Thanks, but Joey and Erin offered to fill-in. I must say; I admire you guys. Most people don't jump off the conveyor belt like you're doing."

"I'd say that you and Wyatt jumped off a few years back."

"Yeah, I suppose you're right. It's a good thing we both have partners who aren't afraid to try something new."

"Actually, I think I'm more the stay at home type than Sienna. She gets island fever from time to time and has to get off the rock."

"I can't blame her, with most of the responsibility falling on her shoulders for raising AJ and the twins. Don't get me wrong, you've done as good a job as you could."

"Dividing things up the way we did made financial sense, but it's something we're both looking to change."

"Here! Here!" Hank slapped Paul on the back as he and Roxanne joined them at the table.

"We were talking about Paul and Sienna's year sabbatical with the girls."

"Oh, that." Hank waved his hand dismissively. "You guys will have a ball. I'll be so busy looking after things, probably won't even miss you at all."

"You're so full of it." Roxanne sat down next to Connie. "Last night he was whining, 'Why do they have to go away for so long?'"

"Well, it's good to be missed, and your Hanky is one sensitive bear." Connie gave Hank a kiss on the cheek as he took his seat on the other side of her.

"Yeah, well it is my sensitive side that drives the ladies crazy." Hank spotted the others coming out of the bar and waved them over.

"See many topless high-dives?" Connie asked Wyatt, as he kissed her on the cheek.

"A couple, but it's hard to appreciate hamburger when you're used to steak."

"A surprising metaphor for a vegetarian animal rights advocate." Barney chuckled and took the seat next to Wyatt.

"So how'd you like the show, Barn?" Brooke asked, joining the group with Joey, and Red.

"I tell you, Sweetheart, if I had tits like that blonde girl, I'd a held onto them when I jumped. Couldn't tell because she was all liquored up, but I think it must've hurt like hell when those babies slapped the water. Sounded like a firecracker."

Brooke rolled her eyes, as she took the offered menu from the waitress.

Joey attempted to move his uncle's train of thought down a different track. "So what's the plan for tomorrow, Uncle Barney?"

"Well, it ain't really my rodeo, but since you asked, I'd say we bust out of here right after daybreak. Pick up some supplies at Road Town, then motor over to Big Dog. Even with the coordinates, I don't think whatever Sherman hid is going to be out in plain sight."

"Sounds good to me, Barney." Paul replied, as he spotted AJ approach with a blonde woman, wearing a bikini that left little to the imagination.

Barney turned to Paul, and mouthed *That's the one.*

"Everybody, this is Eva. She's been abandoned here."

"That's not completely true, AJ. I'm sure he'll be back with his friends. But I don't want to stay on that boat with those assholes another minute."

Sienna could tell the woman was intoxicated. "Hi Eva, I'm AJ's mother, Sienna. Do you live in this area?"

"Nope, I'm from North Carolina. I came here with this rich dude I met at a bar in St. Thomas. He asked me out on his boat for the weekend. Turns out two of his letch buddies were also invited."

"And they left here without you?" Barney asked, incredulously.

"Well, after 6 hours of fighting them all off, I couldn't act nice anymore. I told him what he could do with all his money. While I don't mind taking my top off, I'm not gonna put out for him and his jerk-off friends. I was happy when he left, but then I realized I was stuck here. That's when I met AJ." She took AJ's arm. "You've raised a beautiful man, Sierra."

"It's Sienna," AJ corrected. "I was thinking that maybe we could let her crash with us for the night, then—"

"Hank, we can take her back to St. Thomas in the morning."

Recognizing that Roxanne's maternal instincts had already kicked in, he had no choice. "Sure, not a problem."

"I really appreciate it, you guys. Thank you so much. Maybe one of you ladies might have something I can cover up with. Oh Fuck!"

The three men appeared to be in their thirties. "Thanks for looking after our girl . . . So, are you ready to head back to the boat, Eva?"

"I'm not going back with you, Carl! I'll come by to get my stuff next week."

"Oh? Does Eva have a new boyfriend?" Carl glared at AJ. "So, you like your meat young and dark? Is that it?"

Barney, Wyatt, Paul and Hank stood up, but not before Joey inserted his 6'-6", two hundred thirty pound frame in front of the trio. "You racist pigs need to leave."

"Now!" AJ pushed Carl back into his friends, his eyes blazing.

"OK, OK." Carl held up his hands. "Come on boys, looks like we're outnumbered."

Connie stood and approached Carl, who sneered back at her. "What've you got on your mind, Grandma?"

The next moment he was lifted onto his tiptoes, her hand at his throat. "I just want you to know that you three would be outnumbered by any one of us. Now beat it."

"Yeah, beat it assholes," a man at the next table shouted. The words were repeated by several other diners who'd watched the encounter, as the trio skulked back to their dinghy and putt-putted off into the night.

Barney burst out laughing. "Always knew that Joey could be a bad-ass, but didn't know that about AJ. Looks like we'll be well-protected in our doddering old age, Ace."

"Don't forget about my bad-ass sister." Paul kissed Connie on the cheek, as she sat back down beside him.

"So, you guys are my kind of people," Eva gushed.

Paul watched Sienna grimace as the buxom blonde leaned into AJ, kissed him on the cheek and pronounced, "My Hero."

******

"Quite a day." Paul reached up and turned off the reading light.

"Do you think AJ likes Eva?"

Tired as he was, he chose his words wisely. "I think he was acting mostly as a good Samaritan."

"So, why are they still up on the bow of Hank and Roxanne's boat? I think she's got the hots for him."

"Well, would that be so bad?" Paul knew his mistake as soon as the words left his mouth.

"Oh no, Paul. I'd always hoped AJ's first sexual experience would be with a large breasted woman, ten years older than him, after she'd jumped topless into the Caribbean in front of a crowded bar."

Needing more faculty than he possessed lying down, Paul sat up. "Sienna, AJ's eighteen. Do you really think he's still a virgin?"

"Do you know something, Paul? Was it Kitty Franklin? I never liked that girl or her name."

"I only know that our son's a handsome young man, who has been raised to use good judgement and treat people with respect. If he isn't a virgin, I'm sure he was careful."

Sienna chuckled quietly. "I didn't think I'd ever be like this. It's just hard to let go."

"Even if you could control what he does and with whom, would you really want to deprive him of the opportunity to learn from the mistakes we've all made growing up?"

"I just don't want him to make a mistake that might cost him years, being held back by a bad relationship."

"He's no fool, Honey. He's smart. He's not gonna fall into a trap, no matter how big her boobs are."

Sienna laughed, shaking her head. "You men and your boobs." She took his hand and placed it on her breast. "Think I should have an augmentation?"

He turned into her, their naked bodies pressed together. "Think I should get a penile enlargement."

"How big? Ten inches?"

"I read that a vagina's about 5 inches deep. What will we do with the other 5 inches?"

"Good point. Maybe we should buy a boat instead."

******

Damn hormones and insomnia. She laid awake watching Paul sleep. His still youthful features looked so innocent and peaceful. She felt the slight shift of the boat and thought of waking Paul, but decided to investigate.

"Hey Mom." Wearing only his briefs, she found AJ sitting on a bench in the rear of the boat. ringing out his T-shirt and shorts.

"You swam here? . . . What about sharks? I thought you were spending the night with—"

"Eva? Nope. Come on mom, *Daze* is less than 100-feet away. Besides, I don't think sharks go for dark meat."

"That Carl was quite a piece of work. I don't think I've ever seen you so angry."

AJ's broad smile illuminated the space between them. "Not really. It was mostly an act."

"Well, you had me convinced."

"Nah, let the haters be haters. That's what you and Dad've always said. I saw the look on Dad's and the Uncle's faces when they stood up. With Wyatt going in for knee surgery, Uncle Barney and Hank's high blood pressure and Dad's retinal detachment last year . . . Well, they're all really too old to be fighting. Don't tell them that, OK?"

"I promise."

"Besides, I figured if it didn't go well for Joey and me, we always had Aunt Connie."

"Yeah, she's really something, and so are you."

"AJ pulled his shorts back on. He saw her tears forming. "I love you, Mom. Don't worry about me. You guys have done a great job. I'll always be fine."

"I love you, too, and I'm not worried, AJ. Just proud."

"I'm proud of you guys, too." He stood and kissed her on the cheek. "Ok, so I'll see you in the morning."

"Aren't you going to go with Hank and Roxanne to drop Eva off on St. Thomas?"

"I'd rather get to Great Dog early with you guys and start looking for treasure. G'night, Mom."

"Night, AJ."

Sienna sat smiling for several minutes and replayed their conversation. Now finally tired, she stood and stretched her arms towards the brilliant night sky. "Thank you for my son, my husband, my friends, my life. I am truly blessed." Yawning, she shuffled back to bed and fell asleep, the moment her head hit the pillow.

43

Paul awoke at daybreak and was surprised to find coffee already brewing. Hank and Connie lounged in the morning sunshine on the rear deck in their bathing suits. He poured his coffee and joined them. The buoy *Caribe Daze* had tied up to last night was empty.

"So, you guys are up early." Paul took a seat across from Wyatt. Must have been dark when Hank pulled out. I thought you two were going to sleep in and stay on board."

"Not sure what time Hank pulled out for Saint Thomas, but it was still dark when we swam over." Connie stood and walked down into the cabin.

"You guys swam?"

"Sure, why not?" Wyatt stood and stretched his back. "Red offered to bring us over in the dingy, but it was hot last night and the swim felt great."

Ten minutes later the others joined them. Barney put on some oatmeal and Joey cut into a sweet watermelon they'd stored in the cooler. Grabbing an end piece, Barney took a seat in the captain's chair. "My guess is that if we leave in a half-hour, Hank won't arrive much after us. Hope he at least wakes party-girl up fifteen minutes before throwing her off the boat."

"He's not going to throw her off the boat." AJ sprinkled raisins over his oatmeal, and sat on the steps to the bridge.

"Oh? You sweet on her, AJ?"

"She's actually a very nice person. She really liked all of us; even you, Uncle Barney."

"Really, Uncle Barney too?" Paul feigned surprise. "Well, no accounting for taste, as Andy would say." Paul bumped fists with AJ, after delivering Sienna's oatmeal to her.

"I told you Ace, the ladies like me."

"Can we change the subject please?" Brooke glared at Barney.

"Sure, Sweetheart." Barney moved over to her, grabbing another slice of watermelon on the way. "What would you like to talk about?"

"How about what we're going to do when we get to the Great Dog Island and does anybody know why it was named that?"

"Professor?" Barney nodded at Joey.

"Great Dog and the other nearby Dog Islands were named by sailors who heard loud barking when mooring off their shores. They assumed the barking was made by dogs, but actually the sound was made by Caribbean monk seals."

"Don't think I've ever heard of that species of seal." Wyatt thanked Connie for delivering his oatmeal to him.

"They were hunted to extinction for their meat." Joey explained.

"Crap!" Wyatt almost spit out his first spoonful. "Us fuckin' humans. I just wonder how many animals we've hunted to extinction."

"It's a hard number to pin down, but coupled with the impact of global climate change, it's estimated that 30 to 50% of all species could be extinct by the mid twenty-first century."

After several minutes, Barney finally broke the heavy silence. "Well fuckadoodleleedo. Not much we can do about it today, Mates. The water's crystal clear. The sky's azure blue and there's a treasure out there to be found. I say we get on with it, and if we strike it rich, a share of the loot goes to help our animal friends."

Joey pulled out a map. "The coordinates put the treasure here, about 30 yards back from the western shoreline. There's a day buoy we can tie up to, about 50 yards offshore. The coastline in this area is a solid rock cliff, 50 to 70 feet high. So, Uncle Paul and I were thinking that AJ, Red and I would take the inflatable around the island to the south. We'll pull in at this sandy beach and hack our way through the scrub over this ridge to the spot. We'll bring a pick and shovel and see what we can find."

Paul continued describing the plan. "We'll be in touch using these walkie-talkies. Wyatt, Connie, Sienna and I will wait to suit up, until we find out how the boys fare. The island is known for its underwater caves, so my guess is that our scuba team will have the best chance of finding it."

Brooke jumped to her feet and clapped. "OK, then. Sounds good. Let's get this show on the road, I mean the water, or under the water."

Shortly afterwards, they eased out of the mouth of The Bight, passing Pelican Cay off their port. Once they reached open water, Joey bumped the twin 375 diesel Cats up to 28 knots. Although there was a slight chop as they sped northeast through Sir Francis Drake Channel, the ride was surprisingly smooth. "It's the design of the hull," Barney boasted to

Connie. "When we're trolling, it hardly leaves any wake at all. The Cabo 35's an amazing boat."

"At this rate, Joey says we'll be there in less than an hour," Brooke shouted down from the flybridge.

Paul looked over at Sienna. "Maybe we should get a power boat for our trip. This feels pretty good."

"They're great if you want to get somewhere fast. But we'll have a year. What's our hurry?"

"What'd you say?" Connie pointed at her ears and shook her head. "Can't really hear you over the engines."

"Another good point. I rest my case, and didn't even have to bring up fuel costs."

Connie stood. "I'm heading below. I'll see how Scuba Wyatt's doing with the gear check. We brought some new pistol grip LED dive lights for caving that should really light things up."

Sienna leaned over to Paul and spoke close to his ear. "Don't mean to spring this on you now, but I'm not so crazy about this cave-diving business."

"You don't have to do it. In fact, maybe you shouldn't. This is supposed to be a fun thing."

"No, I want to do it. I'm just telling you not to worry if I start to feel claustrophobic and need to turn back at some point."

"OK. If you feel at all uncomfortable, of course I'll turn back with you. Wyatt and Connie are used to this kind of thing. They'll do fine without us."

As they drew closer, Paul considered telling Sienna about his worries, but didn't think sharing his insecurities would be helpful at this point. Besides, the whole Sherman thing started with him, and he couldn't see bailing out now.

"There she is." Barney pointed through the windshield as they approached the uninhabited island.

Minutes later, Joey cut the speed as they rounded Great Dog's southwestern tip. "There's a familiar boat already tied up to the day buoy," he shouted down from the bridge.

Paul and Sienna stood to look just as Hank gave Red the order to greet the late comers with *Caribe Daze's* air horn. Brooke responded from *The Last Hurrah's* bridge with two short blasts as well.

Joey brought his vessel alongside. "Permission to raft-up, Captain?"

"Permission granted, Captain. What took you so long?"

******

"Fuckin' cheap-ass walkie talkies."

Brooke gripped Barney's wrist, just in time to stop him from throwing the apparently useless communication device overboard. "It might be the ridge between us, that's blocking the signal."

It had been over two hours since Joey, AJ and Red had motored out of view. They had estimated that it would take fifteen-minutes for them to reach the landing beach and another hour to climb through the scrub-brush up to the coordinates.

"Or maybe a tree," Barney grumbled. "What good are these things if they—"

A sudden burst of static interrupted Barney's lament, followed by Red's excited voice. "Ahoy, Family! We can see you. We're here on the top of the island. Listen." The ensuing blast from Red's whistle into the walkie-talkie was deafening. Barney quickly turned down the volume. The whistle continued, directing their attention to the ridge just east of the coordinates.

"There they are!" Shading their eyes, a relieved Sienna and Roxanne waved at the trio.

Joey's deep voice came on next. "It looks like you guys are having a nice time down there while we do all the heavy lifting. Over."

Barney laughed. "Just doing our job. We're supposed to look like tourists, so we don't draw any extra attention. I don't know if you noticed, but we have another boat in the harbor. Over."

"Yeah, we see it. Over."

"What took you so long? Over."

"Google earth doesn't really do the density of this island's scrub justice," AJ responded. "That stuff is thick and thorny. Over."

A concerned Roxanne took the walkie talkie from Barney. "Is everybody OK? Did you get scratched badly? Over."

"No, Mom." Red replied. "We are being very careful, just like you told me to be. I'm wearing the GPS watch. It's very important that I don't break it so Joey and AJ cut down the brush in front of me with machetes. What? Oh, over."

Roxanne passed the walkie talkie to Hank. "That's great, Son. You have a very important job. Over."

"Hi, Dad. I know it. Here's Joey, he wants to talk. Not over." They heard his giggle, as he passed the walkie talkie over to Joey.

"Red's keeping us in stitches. I'm really glad he's along." He waited for AJ and Red's laughter to subside. "So, we're almost to the spot. The topsoil seems pretty shallow here, mostly rock underneath. It's barren and flat. Doesn't seem like a good place to dig, but we'll give it a try. Over and out."

"I don't give it much of a chance," Connie conceded. "At one time, this region was swarming with pirates. I'm guessing that Sherman regarded himself as a modern-day pirate and everybody knows that pirates buried their treasures in caves. If pirates had had scuba gear, I think the caves would have been underwater."

"Well, we should know shortly." Wyatt took a pair of binoculars out of the case and watched as the boys eased their way along the top of the cliff. "It looks like they've arrived. AJ's using the pick."

"How accurate are the coordinates?" Brooke asked.

"Between the initial accuracy of Sherman's coordinates and the accuracy of Joey's GPS watch, I'd say we're hoping within a 10-yard radius." Paul replied.

"What? I didn't know that. That's a big fuckin' hole," Barney exclaimed. "Christ, we should have flown in a backhoe."

Paul snapped, "That wouldn't have drawn any attention." Seeing Sienna's reaction to his sarcastic reply, he stood and leaned against the deck rail. "Sorry Barn, I forgot to talk to you about that. Joey and the boys are looking for some kind of a mark or sign. If Sherman went to all the trouble of hiding a treasure, I don't think he would have left it up to chance that we'd be able to find it within a 2,800-square foot area."

"OK, no problem, Amigo. I know you must have a lot on your mind with your fear of tight spaces and all."

Paul groaned, suddenly remembering that his big-mouthed friend knew of his phobia. Sienna, Connie and Wyatt looked startled.

Clueless to any reactions, Barney sailed on. "They had to break our boy's collarbone to pull him out of his birth mother's vagina." The storyteller mistook his audience's open mouthed silence for intrigue and happily continued. "Yup, he barely squeezed through to the light. I heard the story after he freaked out in a haunted house tunnel they set up in the gym on Halloween at our high school." Barney finally caught on to the implications of what he had just divulged, and approached Paul's wife for absolution. "Sienna, you must have known about this having been married, well, forever and what with being soulmates and all."

"Yes, Barney, you'd think I would have." Sienna replied, looking frostily at Paul.

"Look, Paul. If you have any worries about this dive, Connie, Sienna and I are up to the task." Wyatt cheerfully offered.

"That's right, Ace," Barney interjected. "Facing your fears is one thing, but shitting your Speedo in a dark cave full of barracuda's another."

Sienna was the first to start laughing. When Paul joined in, the entire group erupted, but were abruptly cut off as Red's excited voice came over the walkie-talkie. "We found a message! We found a message! We found it under a big rock. Here's AJ. Not over."

44

"It was pretty obvious. There was only one good-sized rock. It was half buried in the clearing and big enough that we had to dig around it to roll it over. Underneath we found a waterproof plastic brick sized box. Inside was a waterproof container for matches. Inside that was a handwritten message on a small sheet of parchment." AJ read the message. "*Good try, but much too high. Don't mistake one for two. A.S.*"

Sienna pulled Paul into their berth while the scuba gear was being brought up onto the deck. "Why didn't you tell me? Are you sure you want to do this?"

"I didn't want to worry you. It's hard to explain. I feel I have to . . . but you don't."

"By now you should know that I can tell when you're keeping things from me and when you do, it worries me more. Now that I know you're nervous, I'm not letting you go down there without me. We'll be fine."

Barney tapped loudly on their door. "Not a good time for a quickie, guys. All hands-on deck."

Paul shook his head. "His lack of sensitivity still amazes me."

"That's why we love him. So how big of a baby were you?"

"Over ten pounds."

"I'm glad you didn't tell me that before we had the twins."

"Oh? I thought you wanted me to tell you everything."

"OK, Wiseguy, there are exceptions to every rule."

They joined the others topside and pulled on their BCD's and tanks.

Connie checked her dive computer, while Wyatt looked over their valves and spare regulators. Sienna rolled into the water first, then Connie, followed by Wyatt.

Paul was about to join them when Brooke asked, "I'm trying to think of what he might have meant by don't mistake one for two."

"Maybe there's two treasures," Roxanne guessed, "and the first one will lead you to the second."

Paul snorted derisively. "He always regarded himself as the smartest one in any room. I think maybe it's just nonsense that he's using as an obtuse reminder that we can't possibly come up to his level of intelligence."

"Woah. Hang on there, Freud." Barney chuckled, "You'd be better served thinking positive thoughts right now, instead of throwing around clever opinions."

"Thanks Barn. Love ya, Buddy." Paul jumped in. Clearing his mask, he gave Sienna, Wyatt and Connie the OK sign.

"Love you too, Ace." Barney replied quietly, as he watched their air bubbles slowly draw closer to the island.

The four divers reached the base of the island's cliff in 18 feet of water on the longitudinal bearing given for the treasure. As previously agreed, they split up. Paul and Sienna explored to the south with Wyatt and Connie venturing north.

After quickly ruling out a shallow cave, Paul and Sienna dropped lower, shining their lamps into a dark entry that appeared to bend north under the island. Paul tied a nylon rope to his weight belt and headed in with Sienna posted at the entry letting out lengths of rope as needed. This was the protocol they'd all agreed on, to prevent a disoriented diver from heading down the wrong passage while trying to exit a cave.

So far, the bright light from his lantern and a wide, flooded passageway kept Paul from experiencing any traces of claustrophobia. After a couple minutes, he entered a wider vault. Looking up, he noticed that the rock ceiling was now above the surface of the water. Following his bubbles, he broke through the surface and slowly moved his light around the perimeter of a four-foot tall air space. There appeared to be a fissure in the rock near the southeast corner, but nothing close to resembling a passageway. He let out enough air from his BCD vest and sank back down and began finning around the perimeter of the vault looking for an underwater passage that might lead deeper into the island. A shadowy form near the far side of the cave put him on high alert. He was not alone. Turning his light toward the rear of the cave illuminated the gray beast moving toward him. He screamed, spitting out his regulator and spun around instinctively. The creature shot past him out the passageway . . . *Sienna! No!*

Paul caught hold of his regulator and slammed in the mouthpiece. The thirty seconds it took him to reach the cave entry seemed like an eternity. He charged out of the cave, not knowing what to expect, but she wasn't there. He knew it had been a large reef shark. Visions of the love of his life being chomped-in-half filled him with dread. Drawing his attention, a metallic clanking broke through his despair. Sienna floated 10-feet above the mouth of the cave, clanking her dive knife against her tank. She signaled OK, as he rose toward her. Taking her in his arms, he immediately discovered that it's not a good idea to cry underwater.

Seeing his duress, she pushed him up. They broke through the surface. Paul spit out his mouthpiece coughing. "I thought you'd been killed. Oh my god. I can never lose you."

"Settle down. Everything's fine. I think the shark was as stunned to see me, as I was him."

They held each other, silently bobbing in the calm water, until Paul's breathing returned to normal. He kissed her again. "You seem so calm. Didn't that terrify you?"

"I guess with all the spear fishing I did when I was a kid, I got used to diving around sharks. They're OK for the most part."

"They may be OK out in the open water, but sharing a cave with one . . . well, Barney was nearly prophetic."

"Yuck, T.M.I. Speaking of the cave . . .

"I'm pretty sure that one was a dead end."

"You up for going back down?"

Paul put in his regulator and smiled as he let air out of his floatation device. Sienna followed him and after coiling up the nylon rope, they finned north and found Connie, just outside a narrow mouth of another cave. About two-thirds of the 500-foot nylon rope had been played out. Connie signaled that Wyatt had been in the cave nearly 12 minutes. The excitement of the cave's discovery now overshadowed the lingering trepidation Paul had felt from the shark encounter, as they awaited Wyatt's return.

******

From *Caribe Daze's* bridge Red shouted excitedly. "I see bubbles. They're coming back."

"Wyatt found a cave that leads to the coordinates," Connie announced, as Joey helped her up the dive ladder.

"And?" Barney asked.

"Well, one of us sucked his tank dry in less than forty minutes," Sienna explained.

"That wouldn't be Ace here, would it?"

"It would, and I think a little rest for him might be a good idea before we head back down."

"We had a close encounter with a reef shark. Sienna and I are lucky to be alive." Paul took off his equipment and continued to describe the event to the group in vivid detail, even the part where he screamed and lost his mouthpiece, which Barney jumped on immediately.

"Kind of reminds me of the time when two 260-pound University of Idaho linemen broke untouched into the backfield and were about ready to lower the boom on our quarterback here. What stopped them in their tracks and allowed him to overthrow his receiver by twenty yards was his girly scream. Seems like that's gotten you out of a few jams, Ace."

"Why do I tell you anything?" Paul shook his head.

"Go easy on him, Barney. You should have seen him burst out of the cave, knife drawn, ready to do battle." Sienna walked over and kissed Paul on the cheek. "You'll always be my hero."

"I'm glad you weren't eaten by a shark, Uncle Paul," Red called down from the bridge.

Hank raised his beer, "All kidding aside, here's to our Screaming-Paul, a sensitive man who's not afraid to show his softer side, even to a shark."

After the toast, Joey, AJ Hank and Red played poker. Brooke and Barney took a swim together and the divers rested. Paul had almost dozed off, his head cradled in Sienna's lap, when Wyatt announced it was time for the second dive. Wyatt asked Paul to join him down in the cabin for a quick chat, as Connie and Sienna helped each other with their gear.

"Paul, most of the passageway is about 5 feet in diameter and not a problem for single file passage, but there was one section where it did get a bit tight. I just wanted you to know what to expect. You know, with the day you've already had, I wouldn't blame you if you decided to—"

"Thanks Wyatt, but don't worry, after what I just went through, this should be a piece of cake. Besides, you got through all right and I'm about two thirds your size."

"Gee Paul, thanks for reminding me that I'm fat. Your sister put you up to that?"

"No, and I didn't mean to imply—"

"I'm just pulling your chain." Wyatt laughed. "Actually the woman finds me irresistible."

"You and Barney," Paul quipped, as they headed topside.

"Huh? Connie has a thing for Barney?"

"No. Look, just never mind. Let's go find the treasure."

45

Paul focused on relaxed, controlled breathing as they approached the island. After draining his tank so quickly on the first dive, he had something to prove. Besides, he wasn't sure how Zen he'd feel finning through the tunnel to reach the interior cave. Wyatt had described the air in the cave as putrid, but breathable, and calculated that it would take approximately fifteen minutes to reach the cave from the boat. At the depth of twenty-five feet, their fresh tanks should last close to fifty minutes. Paul, however, had experienced how quickly he could burn through his tank when panicked.

They reached the mouth of the cave. Connie started in, her gloved hand sliding along the nylon cord Wyatt had secured to a rock inside the cave. Sienna followed, then Paul, with Wyatt bringing up the rear. The passage was narrower than the earlier one Paul had swam through, but he kept his breathing relatively normal. The tight section required the diver twist like a corkscrew to avoid rocks that projected into the passage. Connie and Sienna made it look easy. Paul felt his scalp tingling, but made the maneuver successfully and gave the OK signal to a relieved Sienna. Wyatt soon appeared and the four divers continued at a slight decline, until the passage widened.

Following the nylon rope upward, they passed through a vertical chimney and broke the surface in a small chamber.

Sienna and Paul pulled themselves onto a large flat rock and took off their scuba gear, while Wyatt and Connie sat on a ledge just below the surface and removed theirs. Once the gear was stowed, they began combing the chamber with their dive lights.

"This rock feels a bit wobbly." Connie tried unsuccessfully to flip it over. Wyatt knelt beside her and put his back to it. The rock tipped over. Connie jumped back. "Shit, spiders!"

"So, my macho ex-FBI agent/sister has a thing about spiders?"

"We all have our fears, Screaming-Paul."

"Hey you guys, I think I found something." Sienna had traversed a ledge to the opposite side of the chamber.

Paul hopped on the ledge and joined her. "Well, he might not have been full of shit after all."

Wyatt picked up his dive light. "What is it?"

"Don't mistake one for two. There's another chamber."

By the time Connie and Wyatt reached the narrow entry into the second chamber, Paul and Sienna were already unstacking a pile of large rocks in the back of the cave.

"Don't take your gloves off, and keep any bare skin from touching the ground," Connie ordered. "This place is full of rat droppings and bat guano."

"Watch out for spiders, too." Paul couldn't help himself.

Sienna and Connie gave him a withering look, as Wyatt plunged the blade of the shovel he'd bungeed to his tank into the ground. His first thrust met with a hollow thud. They uncovered the black plastic after scraping away less than 6 inches of crud. Paul grunted as he pulled the box from the ground. Sienna used her dive knife to slice open the heavy plastic cover.

"Well, open it," Wyatt said excitedly, as Sienna pulled the plastic off the aluminum briefcase.

Paul looked at Sienna. "You know what I'm thinking?"

"We should open it on the boat."

"Exactly."

"OK, fine by me. This place gives me the creeps. Let's get out of here." Connie started back along the ledge.

"Wait a second, Connie." Paul set the case on the ground and picked up the shovel. "Don't mistake one for two." The blade cut through the loose material easily. Ten minutes later, Wyatt took over. They'd widened the hole to about three by four feet, as he dug deeper.

"How deep we goin' there, Wyatt?" Connie whined pitifully, certain she'd already contracted a dreaded disease.

Another hollow thud answered her question.

******

They estimated the weight of each case at 100 pounds. The ledge forced them to return in single file and with Wyatt's bad knee, Paul was the best candidate to Sherpa the cases back to the first cave.

"I'm so glad I married such a strong man." Sienna kissed Paul, as he collapsed next to her, after retrieving the second case.

Breathing hard, Paul shut his eyes to regroup. "I just hope that whatever's in them is worth all this."

"I think that it's already been worth it." Connie put her hand on Paul's heaving shoulders, nodding at Wyatt.

"Absolutely," Wyatt seconded. "This whole trip's been great. It's not the treasure, but the hunt that's important. Right?"

"They're right, Paul. I don't want you to worry about what's in the cases." Sienna took his hand. "I think I was being a little nuts wanting to buy a boat and sail around the world. Even if the briefcases are full of rocks, we'll just have more great memories to share while we're roaming the highways."

"Thanks you guys, I really appreciate you saying all that. Of course, I don't believe any of it, but thanks." Paul stood and picked up Sienna's BCD vest. "Now, let's blow this dung heap."

Their flotation vests made the underwater transport of the cases easy for Connie and Sienna. Paul followed, while Wyatt coiled the nylon rope, as he brought up the rear. The four assembled outside the cave, gave the OK signal and finned back to *The Last Hurrah*.

******

Joey knelt on the swim step to receive the cases. He handed one to Barney and one to Hank, them helped the divers with their gear.

"Christ, these mothers are heavy. We'll need a hammer to bust off the latches. They're rusted shut."

"Hold it, Barney." Sienna stopped him as he headed below. "We need to discuss a few things before opening them."

"OK, like what?"

"Well, there's something to be said that if we don't open the cases, we won't have to declare what's in them. I mean, it could be full of rocks."

"Is that what we tell the judge?" Hank joked.

"I don't think that excuse has worked too well for smugglers in the past," Connie said, toweling off her hair.

"We're not smugglers, we're buccaneers. Johnny Depp never had to deal with customs." Barney rattled one of the cases. "Sounds like metal, not rocks."

Connie grabbed a bottle of water from the cooler. "Assuming the treasure represents a significant value, and since all or part of it was gained illegally to serve the interest of a felon, I doubt that we'd see any of it, if the authorities got wind of it."

Barney nodded. "Listen to her . . . Agent Hunter would know." Adding sarcastically, "Sure, let the feds have it. That'd be great. More money for bombs. Your tax dollars at work."

Paul broke in. "OK then, if we're going to keep this away from the authorities, I think we should clear British Customs at Great Harbor on Jost Van Dyke. It's less formal than Road Town and there's not much chance of an agent boarding the boat."

Joey looked concerned. "I can't believe we didn't think of this before. I even checked out the price of gold and silver without considering how we'd bring it home. We suck as pirates!"

"Easy, Matey. Uncle Barney has a plan."

"Oh great," Joey groaned. "I feel sooo much better."

"It's simple," Barney continued, "Paul's idea of clearing through Jost will work for British customs and we can drop the cases onto the northern reef off Buck Island, before we clear U.S. customs in Christiansted. There's no boat traffic there and no way anyone will spot the cases before we pick 'em up the next day."

"Yeah . . . I guess that'll work. Everybody on board with the plan?"

The agreement was unanimous.

"So, let's bash off these rusty latches and find out if we even need a plan." Barney retreated into the cabin and reappeared with a large screwdriver and hammer.

"Hold up for a minute, Barney," Paul said, looking over the cases carefully. "There's some kind of paraffin or waxy substance over the latches and hinges. Also, there's more between the upper and lower lids. Andrew apparently went to some trouble to waterproof the cases. If we open them now and break the seal, we might damage what's inside when we dump them overboard."

"Christ, Amigo," Barney picked up one of the cases and shook it. "Listen . . . it's metal. A little wetness for a few hours won't hurt."

"Paul's right, Barney," Connie weighed in. "There could be documents or bank notes in there as well. Why take the chance?"

"Uncle Barney," Joey said, "I'd feel better waiting. I like the idea of not knowing what we have until we're through customs."

"All right, all right. Shit, no need to take a vote."

Paul and Barney carried the cases below. As Paul finished sliding the second case behind the engine block, Barney patted him on the shoulder. "Well, Ace, from the look of things, you've got a pretty good chance of taking that round-the-world cruise after all."

"Yeah, I guess . . . We'll find out soon enough."

"Wow, that's quite a reaction. You seem about as happy as if I'd sat on your guitar."

"Not my Gibson!" Paul cracked a smile.

"You sure as hell don't look like someone who may have had a large sum of money just drop out of the sky."

317

"Yeah, I know. It's how I felt when Sherman set up the account for AJ's college; but I didn't have a choice then. It was in his name, so I went along with it. Now, Sienna's excited about taking a sailing trip and—"

"You feel you owe it to her, with all the crap you've drug her through."

"Wow, I guess you had that one ready to fire, but yeah, that's exactly right."

"Thought so . . . You know I love you, Ace. But when it comes to common sense, you definitely score on the low end of the curve. You're all about right and wrong, black or white." Barney lowered his voice. "Shit, I even had to talk to you about not turning yourself in for killing Falco. Think of what that would have done to Sienna and your family."

"I know, Barney. That was good advice, but this seems different. Yeah, there's an ethical side to it, but practically speaking, I worry that nothing good can come from anything connected with Andrew Sherman."

"What? You're worried about your round-the-world cruise going down in a typhoon or something?"

Paul shrugged his shoulders.

"Maybe Somali pirates?" . . . Barney shook his head and stood up. "OK, I give up. And people say I'm pig-headed."

After Barney left, Paul realized that he'd been so busy planning and carrying out the treasure hunt that he hadn't noticed his growing ambivalence over actually finding a treasure. The first hint he'd gotten was the moment of relief he'd felt when Sienna joked that the cases might be full of rocks. Not ready to join the others, Paul opened the door to their berth and was startled to find Sienna.

"Hey Honey, I'm just taking a few minutes to rest. It's been quite a day."

"You talked with Barney?" Paul asked.

"No, why?"

"He and I just had a discussion about the treasure."

Sienna sat up in the bed, a serious expression on her face. "Paul, I need to say something. Whatever's in those cases . . . I'm just not sure we should keep it."

"You aren't?"

"No. If it turns out they're full of money, I don't want it. We're not rich, but we're certainly not poor. We have friends and family. We live in a beautiful home on a beautiful island. We have everything we need. Plus, I know you've had reservations in the past about anything to do with Andrew Sherman. Tell me truthfully . . . Weren't you a bit relieved when Pascall lost AJ's college fund?"

"Sienna, it's not just about me. What about your dream of going on a world cruise?"

"Honey, traveling with you and the girls for a year in a VW van would be more than enough for me. Think of how much fun we'd all have. We'd could start in Miami, then head west along the gulf coast . . ."

46

Paul and Sienna appeared on deck just as Joey guided *The Last Hurrah* into White Bay. Hank and Roxanne had already tied up *Caribe Daze* to its buoy. Joey brought the Cabo36 along *Daze's* port side. Wyatt and Barney rafted the two boats together and laid out an anchor to keep the vessels from drifting.

"You guys OK?" Barney asked, noticing their arrival.

"Better than OK, Barn." Sienna replied.

"Well, that's a relief. As much time as you were taking down below, I figured Ace had finally pushed your patience over the edge."

Paul had told Sienna about his earlier conversation with Barney. "No, as a matter of fact, it turned out we were on the same page. Before we head in for dinner, can we get everybody together. We'd like to discuss what we've come up with."

Barney gave them a curious look, then shouted, "All hands-on-deck. The newly-rich couple have returned from their ruminations and want to bring us all up to speed."

Wyatt was the last of the group to arrive. "Sorry guys. Nature called."

"No one asked, Sweetheart, but thanks for sharing." Connie patted the bench next to her.

"First off, Paul and I want to thank you for joining us on this treasure hunt. When we were in the cave, Wyatt said that it was the hunt and not the treasure that's important, and he's right. Having—"

"Yeah, but that was when you guys thought the cases might be filled with rocks," Barney interjected. "How does that work if the treasure turns out to be worth a bundle?"

"It works the same, Barney. Having all of you alongside us, has been the best part of this adventure . . . Paul and I have realized that we don't feel right using any part of this treasure to sail around the world."

Barney groaned.

"It would feel right, however, putting it toward a noble cause," Sienna added, a smile blossoming on her face.

"Like a charity for retired pot farmers?"

"Uncle Barney, this is one of those times we've talked about." Joey made the familiar zipping the lip shut motion.

"Right Champ. Sorry, my bad."

"We have a wonderful life and we can't see how money would make it any better."

"Well, for one thing, Honey, money gives you options," Roxanne volunteered. "You can spend your time doing exactly what you both want to do. Paul wouldn't have to be away from you and the kids, working as much."

"There's other ways you can make that happen," Connie interjected. "Also, we've all been so caught up in the hunt, we've avoided looking at the difficulties hiding a potentially large sum of money from the IRS. Tax laws would have to be broken to keep from explaining where the money came from and we've already discussed the downside of that."

"Excuse me, but are all of you nuts?" Barney loomed over them, red-faced.

321

"Sit down, Barn." Brooke took his hand and pulled him beside her. "You don't need to bellow. We're all right here."

"Sorry, you're right." He took a deep breath. "If what's in those cases is what we're all thinking it might be, then that's a shit-pile of money you guys are walking away from. Now, excuse me for not buying this bullshit about money being the root of all evil. Money isn't good or bad. Other than this little bout of craziness, you two have your heads on about as straight as anybody I've ever met. You'd put the money to good use."

"That's exactly what we're talking about, Barney, putting it to good use," Paul explained.

"Look, you guys do what you want to do. I've said my piece."

"Oh Jesus, Barney, please don't pout," Brooke pleaded.

"Yeah, come on, Big Guy," Hank pulled out a couple bottles of champagne from the cooler. "Let's toast our good fortune, then head in for some food before the bars close."

******

After dinner the buccaneers walked down the beach to The Soggy Dollar Bar. When the bartender announced last call, they swam under a full moon, back to their ships.

Once aboard, Paul and Sienna showered. Wrapped in blankets, they sat together on the bow of *The Last Hurrah*, while the others prepared for bed. Soon, the clanking riggings and waves slapping against the hull were the only early morning sounds.

Sienna laid back in the crook of his arm. "Paul, do you remember when I asked you how it would feel when AJ headed to college?"

"Yes."

"I think I was asking because I felt lost. Now if you asked me the question, I know what I'd say."

"Yeah, what's that?"

"Well, I'll miss seeing AJ every day, but I have you and the twins to wake up to. Maybe I'll start another restaurant when we get back. Who knows, but I'm really excited."

"Kind of like, when one door closes, another door opens?"

"Exactly."

"You know, Andrew Sherman closed a door on me when he destroyed our business, and look what I have now."

Snuggling into him, she replied, "You're a very lucky man."

After ten minutes of silence, Paul realized that Sienna had fallen asleep. Careful not to wake her, he shifted positions, so they were both lying down.

He reflected on the loss of their unborn child and subsequent killing of the three men. Neither would have happened if it hadn't been for Andrew Sherman.

Nearly a decade ago, even though Andrew was racked with guilt for the damage his disappearance had caused Paul, he hadn't asked for forgiveness during their chance encounter. If he had, Paul wouldn't have given it.

He recalled his own period of guilt and self-loathing and the pain he'd inflicted on Sienna, AJ and his friends. Chui had taught him that his pain was trapped energy and could only be unlocked with forgiveness. Andrew had tried to make things right. He'd left money for AJ and even from the grave he'd led Paul to a treasure.

Tears filled his eyes. He visualized Andrew in front of him. A weight lifted as he spoke, "I forgive you, Andrew. Be at peace."

Paul searched the sky and found the Southern Cross; a heavenly signpost promising more oceans to sail, more roads to travel, and more life to live. He pulled Sienna close and before drifting off, thanked his lucky stars.

47

Like a shot, the twins broke through the door from the tarmac into Connie and Roxanne's arms. Paul, Sienna and AJ followed and were immediately engulfed with hugs and kisses by the welcoming throng.

"Welcome home, Reed, Phoebe, Ace and Little Ace," Barney shouted, as he picked Sienna off the ground in a smothering bear-hug.

"Happy holidays, Little Brother." Connie walked beside Paul to the truck. "I can't believe it's been six months. Where has the time gone?"

"We didn't want to go any longer without seeing all of you. Has everybody made it down?"

"Yeah, surprisingly everyone's flights were on time and no one missed their connections. The place has filled to overflowing, the past couple of days. It's gonna be a great Christmas."

"Is it too much for Andy and Aunt Charlotte?"

"Paul, are you kidding? They're in heaven. They're overseeing Red and the others with the meal prep right now."

"How was the trip down-island?"

"Mission accomplished. It's all set up."

"Great news!"

******

The immaculately dressed Bajan smiled warmly, but declined the director's offer to take a chair. Instead, he pulled the sealed envelope from the breast pocket of his white sports jacket and handed it to her. This was his twenty-fifth meeting since arriving on Saint Croix two days earlier.

Of course, he hadn't shown it at the time, but when the bank president had notified him of this assignment, he was royally pissed off. Directed to leave his island, his family and his children, four days before Christmas . . . He almost quit on the spot. But, that all changed when the third recipient of the envelope, the president of the island's battered women's shelter, ran out of her office with tears streaming down her face and hugged him.

Two days and twenty-seven appointments later, he sat in the make-shift waiting area for his last appointment. Not a dog lover, he nonetheless felt compassion as the frenetic creature's barks reverberated through the wooden door that separated him from the kennel.

"Mr Thompson?" The man looked like he'd slept in his clothes.

The Bajan hesitated before taking the offered hand. *Remember to wash your hands before boarding the plane back to Barbados.* "Yes, thank you for seeing me, Mr. Limrick. This won't require much of your time, but I would like to speak with you in private."

"Call me Lew. Of course, of course, come in." Limrick stepped back as Thompson passed into the small office. "Here, let me clear this off the chair. Please have a seat."

326

Resistant to extraneous interactions, he accepted the offer. *Why not? I'm early for the flight. I've probably already caught whatever disease inhabits this pigsty.* "Thank you." David sat down and pulling out the envelope, handed it to Lew.

"What's this, a subpoena?" . . . If that witch wants any more from me, tell her good luck. This well has run dry."

"This is not a subpoena, Mr. Limrick."

"What then?"

"It would be best if you saw for yourself."

Limrick tore open the envelope. He read the contents. "What the fuck? Is this some kind of sick joke?"

"Sir, I can assure you that this is not a joke. I've spent the last two days giving varying amounts to the directors and presidents of thirty non-profit organizations on your island of Saint Croix."

"Who is this from?"

"The donor has insisted on anonymity. I don't even know who it is."

Limrick looked down at the cashier's check. "Five hundred thousand dollars. Five . . . Hundred . . . Thousand . . . Really? Do you have any idea what we can do with this?"

"Find homes for the poor creatures I hear barking in the back, I hope."

"Oh we will, and so much more." Limrick rushed over and hugged the surprised Bajan, uncomfortably pinning him to his chair.

"Ah, Mr. Limrick?" David tapped the man on his shoulder. "Please let me up."

"Of course, sorry . . . We've been fighting an uphill battle for so long and now . . . You have no idea what this means to us."

327

******

"Oh Great Spirit, thank you for granting me another day on earth with my family. Thank you for keeping them all safe and please remind them that I'm not getting any younger and to check in from time to time as they travel all over hell and gone."

From his bowed-head position, Paul caught Sienna's wink, as Andy concluded his pointed grace.

"Now dig in damn it, before it gets cold."

They didn't need to be asked twice, as steaming platters of roast beef, mashed potatoes, green beans and kale from Andy's garden were passed between the 24 diners.

"How's our college man?" Hank asked, topping off AJ's wine glass. "The ladies leaving you with enough time for your studies?"

"Not really into the ladies right now, Uncle Hank. I barely have enough time for my classes."

"That's alright, Little Ace," Barney said, overhearing from across the table. "Plenty of time for that down the road. Your Uncle Barney's had to be firm with plenty of women. Not always easy to resist their wiles, but necessary at times." Brooke's groan caused him to take her hand, adding, "Of course, one day, you'll meet one that's too wily to resist."

"That was quite a recovery," Carmen noted, passing the mash potatoes to Kate. "Barney's gotten so much smoother in his old age."

"Old age? I can still dance you under the table."

"That's just a saying. It's not as silly as it sounds," Red explained to Kate's confused daughter, Brianna.

"It's good to be home again . . . even if it's just for a week." Paul took the bread basket from Sienna.

"Where are you guys headed next?" Sally asked.

"We left the van in Miami, so we'll drive AJ back up to school, then head north for Prince Edward Island. After that, we'll play it by ear."

"When can we take off like that, Tex?" Sally asked.

"Now don't give the Sheriff here a hard time," Andy jumped in. "He's still the law in his parts and a lot of people depend on him to keep them safe."

"Thanks Andy. Remember, I've got a deputy star in the office to pin on you anytime you want the job."

"Ha! Can't you just see that, Char? Sorry Tex, but I haven't shot a pistol in years."

"I think he was kidding, Dear."

"Well, of course he was. I'll tell you Sheriff . . . Getting old ain't easy. I still feel like I could put up a good fight if need be. The mind says go, but the body says no."

"I just hope I have half as much go in my body when I get to be your age."

"Well, that's very sweet of you, Kate."

Paul was still a bit tired from the trip and was content to sit back and enjoy the company. While Sienna retied Phoebe's hair ribbon, he watched AJ and Joey share a laugh, Barney kiss Brooke, Carmen kiss Kate and Andy kiss any woman within arm's reach.

The sun had already set by the time they finished their meal. Sienna and the twins left to help build a bonfire. Andy brought down a bundle of saplings for Barney and the girls to be used as skewers for their s'mores.

"Hey, Uncle Paul," Joey called out. "Erin and I are headed back to our cabin to grab a sweater for Clarabelle. I have a big-bodied Martin I just bought off the internet, if you're interested in jammin' later tonight."

"Sign me up," Paul shouted back, still working on his strawberry shortcake. A few minutes later, he pushed away from the table and followed the path to the lookout. The Christmas winds buffeted him from the east, as he stood at the guardrail, facing the dark expanse of the Caribbean.

Paul recalled years ago, walking through the ruins of a tungsten mine in the Pasayten and wondering, *What will be my legacy?* He knew that it wouldn't be in the buildings he'd designed, but in the bonds of family and friendship.

Barney's booming voice and loud shrieks of the girls' laughter reached him from the fire pit. The light of the bonfire flickered high above, in the canopy of the surrounding mahogany trees.

He imagined a future traveler kicking through Windsol's ruins. Would that person feel the soul of the place; the force that gave life to the concrete, steel and rubble strewn over the ground before him? Would he hear, across the centuries, the echoes of their children's joy-filled laughter? Would he feel the love that bonded them all for life?

Paul knew the answer. The heart of their family would live on . . . It's pulse forever beating in the crashing waves on the beach below.

The End

Made in the USA
Middletown, DE
24 March 2017